A CHARMED LOVE

Reaching under the center support of the bench, Tom's gloved fingers found an envelope taped to the underside. Carefully breaking the seal, he pulled it forward and into view. On the front, the murderer had written only Denise's name in the same elegant black script.

Opening a plastic evidence bag, Denise said, "I think we should take this to the nearest NYPD station. Let's have them dust it for poison and fingerprints."

"Agreed," Tom replied as he gingerly placed it inside.

Easing into the crowd once again, they rode to the first floor. This time, the trip seemed slow and plodding despite the popping eardrums. Curiosity about the contents of the envelope filled Denise's imagination as much as the prospects of seeing the panoramic view of Manhattan had on the ascent. Tom, however, could hardly wait to reach ground level.

After speaking with an officer on the corner of Fifth Avenue, they walked toward the station. They did not linger as they passed people enthralled with the spectacle of New York. They had a purpose and an envelope to inspect.

The New York Police Department office looked similar to theirs in Maryland. The only difference appeared to be the noise level. Crowds of shouting, pushing people filled the entryway. Some of them were lost and in need of directions, others were reporting thefts or muggings, and still others were under the protection of attentive officers.

A CHARMED LOVE

Courtni Wright

BET Publications, LLC
http://www.bet.com
http://www.arabesquebooks.com

ARABESQUE BOOKS are published by

BET Publications, LLC
c/o BET BOOKS
One BET Plaza
1900 W Place NE
Washington, DC 20018-1211

First Printing: September 2002
10 9 8 7 6 5 4 3 2 1

Printed in the United States of America

One

The buzz in the squad room was almost deafening as the detectives milled around the coffee machine, made phone calls, and clustered in groups to share their weekend activities. Their energy added animation to the dull, lifeless, gray walls and the sterile cubicles. Each desk looked like the next—cluttered with open cases strewn chaotically amidst the half-empty coffee mugs. Gum wrappers littered the ashtrays that once held half-smoked cigarettes but now served as trash cans. Old-fashioned Rolodex files augmented computer directories. The job and the people who performed it had not changed much in decades. Intuition, insight, and elbow grease still solved crimes.

Denise Dory sat at her desk. The lamp with its green shade shined light on the open file. Absentmindedly, she played with a pencil that slid over and under the thin, delicate fingers of her left hand. She wore only a watch on her left arm, preferring to keep her jewelry to a minimum.

Denise wore her hair short-cropped and no-nonsense. She did not feel that she had time to primp or fuss over her appearance and preferred the natural, unadorned look of freshly scrubbed soft brown skin to makeup. She maintained her tall, lean appearance by jogging and lifting weights, but she did not consider herself athletic or an exercise addict. She took life as it came and did not sweat the missed exercise sessions, the chipped nails, and the runs in her stockings.

Her once steaming coffee sat cold in her cup. Unlike her

colleagues who were only now arriving at work, Denise had been on the job since seven o'clock. She enjoyed the silence of the early morning hours during which she was alone except for the presence of one other detective who sat slumped at the desk behind hers.

Tom Phyfer had been poring over his cases since six. He was an early riser who enjoyed arriving before anyone, even Denise. He started the extra-strong coffee, scanned the newspaper, and checked the morning blotter before anyone else arrived. He stayed away from office gossip, preferring to put in a hard day's work and go home. He exercised by running with his new canine partner, who Denise considered more of a nuisance than an asset, and working out with weights to keep his muscles at their peak. His suits barely concealed the bulk that lurked under the fabric. Tom hardly noticed the women who smiled appreciatively as he ran past them with the sweat glistening on his warm brown skin.

By the time Denise slipped into her chair, Tom had already planned his day. They had been partners long enough for both to know that neither would change. They enjoyed each other's company and respected each other's opinions professionally and personally.

Their professional partnership resulted from Tom's reputation as a gruff, uncooperative grouch. Knowing his detective skills, Denise decided to focus on the investigative intellect that lay under the rough exterior. When Tom needed a partner, she was the first person to step forward. She had never regretted the decision and could think of no other partner she would rather have at her back despite Tom's initial reservations. Although everyone on the force knew Denise's reputation for being one of the best detectives in the country, he was skeptical about having a woman as a partner. However, after seeing her in action as his backup, he quickly changed his mind.

The tension, the energy, the simpatico exchange of ideas and thoughts helped their professionalism to grow into something legendary on the force. No one ever expected to see

one without the other. Wherever Denise went, Tom was sure
to follow. Whenever Tom left the room, Denise was close
behind him. Together, they had solved more cases than anyone on the force; singularly, they were almost as impressive.

Denise stretched and lifted the cup of coffee to her lips.
"Cold!" she muttered and rose. Her skirt fell gently over her
trim calves as she walked toward the crowd at the machine.
Long ago, she stopped noticing the appreciative whistles of
the male detectives as they gazed at her backside. Keeping
her shoulders level, Denise allowed the almost sensuous
natural rhythm of her walk to propel her.

"Refill, Denise?" Barry Newman asked as he stepped
aside for her to pour the cold brew into the nearby sink.

"It's good this morning, isn't it?" Denise replied as she
poured another cup of the steaming, thick concoction that
Tom called coffee.

Laughing, Roger Daily replied, "It is if you like tar. That
partner of yours hasn't learned to count in all these years.
You need to set him straight, Denise. It's one scoop per cup
not ten."

"Hey, you deal with him," Denise replied as she added a
little sugar to the sludge in her cup. "He won't listen to me
either. Add some hot water to it if it's too strong. You know
that Tom won't change. He thinks that it's not coffee unless
the spoon could stand unaided in the cup. I think he got it
right this morning."

The good-natured bantering continued with Tom's coffee
and his sleeping canine partner the brunt of the jokes. Tom
did not mind and neither did Denise. Both of them had listened to the same comments every morning for more days
than either wished to count. Besides, if they hated the coffee
so much, any one of the other detectives could come in early
to turn on the machine.

"Break it up, you guys. I need to talk with Denise," the
captain stated as he motioned for her to follow him to his
office at the end of the hall.

"Just giving her the usual ribbing about her partner, Captain," Roger replied with a hearty laugh.

"I know," the good-natured captain nodded. "I could hear you guys in my office. Is this why we're paying you? Get to work, you guys, before I replace all of you with canine officers."

Tossing his cup toward the closest trash can, Barry responded, "That'll be the day. Can you imagine the mess around here when all those supposedly housebroken 'officers' let go? I think you'll need us for a while yet."

Laughing, Denise pointed to the litter on the floor and replied over her shoulder, "Looks to me as if you're not too well trained yourself, Barry. Missed again."

The uproar followed her down the hall. Sinking into a worn, colorless leather seat in the captain's equally gray office, Denise waited. The last time Captain Morton called her to his office without Tom, he had assigned her to a murder case on Capitol Hill. Trying not to appear anxious, she wondered what he had in mind this time.

"Denise, I've got an assignment that's right up your alley. It requires feminine wiles, smarts, and savvy," Captain Morton began as soon as she was as comfortable as possible in the chair with burst springs that poked into her backside.

Turning her head slightly to the side, Denise asked, "Are you being sexist, Captain? What's this 'feminine wiles' stuff? By the way, you need to get this seat fixed."

Laughing heartily at the expected reaction, Captain Morton replied, "I like it that way . . . keeps my detectives on their toes, so to speak. And no, I'm not being sexist . . . just wanted to get your attention. Read this."

Captain Morton watched as Denise scanned the memo from their chief that detailed the nature of the crime, the eyewitness accounts, and the lack of evidence. From what she read, Denise could tell that the case was fresh and would be difficult to solve. The lack of clues, real information, and motive would make her job difficult.

"Why me?" Denise asked as she handed the sheets of paper back to him.

"You're good . . . OK, the best," Captain Morton replied, waving her off. "Besides, the chief asked for you again. The jeweler was one of her best friends."

With a lift of her eyebrows and a sigh, Denise commented, "The chief certainly moves in impressive company. According to the dossier, the victim was one of the most famous designers in the world. Who would want to kill a jeweler? I could understand robbery, but that doesn't appear to have been the motive."

Smiling, the captain said, "I thought you'd find the case intriguing. That's the question for you to answer. Who would kill him and why? When the designer in Florida was killed a few years ago, everyone suspected drugs or homosexuality as the reasons. This Mr. Worldly, according to the chief, was straight and a deacon in his church. Go figure."

"Could Tom join me on this one? He was a lot of help on the Hill case," Denise asked as she collected the sheets of paper that comprised the only information available.

"No, you go it alone. I want him to stay with that canine study. He and that dog are doing great work and getting good press," Captain Morton replied as he started flipping through the call-back slips on his desk. In his mind, the meeting had ended now that Denise was on the case.

"But, Captain—"

"Good-bye, Denise," Captain Morton replied without looking up. His fingers were already busy dialing the digits of the first caller's phone number.

Denise left the office with the sound of his voice in her ears. Once again, she would have to tell Tom that their partnership would have to go on hold for a while. At least this time, the presence of the slumbering German shepherd under his desk might keep him company and out of trouble. Sadly, nothing would keep her from missing him.

Returning to her desk, Denise avoided Tom's eyes. She knew that he suspected something but would not ask. He would respect her privacy and professionalism until she decided to share the information with him.

Denise spent several minutes carefully reading the sheets of paper. The jeweler, Joseph Worldly, had been well respected in his profession as one of the premier designers of very trendy expensive gold and diamond items as well as a line of unique, affordable engagement rings. He lived with his wife in Potomac, Maryland, but maintained apartments in each city in which he did business. He had shops in Bethesda, Maryland; Tysons Corner, Virginia; San Francisco; Los Angeles; and New York and had recently teamed with one of the most famous jewelry firms in Paris and had planned to open a shop on the Rue de la Paix.

Nothing in his dossier could explain the murder. When Mr. Worldly was at home, he attended the historic Episcopal church in Bethesda and served as a deacon. He gave generously to civic causes, supported his political party, mentored new jewelry artists and struggling businesses, and, according to the "Style" section of the *Washington Post,* threw elaborate parties. His friends, family, and associates loved and respected him. In short, Denise could find nothing in the dossier to explain his murder.

However, someone had killed Mr. Worldly, and not for his money. His wallet had contained numerous credit cards and enough cash to purchase a ticket to almost anywhere in the world. Mr. Worldly had died at the hands of an unknown murderer for reasons equally unknown. Denise would have to find the clues that would lead to the killer.

Returning the sheets of paper to the folder, Denise slowly turned toward Tom's desk. As she'd expected, he was busy on one of his canine cases. Despite his initial hesitation to pair with the German shepherd named Molly, he had earned quite a reputation by cracking several tough drug-related cases. Molly, as always, snoozed under his desk with her muzzle resting on his foot.

"Got a minute?" Denise asked when Tom did not look up.

"I was wondering when you'd turn around," Tom stated

in his usual gruff tone. "I've read this same report at least five times. What's up, Dory?"

Denise smiled as she rested her hand lightly on his muscular brown arm. Even though their relationship had changed since the Capitol Hill case, she liked being called by her last name, a sign of camaraderie between them, and was glad that the new romantic tension between them had not affected their work. She enjoyed his dry wit, his seemingly sour disposition, and his lay-down-his-life loyalty. Denise understood and trusted Tom in a way that she had never felt toward any other partner.

Clearing her throat, Denise stated, "The captain assigned me to a new case . . . no leads, just a body. It's high profile. I'll have to beg off some of our other work. OK?"

"It'll have to be," Tom replied with his usual, slightly bored tone. "Can't do anything about it now. Once the captain makes up his mind, there's no changing it. Tell me about the case."

"There's nothing to tell," Denise responded, "I have a dossier on a very nice but very dead man who was liked by everyone. There's no apparent motive and no known enemies. All I know is that the man died at the hands of a killer using an unidentified substance."

"Not much to go on," Tom commented as he reached down to scratch Molly behind the ear.

Watching Molly's obvious enjoyment, Denise asked, "Do you think she's jealous? Every time I turn around to talk to you, she wakes up."

Chuckling, Tom said, "I guess it's one of those feminine things. She senses your interest in me and wakes up to annoy you."

"My interest in you?" Denise asked incredulously as she moved her hand away from him and crossed her arms. "How could she sense that when I'm talking with you about something totally unrelated to us?"

"I guess she can sense the heat between us," Tom joked with a lift of his eyebrows.

"You're full of it," Denise chuckled. "She just doesn't like me. Didn't she chew up the sweater I left at your apartment? It was on the sofa next to yours, but she selected mine for a snack."

"Like I said, it's a feminine thing . . . protect your turf thing," Tom replied, quite content to be the center of the battle between his two favorite females.

"Anyway," Denise commented, changing the subject back to the case, "I'll have to do some traveling on this one. The deceased lived in Bethesda, Maryland, but had a number of shops around the country and a new one set to open in Paris."

Handing Molly a biscuit, Tom stated, "I won't be lonely, might even go on an occasional date . . . live the life of an unattached man."

Looking with disgust at the contentedly chewing dog, Denise replied, "Not with that dog, you won't. She ate my sweater, but I survived. The next woman in your life might not be so lucky. She might become the snack. Besides, before I came along, you had enjoyed a long, dry spell of nothing much. Don't push your luck. You might find yourself snuggling with that dog permanently."

To Denise's back, Tom remarked, "At least, Molly doesn't give me all this mouth."

"Whatever," Denise replied over her shoulder.

A grunt was Tom's comeback. He hated that one-word rejoinder that seemed to silence forever anything else he might have to offer. He'd lost many arguments, professional and personal, with Denise as a result of that one word.

Denise spent the next hours on the phone making arrangements to visit the coroner and meet the widow. Perhaps one of those two people would offer a possible motive not stated in the dossier. She certainly had little enough to direct her efforts now.

As was her habit, Denise gathered her sketchpad and pencils and prepared to leave the precinct. The coroner's office would be her first stop. He might have a lead for her to follow now that he had conducted a thorough examination of the body. Knowing only that the victim had died from violent convulsions and fever was not enough. High-profile case or not, Denise needed more.

"This package just arrived for you, Denise," Ronda, the precinct secretary, announced as she placed the small, wrapped box on her desk. "Secret admirer?"

"Yeah, top secret. So secret that I can't even guess who it is. Thanks," Denise replied as she donned gloves and prepared to unwrap the white paper with the thin gold lines running through it. The precinct always X-rayed packages as a precaution, but she felt the need to protect her hands from poisons.

"What's that?" Tom inquired as he joined Denise at her desk.

Looking at him with a hesitant smile, Denise asked, "Did you send me this as a peace offering?"

"No," Tom replied emphatically. "You know I don't do stuff like that. My mind goes mostly to food . . . dinner at the diner or the pizza place tonight."

Chuckling, Denise commented, "Excuse me! I forgot about the direct link between your stomach and your heart."

Denise turned the box over to examine it from all sides. The top carried the name of a jeweler in New York City in gold letters but nothing else. Lifting the lid of the rectangular, red velvet box, she found inside a sparkling, gold bracelet nestled among the satin folds.

"Is this some kind of joke?" Denise asked the group of curious detectives who had gathered around her desk. She lifted it out and held it in the air.

Taking it from her fingers, Ronda replied, "All 18k of it. Is there a note?"

Pulling the fabric from the box, Denise discovered a gift card on which the sender had written: "Consider this an add-a-clue bracelet. More later."

"A bit cryptic, isn't it?" Denise remarked as she returned the card and the bracelet to the box.

"And mysterious," Ronda added. "I'd love to have a secret

admirer who would expose his identity through clues. This is very romantic."

"It would be romantic if I could think of someone who might have sent it," Denise responded, looking at Tom's blank expression.

"Don't look at me. That would have set me back big time. I'm as confused as you are," Tom commented.

"Well, he promised a clue. I guess I'll have to wait," Denise concluded as she tossed the box into the drawer.

Ronda looked shocked as darkness engulfed the box and asked, "You're not going to wear it? If someone had sent me an 18k gold bracelet with promises of more to come, I'd sure wear it."

Popping into the thick crowd, the captain interjected, "All right, everyone, back to work. Denise, could I see you in my office?"

As the crowd thinned, Denise lifted the box from her desk and followed Captain Morton down the hall. She hoped he might be able to shed a little light on the arrival of the bracelet and the meaning behind the note. Looking over her shoulder, she saw that Tom sat with his hands folded across his stomach, thumbs tapping together. Denise knew from past experience that Tom was not happy at the intrusion of the case into their regular pattern. By sending the bracelet, the perpetrator had entered the squad room where he definitely did not belong. That violation was unnerving to everyone who worked there.

The captain quietly examined the box and the bracelet as Denise sat patiently in the chair opposite his desk. His long, thin fingers gently manipulated each link as he looked for a weak connection. Denise could tell that he was running through the various meanings behind the bracelet.

Returning it to her, Captain Morton remarked, "If you find out that this is more than a sign of admiration, mark it as evidence. I received this unsigned letter this morning at the same time that the package arrived for you. What do you make of it? I've never had a perp advertise his intentions the way this one has. It's one thing to drop clues, it's another to inform everyone of the intent."

After reading the captain's letter, Denise quickly responded, "This is definitely a downer. My secret admirer is the jeweler's killer. He must be well connected with the force because he knows that I've been assigned to the case. I wonder who leaked the information."

Easing into his chair, Captain Morton replied, "There's always the possibility that it was a slip rather than a leak. Someone might have mentioned to a friend that you had been assigned to the case without realizing that the friend was also a killer. I don't want to think that there's a leak in the department."

Finding the inactivity and the conversation boring, Denise impatiently stated, "All right. . . . Someone very quickly and inadvertently spilled the beans. Now what? I had planned to visit the coroner this morning and the widow this afternoon. Any objections to my plans?"

"None," Captain Morton responded, aware of Denise's inability to sit idle when there was work to be done. "Let me know what you find out."

The squad room was alive with gossip and speculation when Denise returned from the captain's office. People from other units had descended on them to check out her bracelet and wonder at the identity of the sender. She had to push past the crowd to get to her desk.

"OK, folks, enough's enough," Denise announced as she removed the bracelet from Ronda's wrist, placed it in the box, and closed the lid with an angry snap. "Am I the only one around here with work to do?"

"Nah, but you're the only one with a $3,000 bracelet," smirked Ben from accounting.

Looking incredulously from Ben to the others gathered around, Denise asked, "How do you know the price? I didn't see a tag."

Grinning broadly, Ronda announced, "I phoned the jeweler in New York. He said that if you don't like it you should feel free to exchange it for another one. The gentleman who picked it out wanted simple elegance to highlight the charms, but he sells more elaborate designs as well."

Growling from his desk surrounded by a crush of police employees, Tom demanded, "What charms? This guy is planning to send Denise charms, too?"

Ronda, happy to be the center of activity and knowledge for once, continued gleefully, "From what the jeweler told me, Denise's mystery man plans to send a number of them. The guy didn't say what kind, but I bet they'll be beauties."

Picking up her things, Denise said, "He's not a mystery man, he's a murderer. He killed a local jeweler. I think he's planning to communicate with me using the charms as clues."

Ronda looked deflated at the news. A mystery man was romantic, a murderer was not. Slipping from the thinning crowd, she eased down the hall toward her desk outside the captain's office. She had enjoyed enough excitement for one day.

"A murderer, huh?" Tom growled as the others returned to their work. "You'd best be careful, Dory. Anyone who would go to these lengths to stage a murder and drop clues that might lead to his own arrest is dangerous."

"Don't worry," Denise commented with a smile as she stuffed her sketchpad into the valise. "I'll be very careful. I don't like it that he already knows that I'm on the case. I don't appreciate his little charm bracelet idea. He sounds like one sick pup to me."

"I don't like having another man watch my girl." Tom sulked angrily with his arms still folded over his chest.

"Your girl? Since when am I your girl? I hate that term. I'm not a teenager," Denise teased.

"Since the Capitol Hill case and don't you forget it. I don't care how you refer to yourself. You're my girl, *my woman,*" Tom advised as he studied her sweet face. "This isn't a casual romance for me, Dory. Take care of yourself."

Placing her hand lightly on his shoulder, Denise replied, "Do me a favor while I'm at the coroner's and the widow's.

Phone the jeweler in New York for a description of the man who purchased the bracelet and run it through the FBI files. You might even want to call your contact at the Bureau to see if he knows anything. I have a feeling that I'll need a lot of help on this one."

"That's at the top of my 'To do' list," Tom responded. "I'll see you when you return. I should have some information by then."

"And think of another term of endearment for me," Denise added as she turned away.

Tom's sturdy warmth radiated through Denise's body and enfolded her in confidence. Balancing her things, she walked from the squad room and down the stairs to the street. The coroner's office was only two blocks away and she could use the walk. She needed time to think, time to put herself in the killer's shoes, time to understand his need to use the bracelet, charm, and clues as a means of contacting her. Denise knew that she was on a perilous assignment, for any man who would taunt his tracker was playing a potentially lethal game . . . for both of them.

Two

The county housed the coroner's office in a building two blocks from the police precinct. Actually, official expansion of the surrounding buildings had connected the structure to the precinct but had not provided access from one building to the other or from any of the interconnecting ones. Denise had to walk two blocks north and then another two blocks east before she could enter the coroner's office.

Usually, Denise would have walked briskly to the coroner's office. However, she strolled this time. She needed the time to digest the little she already knew about the case and to try to figure out the killer's reason for making contact with her, especially through a charm bracelet. In her career, she had received poorly typed, cryptic messages from thieves and amateurishly clipped and pasted magazine letters forming messages from rapists. However, never had she received jewelry from any of them.

Denise contemplated all the possible reasons behind the charms. They might represent places in which the murderer intended to commit crimes or places in which he had already left undiscovered evidence for the current one. They could signal potential victims or ones not yet discovered. They might even be red herrings to throw her off his track. Reaching the door to the coroner's office, she decided that she would have to wait and see.

The coroner barely looked up as Denise tapped on his office door. Papers were strewn everywhere, protruding from folders in open file cabinet drawers, overflowing his desk, and lying stacked in corners and the only other chair in the office. She could hardly enter without stepping on a photograph, a memo, or a hastily handwritten note.

"Dr. Bird," Denise began when the knock produced no response. "May I have a few minutes of your time? It's very important to this case."

Removing his cracked glasses from his weary, bloodshot eyes, Dr. Bird replied, "If you must, but I'm up to my neck in work. In this business, everything's always very important. Nothing can wait. The deceased aren't going anywhere, neither is the evidence in their corpses. No one can ever wait for anything. I've never worked on anything that isn't very important, vital, and necessary to have at this moment and not a second later. What is it you want, Detective Dory?"

Standing on the only clear spot she could find, Denise responded, "I've come to ask you about the Worldly murder. It's high profile, and I thought you might have finished the autopsy. I need motive, method, anything."

Shaking his head and hunting through the mess on his desk, Dr. Bird commented, "Yeah, I understand the chief is all over this one. I hate high-profile cases. The higher the profile, the more mess the brass makes for me. The constant phone calls keep me from doing my job. Yes, I've finished the autopsy, and, no, it won't help you."

Looking quite confused at the atypical tirade, Denise said, "Why won't it help?"

Flipping the pages of the typed report, Dr. Bird stated, "The autopsy uncovered nothing that the initial pathology data had not already produced. Mr. Worldly died of fever and convulsions produced by an unknown and possible biological cause. He had consumed a hearty meal prior to encountering the killer. We don't believe that anything in the food contributed to his death. However, he showed signs of hardening of the arteries and excessive fat around his heart that would have been his downfall eventually. For an overweight sixty-year-old whose lifestyle was obviously very sedentary, he was in typical condition. No sign of blunt force trauma or struggle exists on the corpse. He probably contracted a virus on one of his trips abroad, plain and simple. His passport showed that he had just returned from South Africa, Malaysia, and Brazil. Perhaps he contracted something there. At any rate, I don't have anything to suggest that someone killed him except the chief's determination that this is a murder case. Find me something and I'll check into the possibilities. I'm stumped."

"Oh, was the only response that Denise could utter.

Relaxing a bit, Dr. Bird continued, "I told you, Detective. Nothing. Now if only the brass would believe me and leave me alone, I could finish some of these other cases so that I wouldn't have to work late tonight as usual. Anything else I can do for you?"

Holding her unopened sketchpad to her chest, Denise replied, "I'd like to see the corpse, if you don't mind. Thanks for the help."

"Sure," Dr. Bird said as he returned to his work. "You know the drill. See Tommy at the door. He'll help you."

Tommy Grimes was Dr. Bird's pale, bent assistant. Whenever Denise saw him, she thought of the sidekicks in the old horror flicks. Tommy looked as if the sun and fresh air never touched his skin, and he had the dull personality to match.

Tommy raised rheumy eyes to meet Denise's face. His lips slowly spread into his version of a smile. He rose and, without speaking, collected the key to the vault in which Mr. Worldly's corpse lay. Leading her into the cool autopsy storage area, he wordlessly unlocked the vault, pulled out the shelf, and stepped back. He turned his attention to other matters in the room while she worked.

Denise took a deep breath, stepped closer, and lifted the sheet. She hated looking at corpses but knew that they sometimes told an interesting and valuable story. This one, however, did not.

Mr. Worldly had been a heavyset man of too little exercise. Although of average height, his bulk made him seem shorter.

His hair had once been a deep brown, now heavily mixed with color-enhanced gray that sparkled under the glaring lights. His nails were freshly manicured and his hands meaty and soft, showing no sign of manual labor. His skin showed signs of a recent trip to the islands rather than time spent under a sunlamp, resulting in a slight leathering of the forehead and nose from a light burn. There was no bluing around the mouth that usually suggested poisoning. As Dr. Bird had said, the corpse told no tales.

As Denise quickly sketched the face and hands, she noticed the depression left by his rings. She would ask Tommy about the deceased's possessions as soon as she finished her drawing. The chunky right wrist carried a suntan line from a thick bracelet and the left from watch and perhaps another bracelet. Upon closer examination, Denise saw that the neck and chest also contained suntan marks from jewelry, perhaps a chain with a pendant. His ears, however, had also been pierced and showed signs of a fairly large earring. Mr. Worldly certainly liked his trinkets.

Closing her sketchbook, Denise turned to Tommy and asked, "I'd like to see Mr. Worldly's personal belongings, please."

Grunting his concurrence, Tommy led Denise to the safe in which the coroner kept the victim's belongings until the police released them to the family. Extracting the bag marked "Worldly," he stepped to a small table and pulled out the contents. Again, without speaking, he moved aside so that Denise could have a closer look.

Lifting the well-tailored, summer-weight wool trousers, Denise saw that Mr. Worldly had indeed been a large man. The charcoal-gray pants had to have been fifty inches in the waist and thirty-four in the inseam. The fabric was incredibly soft, appearing to contain not only wool but a touch of silk as well. The size of a small sail, the light blue silk shirt had been ruined by being ripped off Mr. Worldly's body during his convulsions. Enormous sweat stains further discolored the delicate fabric.

The shoes were a size thirteen, heavy, and barely worn. The heels showed no sign of roll over and the soles had hardly been scuffed. Denise sniffed them to find that Mr. Worldly either did not have smelly feet or had just purchased the shoes or a combination of the two. The black silk socks were equally as fresh. Knowing that he had been killed in the evening, Denise wondered if he had just showered, perhaps for a quiet night at home.

Denise continued to sketch the belongings and make notes around the edges of the questions that she would ask his widow. Already, she was fascinated about the evening plans that might have caused Mr. Worldly to dress in freshly pressed clothing of exceptional quality. She wondered if, perhaps, he had planned to play cards with friends, watch the television with his wife, join colleagues for drinks at the club, or simply relax in style at home.

The plastic bag containing the contents of his pockets showed that Mr. Worldly had been carrying neither a driver's license nor loose change. He had been wearing a Presidential Rolex with diamond bezel and two 18k gold bracelets, one of Greek key design and the other a panther. She assumed that the panther had been the watch's partner on the left arm, which would explain the thin suntan line with the larger watch imprint. Around his neck, he had worn a twenty-four-inch snake length chain on which hung a Roman coin encircled by twenty white diamonds. Continuing to examine the contents of the baggie, Denise discovered a large white diamond earring of at least a karat; a thick, plain gold wedding band; a gold signet pinkie ring; and a diamond ring with a blinding center stone. Mr. Worldly had been a walking display case for his jewelry business.

Finishing her sketches, Denise returned the contents to the larger bag that Tommy locked in the safe. Following him to the front desk, she thanked him for his help and left. As usual, he had not spoken a single word during her time with him.

Breathing deeply the fresh air, Denise felt relieved to be outside again. Although well- lighted, the coroner's suite smelled of chemicals, blood, and death. She was glad of a gentle breeze that rustled her short hair and clothing, removing the lingering smells.

By the time Denise returned to the squad room, most of the detectives had left either on cases or for lunch. Tom still sat at his desk with Molly staring lovingly and pleadingly into his face. The dog was either hungry or in need of a walk.

As Denise advanced, Tom stood and announced, "It's about time you got back. We're hungry."

"We? We're going to lunch with a dog? I thought we had this discussion last week," Denise replied as she laid down her things.

Slipping into his suit jacket and picking up Molly's leash, Tom stated as he started toward the exit, "You know I can't leave her here unattended. Besides, the project dictates that I take her with me everywhere. I've made arrangements for us to have a table at the back of Luigi's. No one will know she's there."

Rolling her eyes and charging after the fleeing pair, Denise muttered under her breath, "Whatever, but I'll know."

Settling into a table at the back of the restaurant near the kitchen, Denise perused the menu. She was irritated by having the now content dog sleeping on the floor between them and by the usual sprint to keep up with Tom. Regardless of the number of times that she had complained about both, they were always a speedy threesome.

After placing her order for linguine with clams, Denise shared the information she had gained with Tom. He listened so attentively that she almost forgot to be annoyed at having to share her lunch break with a dog. She was almost glad they'd gotten the table near the kitchen because no one could eavesdrop on their conversation. Until she apprehended the criminal, she could not be too careful; he could be anyone.

They ate as the dog slumbered. Occasionally, Tom would offer a suggestion or ask a question for clarification, but mostly they ate in silence. Denise loved the quiet time. Never in any relationship had she felt so comfortable in saying nothing. With Tom, she could sit and think without worrying that he would misunderstand her silences.

By the time they had finished their salads, Denise had the rudiments of a plan. Following her afternoon appointment with Mr. Worldly's widow, she would board the train for New York. The jeweler who sold the murderer the bracelet might be able to provide her with a sketch of the man.

Digging into her linguine, Denise asked, "Do you think the wife of a man that rich and famous would know all of his little secrets? I wonder if Mr. Worldly kept information from her."

Looking under his eyebrows, Tom commented, "He'd have been a fool if he didn't."

"What?" Denise asked with her fork paused in midair.

"No man should tell his wife everything," Tom stated flatly. "He should keep a little something to himself."

"You're joking, right?"

"No," Tom replied. "I wouldn't tell you everything if we were married. Some of this stuff is my personal business."

Bristling, Denise retorted, "Well, you don't have to worry about keeping anything from me. You're the last man I'd consider marrying. Great partner but too moody for a permanent relationship. And secretive too? No way."

Looking peeved that Denise had put down his offhand reference to marriage, Tom said, "You just don't understand. A man needs his space. A wife doesn't need to know everything."

Easing the linguine and clams onto her fork with a crust of bread, Denise postulated, "And a woman doesn't need her space, I suppose. A woman has to tell her mate everything, have no secrets, and be an open book that he and the myriad of kids can read without any trouble."

Looking at the ceiling helplessly, Tom tried to defend himself by saying, "If a woman wants her man to protect and defend her, then she needs to be open and above board so that he'll know what he's getting into. I'm not saying that she can't have private thoughts. I'm saying that her life needs to be more . . . open."

Pushing aside her half-eaten meal, Denise replied stiffly, "I don't know any women who want to be protected and defended. All of my female friends and colleagues do a pretty good job of taking care of themselves, thank you. However, if such women exist today, then, while taking care of the kids and doing the housework not to mention being barefoot and pregnant in the kitchen, I still maintain that they're entitled to have thoughts and dreams that they don't share with their hunter-gatherer mates. They would go mad if they couldn't dream of something beyond dirty diapers and carpools."

Realizing that he had stepped into a sensitive arena, Tom tried to extricate his foot from his mouth by saying, "Maybe I misspoke. I would never deny my wife the right to dream, but I'd need to understand her thoughts if I'm to do my job as husband. I can't be a good partner to someone I don't understand. It's like with us. I understand you and can anticipate your moves when we're in a tight situation. I need the same from a wife, that's all."

"Women expect the same simpatico existence from a husband," Denise added.

"Exactly."

Waving off the dessert menu and picking up the check, Denise replied, "Good save."

As they walked from the restaurant, Tom breathed deeply. Even breathing the carbon monoxide–laden air at lunchtime was preferable to getting into an argument with Denise. He had learned that religion, politics, and women's rights were three issues not to touch with her. Momentarily, he had forgotten, and she had almost handed him his head.

Leaving her in the parking lot as he returned to the squad room, Tom thought about their heated discussion. Her ability to hold her own against anyone was what made Denise an ideal partner. She was hesitant about nothing and afraid of no one. Watching her drive away, he wondered if that confidence would interfere in their love life if he managed to do more than strike the flint.

Denise was thinking, too, about their luncheon conversation as she drove to Mrs. Worldly's house in Potomac. She knew that Tom had a strong chauvinistic streak, as did many of the men on the force, but they had never discussed his feelings on women's rights. She knew that he respected her as a competent equal partner, but she wondered if he would expect her to walk three paces behind him if their relationship developed.

Their relationship had taken a new direction while they worked together on the Capitol Hill case. They had found that they did not like being apart and that they functioned at their peak when they could work together. They had also discovered that the affection they held for one another was based on more than simply their professional relationship. However, their budding romance needed a lot of work and attention.

Driving down the tree-lined streets, Denise reflected on the first time they had kissed and their first romantic evening. Tom was as attentive as a lover as he was as a partner. She only hoped that their personal involvement would develop the strength of their professional one. However, time alone would tell.

Time. . . . Denise wondered if Mr. Worldly had known that he would meet his maker. Although his body had not shown any sign of struggle, she wondered if the murderer had warned him of the imminent attack or if he had suspected that his end was near. Because this killer liked to signal his intentions, Denise speculated about the type of warning he might have given Mr. Worldly.

The Worldly house rose from the midst of the Potomac rolling horse country. It was one of the older, more expansive homes on a massive lot that offered a ten-stall barn, paddock, and grazing area. The white house itself with its stately columns and flawlessly maintained grounds was reminiscent of the old estates of the antebellum period. Having stopped only briefly to search for information in the library, Denise arrived in record time.

From the brick walk as she peeked through the front windows, Denise could see the sparkling chandelier hanging in the dining room with the massive mahogany table, gleaming silver candelabra, and the twelve upholstered high-backed chairs. To the right stood the sideboard, heavy with a huge six-piece silver tea service and the china cabinet laden with china and crystal. Tall plants broke the monotony of the corners and added color and texture to the room. The living room was equally impressive with oriental rugs, heavy furniture, intricate tapestry upholstery, and decorative wall sconces. Antique bureaus, candlesticks, and wing chairs flanked the side window and immense hearth. Vases worth more than her annual salary held flowers that trailed greenery amidst the brilliant blooms.

The front door opened on the first ring, and Denise stepped into the room-sized marble foyer. The round table in the circular expanse held a gigantic vase of flowers of every description. She did not doubt that the silently waiting butler or a maid changed them daily.

After showing her shield and announcing the intent of her visit, Denise waited in the living room as the butler vanished into the depths of the house. She sniffed appreciatively of the myriad of blooms and gazed at the original artwork before settling into the luxurious sofa that was so deep her feet barely touched the floor. The people who lived in this house definitely never ate from paper plates or the Chinese food container.

Denise did not have to wait long, although she would not have minded because the classical music playing softly in the background was a delightful treat. Ester Worldly soon appeared, dressed in a black silk shirt, slacks, and pumps. A single strand of pearls adorned her neck and a matching pearl shone its luminescence in each ear. She was about forty-five with stylishly long hair held from her face by a black velvet

headband. Her manicurist had applied a very pale shade of
pink to her medium-length nails.

"Detective Dory," she said extending her very soft hand
in a surprisingly strong handshake.

Sinking again into the sofa in response to the widow's
gesture, Denise said, "Mrs. Worldly, thank you for seeing
me. I won't take much of your time. I just need to ask a few
questions."

"Your chief called to say that you'd come by. I'll do anything I can to help, Detective," Mrs. Worldly offered. "What
would you like to know about my husband?"

Opening her sketchpad, Denise asked, "I suppose my first
few questions will be rather obvious. May I sketch as we
talk? Instead of using a tape recorder, I draw. Do you know
anyone who would have wanted to kill your husband? Did
he have any enemies?"

Shaking her head, Mrs. Worldly replied, "Feel free to
sketch. As to enemies, none come to mind. As with any person of influence, my husband was not necessarily everyone's
favorite. However, I can't think of anyone who could have
disliked his politics enough to kill him. My husband was
conservative but fair and just."

Looking for any sign of sorrow in the woman's composed
and well made-up face, Denise continued, "With the stock
market in almost constant turmoil, might he have suffered
any unusual bad debt that might have thrown him into un-
savory company?"

"No," Mrs. Worldly answered without hesitation. "His
portfolio has taken a hit of late but nothing from which it
would not have rebounded. The stores are doing so well, even
in this troublesome economy, that my husband was planning
another store. As a matter of fact, the Paris shop will open in
a few weeks with me cutting the ribbon in his place."

Hoping to get a reaction from Ester Worldly, Denise commented, "No enemies, no financial trouble, then who killed
your husband? Friends don't murder each other."

Mrs. Worldly moved almost imperceptibly to the question.

However, Denise observed the slight tightening of the skin on her cheekbones and the flinch of the fingers on the widow's left hand. Denise wondered if Mrs. Worldly were shocked by the question or hiding something.

"I don't know what you could mean, Detective," the widow Worldly responded firmly.

"Let me be direct," Denise replied with equal resolve. "Were either you or your husband engaged in extramarital affairs? There's an age difference; these things happen."

Sitting even straighter, Ester Worldly replied, "I loved my husband. Nothing and no one could turn my affections from him. He was a good provider and a pillar of the community. We enjoyed a very close, loving relationship."

Watching for the next reaction, Denise asked, "I understand you've been married for twenty years. Do you have any children?"

Gazing from lids that had narrowed slightly, Mrs. Worldly responded, "No, my husband has grown children from a previous marriage. I was very involved in my work when we first married and didn't think that I could give a child the time it needs."

"How do your step children feel about you? Don't you inherit the business, house, and interests in the race horses now that Mr. Worldly has been murdered?"

Bristling even more, Mrs. Worldly stated coldly, "Those questions are too insulting and coarse to merit response. I think this session has ended."

Rising, Mrs. Worldly stepped away from the sofa and glared down at Denise. Slowly gathering her things, Denise commented, "I seem to have struck a nerve. I am sorry. It's just that I stopped at the library on my way here. According to the microfiche, considerable tension exists between you and the deceased's children. As a matter of fact, last year when their father was ill with cancer, they tried to convince him to change his will in their favor. It seems that they weren't too happy at not being left the house and other holdings."

Mrs. Worldly turned on her three-inch heels and stormed

from the room. At the door, she muttered, "John will show you out."

Almost immediately, the butler appeared to help Denise carry her sketchbook to the car. As he held the door for her, Denise could see the angry face of Mrs. Worldly scowling at her from the upstairs bedroom window. She had definitely struck a nerve.

By the time Denise returned to the squad room, most of the detectives had left for the day. Tom, however, sat hunched over his desk, almost as if he hadn't moved. Even Molly appeared frustrated at waiting, for she paced the area between Tom's desk and the exit to the parking lot.

"Why are you still here?" Denise asked as she tossed her sketchbook onto the desk.

"Waiting for you and putting the finishing touches on this report," Tom mumbled as he looked up from the greatly diminished stack of papers.

"That's nice," Denise commented warmly as she smiled into his eyes.

Moving quickly from what he called "the mushy love stuff," Tom asked, "Learn anything from the widow?"

"You mean the ugly stepmother?" Denise began with a chuckle at his discomfort. "There's considerable turmoil within that little family. It sounds as if the grown children aren't too thrilled with the idea that mommy dearest will receive all of the money. She didn't come out and say it, but her face certainly tightened at the mention of it."

Laughing, Tom replied, "A society scandal! You've certainly landed a live one. Not only was the man famous as a jeweler and renowned for his philanthropic and political activities, he has a sweet young widow."

"She's probably forty-five, but I'd guess that at seventy Mr. Worldly has children almost her age," Denise replied chuckling.

"Remind me not to remarry," Tom commented as he closed the last folder and collected his keys.

Slipping her purse strap over her shoulder, Denise retorted,

"Remarry? In case you've missed it, you have to marry before you can remarry."

"That's a technicality," Tom replied as he started toward the door with the overjoyed Molly trotting beside him.

"Fairly important one, I'd say." Denise laughed as she struggled to keep up.

Turning abruptly and almost charging into the advancing Denise, Tom quickly returned to his desk. Opening the top drawer, he said, "I forgot to give this to you. Another present?"

Walking slowly toward him, Denise replied, "No . . . another clue."

Denise quickly stripped the brown paper from the small square box to reveal the familiar white paper with thin gold lines. Looking from Tom to the box, she ran her finger under the tape and slowly discarded the paper. Resting the red velvet box in the palm of her hand, Denise paused for a minute to collect her thoughts.

"We know it's not another bracelet," Denise commented quietly.

Watching her intently, Tom stated, "You're right; it's not. You can open it. It won't explode. We X-rayed it when it first arrived."

"So you already know what it is?" Denise asked without opening the top.

"I know that it's not an explosive. Ronda described the shape. Open the box, Dory," Tom insisted, growing impatient to go home.

"Don't rush me. It's not every day that a woman receives gifts from an admirer," Denise stated tongue-in-cheek as she stared at the box with the name Charming Charms embossed on the top.

"A murderer you mean. Open the box," Tom snarled impatiently.

The silence in the squad room was thick and dense. Denise could hear the old clock ticking on the wall. Even Molly sat without moving her usually lively tail. The entire room appeared to be waiting to see the contents of the box.

Turning slightly away from Tom and aiming the top away from her face, Denise carefully opened the lid. Although the box had been checked, she did not wish to take any chances. The overhead lights glinted brightly off the gold surface as she turned the box toward her.

"It's a charm," Denise announced.

"Of what?"

Holding the gold charm by its *O*-ring, Denise gazed at the intricacy of the craftsmanship. Although she knew that it was not an original design, she could tell that the artist had spent considerable time crafting the details of the tiny replica of the Empire State Building. Denise could almost see the visitors on the observation floors.

Showing Tom the charm, Denise stated, "I had already planned to go to NYC to interview the jeweler who sold the murderer the bracelet. Now I see I'll have to ask Charming Charms about this little number. Our killer's crafty . . . buying the items from different jewelers."

Tom turned the delicate replica of the Art Deco skyscraper in his hand. It looked even smaller nestled against his massive palm. The artist had captured the massive height, television antenna mast, and carvings of the original.

"Where's the bracelet?" Tom asked as he moved toward Denise's desk.

"Top drawer, right. Why?"

"I think you should wear it," Tom replied as he fastened the little charm onto the link.

"I will not; it's evidence!" Denise objected. "We might need it in the case, and I don't want to lose it. This isn't a token of the murderer's affection. He's tempting me to follow him to New York."

Running her finger over the satin fabric of the tiny box, Denise felt an almost unnoticeable ridge. Lifting it gingerly, she discovered a neatly folder piece of thin rice paper, the kind that people once used for air mail letters. Carefully opening it, she read the note printed in incredibly neat black letters.

"What's that?" Tom asked as he handed the long box that contained the bracelet back to her.

Reading slowly, Denise replied, "A note from the killer. Listen. He says that I'll find a clue to his identity under the third bench on the right of the number 15 telescope."

"When are you leaving?"

Picking up both boxes and stuffing them inside her purse, Denise said, "Tomorrow."

"Good. I'll go with you," Tom stated as he charged toward the door with his usual burst of energy.

Trotting to keep up, Denise chuckled to his retreating back. During all of their relationship, seldom had Tom walked at a leisurely pace when it was time to go home or to a meal. Now, chasing him into the parking lot, Denise wondered if she would spend their trip to New York at the same pace.

Three

Although Denise and Tom arrived in Grand Central Station at eight o'clock Saturday morning, the station hummed with activity. Food and souvenir vendors were already doing a bustling business as tourists flowed from the bowels of the station—hungry and ready to see and taste all that the Big Apple had to offer. Joining the queue that filed from the massive doors, they added their number to the teaming throng that would swell Broadway, Central Park, and Fifth Avenue.

Deciding to walk from the station to their hotel in the area of Times Square and Broadway, they strolled past restaurants selling sumptuous deli sandwiches whose fragrance made them hungry. After stopping for some take-out food, Denise and Tom chewed contently as they passed historic landscapes and commercial centers. The congestion on the sidewalks managed to reduce Tom's long strides to much more manageable ones.

Their hotel sat in the center of Times Square surrounded by some of the most famous theaters in the world. Denise could almost hear the tapping feet of *A Chorus Line* as they passed the darkened theater. She could smell the excitement of the people standing in line at the "same day" ticket stand.

"Do you like plays?" Denise asked as she eyed the crowd that waited for a reduced ticket to a major Broadway show.

"They're OK," Tom replied, sensing her motive. "I like movies better. For the money, give me a movie any time."

"But you wouldn't mind going to a play while we're here if we can get a reasonable ticket?" Denise continued as she eased toward the line.

Tom chuckled, "No, but try for a musical. No one will hear me snore over the singing and the orchestra."

"You're not going to snore," Denise retorted with a chuckle. "You couldn't possibly fall asleep at a New York play."

"That's what you think," Tom replied as he paid for the tickets for what he knew would be a nice nap.

The hotel contained a charming lobby and quaint rooms. Although recently redecorated, the style was heavily Art Deco with simple, clean lines, geometric ornamentation, chrome, and Bakelite. Everything was clean and crisp, just the style that would appeal to weary travelers on business.

Their room had two double beds. Eyeing them, Denise set her bag on the one closest to the bathroom, leaving the one with the sun streaming across it for Tom. There was plenty of space for each to have privacy.

After unpacking quickly, they decided to hit the streets. Before the crowd grew too unwieldy, they wanted to arrive at the Empire State Building. Denise was sure that the killer had left something for her amidst the columns and girders of the structure.

"Hey, cheesecake!" Tom announced as they hurried past one of the most famous restaurants in the city.

"You want to eat now?" Denise asked incredulously.

"Well, considering the way you're looking at me, I guess I'm not hungry after all," Tom replied when Denise did not seem inclined toward stopping.

"We'll grab something to eat there later. We're in a hurry remember," Denise commented as they continued to move with the traffic in the direction of the Empire State Building.

Rounding one corner after the other, they finally arrived at one of New York's most famous monuments. The Empire State Building rose 1,454 feet above them on Fifth Avenue at 34th Street. At the base of the famous skyscraper, vendors selling T-shirts were almost as prolific as the tourists that filled the lobby and waited for one of the famous elevators to lift them to the observation tower.

Joining the crowd, Denise and Tom purchased their tickets and eased into the next available elevator. As they ascended, they swallowed to relieve the popping in their ears. Although Denise could barely contain her excitement at being in the historic structure, Tom looked totally unimpressed by the famous shops that lined the entrance, the massive marble foyer, or the speed of the ascent.

"Look at that view!" Denise remarked breathlessly as they walked toward the overlook. All of Manhattan lay below them. Through the clear air, they could see the different bridges to the left and right. However, the most impressive sight was straight down.

"Looks like a toy town, doesn't it?" Tom remarked as he glanced quickly at the minuscule town below and then backed away from the railing.

"Are you afraid of heights?" Denise asked as she studied the pinched expression on his face.

"Maybe a little," Tom admitted as he stepped toward the middle of the observation deck.

Tearing herself away from the stunning vista, Denise joined him and said, "Why don't you help me find the number fifteen telescope. Remember, the clue is under a bench near it. We can enjoy the view later."

"Let's find the clue and then you can enjoy the view later," Tom rebutted crisply. "I'm heading for terra firma and a piece of that cheesecake to celebrate my survival. If God had wanted me to fly, I would have been born a bird. This is too high up for me."

Chuckling, Denise led Tom on the search for the telescope, saying, "I'm surprised at you. I've finally found your Achilles heel. You're afraid of heights."

"If you look carefully, you'll find a few more, too," Tom confessed as he plodded along beside her. For once, he was not leading the way at a gallop.

"Here's number forty, forty-six," Denise announced. "We're going the wrong way. It's around that side."

"Is this thing swaying?" Tom asked with growing anxiety sounding in his voice. "If it's swaying, I'm leaving."

Speaking absently, Denise replied, "It's your imagination. Here it is . . . number fifteen. Now let's find the bench."

"Here's the third bench, but I don't see anything," Tom commented, as he rose from his hands-and-knees position.

Pointing in the opposite direction, Denise suggested, "Let's look under the other third bench. His approach might have been different."

Tom sank to his knees again amidst curious stares from tourists. He almost looked as if he were proposing to Denise except that she, too, was gazing under the bench. Wandering away, the gawkers decided that they must have dropped something that rolled under the metal structure.

Reaching under the center support of the bench, Tom's gloved fingers found an envelope taped to the underside. Carefully breaking the seal, he pulled it forward and into view. On the front, the murderer had written only Denise's name in the same elegant black script.

Opening a plastic evidence bag, Denise said, "I think we should take this to the nearest NYPD station. Let's have them dust it for poison and fingerprints."

"Agreed," Tom replied as he gingerly placed it inside.

Easing into the crowd once again, they rode to the first floor. This time, the trip seemed slow and plodding despite the popping eardrums. Curiosity about the contents of the envelope filled Denise's imagination as much as the prospects of seeing the panoramic view of the Manhattan had on the ascent. Tom, however, could hardly wait to reach ground level.

After speaking with an officer on the corner of Fifth Avenue, they walked toward the station. They did not linger as they passed people enthralled with the spectacle of New York. They had a purpose and an envelope to inspect.

The New York Police Department office looked similar to

theirs in Maryland. The only difference appeared to be the noise level. Crowds of shouting, pushing people filled the entryway. Some of them were lost and in need of directions, others were reporting thefts or muggings, and still others were under the protection of attentive officers.

"Looks familiar, doesn't it," Denise commented loudly as they waited their turn.

"Too familiar," Tom yelled. "Makes me want to roll up my sleeves and help. They're even slower than we are at this."

"I don't think we ever see this many people in a day. It's a madhouse in here," Denise shouted as she defended the slow progress.

By the time they reached the desk sergeant, Denise had seen angry call girls, irate cabbies, and frightened teens in numbers like nothing she had ever experienced. Her precinct and most others in the suburbs of Maryland seldom saw that much volume. Even with five men working, it took twenty minutes of waiting for them to reach the front of the line.

"Next?" the desk sergeant demanded in a very tired voice.

Extending her hand and badge, Denise replied, "We're Detectives Dory and Phyfer from Montgomery County, Maryland. We're investigating a murder case that has led us to New York. We'd like to request your help in X-raying some potential evidence."

"Follow me. I'll take you to the captain," the too-lean and very tired corporal directed as he motioned toward the back of the room.

Walking behind the stooped young man, Denise and Tom entered the inner sanctum of the police precinct and found little difference between its appearance and that of their office at home. Half-empty coffee cups, discarded pieces of uniforms, and gum-wrapper-filled ashtrays were everywhere. Molly, the police dog, was the only missing element, and Denise knew that somewhere there was a canine corps.

The captain, also haggard and tired, advanced toward them with an extended hand. Smiling broadly, he greeted them saying, "I understand you're from Maryland. Welcome to NYPD 415. What can I do for you?"

Clasping his hand, Denise replied, "We're investigating a murder of a jeweler in Maryland. The killer has started sending me clues to his identity through jewelry and now a note that we found under a bench at the Empire State Building. Before I open the note, I'd like to have it dusted for prints and poison, if possible."

"Gladly," the captain responded extending his hand again. "Why don't you give it to me, and I'll have one of my people take care of it for you. Rest yourselves in my office while you wait."

Denise quickly extracted the evidence bag from her purse and handed it to him. With a nod and a motion toward the coffee machine, the captain vanished into the squad room. Before he was completely out of sight, Tom had a cup of the thick brew in his hand.

"Is it as good as yours?" Denise asked as they sat on the sofa together and waited.

"Almost," Tom mumbled between sips. "They know how to make a decent cup of coffee. If I only had a piece of that cheesecake, I'd be set."

The captain returned in a few minutes with the report. Handing the bag to Denise, he stated, "Your killer is a very careful man. He wore gloves and dusted the envelope to prevent our finding anything. It's clean . . . no traces of anything toxic and no prints. I only saw a small metal object inside."

Carefully opening the envelope, Denise read aloud the cryptic note saying, "You'll find me hanging around the necks of the rich and famous as well as the ordinary folk. The glory of my flowers welcomes all visitors. You'll find your next clue at the site of a watery grave."

As the others puzzled over the message, Denise again tipped the envelope. Into her palm tumbled a tiny wrapped package. Opening the white and gold tissue paper, she uncovered a miniature gold lei. The detailing was so intricate that she could almost smell the fragrance of the orchids and hear the sound of the waves on the Hawaiian shore.

"What's that? A charm? Your murderer sends you charms?" the captain asked incredulously as he inspected the lei.

With a slight chuckle, Denise replied, "He claims that I'll be able to uncover his identity if I follow the clues, but, so far, he has only brought me to New York. Although it looks as if I'm going to Hawaii next. He's certainly adding interesting charms to the bracelet. I might get to travel a bit on this case."

Shaking his head, Tom commented, "Hawaii's a big place. This is like looking for a needle in a haystack. This man is probably laughing up his sleeve right now."

"Maybe, but you're getting nice trips out of it," the captain remarked as he returned the lei to Denise. "I hope your captain's budget can support this man's idea of fun. While you're here, let me know if I can be of any assistance."

Smiling Denise replied, "Thanks, but after I interview the jewelers from whom he bought the bracelet and Empire State Building charms, I should be about ready to go home. I'm sure I'll have to prove to my captain that I need to go to Hawaii."

"You certainly would if you were my detective," the captain commented as he returned to his office.

As Tom added the newest charm to the bracelet, he asked, "Are you really planning to go to Hawaii to follow this guy's clues? This nut might lure you into a dangerous situation without proper backup. I don't like the sound of this, Dory."

"I'm not really sure what I'm doing yet, but if I have to go, I'll do it," Denise stated as she slipped the box into her bag. "A lot depends on the interviews this afternoon. Let's go. The jeweler's expecting me."

"Sounds to me like you're enjoying this attention. Just be careful," Tom advised as he lumbered along beside her. His usual speed was slowed by the crowd on the sidewalk and his growing discomfort over Denise's involvement in the case.

"You sound just like my mother. Relax," Denise commented with a quick glance at his long face.

Tom's stony silence continued until they reached the first jewelry store on Fifth Avenue and then his mood changed to disgust. He was a man of simple tastes and found the display cases overflowing with glittering diamonds, gold, and platinum more than he could take. The pompous manner of the carefully and expensively dressed sales associates also made him feel ill at ease in his inexpensive, wrinkled, off-the-rack summer suit. He was also aware that most of the patrons and all of the sales personnel were white. He felt very uncomfortable under the glare of the shimmering chandeliers and the eyes of the people in the room. He knew that everyone thought he would soon pull a gun and rob them.

While Tom sulked in a chair near the door, Denise advanced into the sweetly scented room. Although she was aware of being one of the few black women in the famous shop, she ignored the stares of the richly dressed matrons and proceeded with her plan to uncover the identity of the killer.

"May I help you?" a sales associate behind an expansive counter of exquisite diamond bracelets asked condescendingly as she assessed Denise's slightly wrinkled blue linen suit, white blouse, and sensible blue pumps.

"Mr. Burrow, the manager, is expecting me. Kindly tell him that Detective Dory is here," Denise replied without glancing at the sparkling trinkets.

With a raised eyebrow as the only response, the sales associate dialed a two-digit number. She spoke her message softly and hung up. Dismissing Denise as a waste of valuable sales time, the woman walked to the other side of the counter.

Almost immediately, a short, plump gentleman dressed in a black-on-black suit appeared. As he approached Denise smiling, he seemed the only personable employee of the renowned establishment. He extended his hand in welcome as he faced her.

"Detective, it's nice to meet you," Mr. Burrow beamed.

"I've pulled together all of the information you requested. If you'll follow me to my office, I'll give you a copy of everything I have."

"Thank you, Mr. Burrow. I'll get my partner and follow you," Denise replied as she motioned toward Tom.

Shaking his head, Tom indicated that he intended to remain in the chair. He had found a current copy of a sports magazine and was reading, or pretending to read, the lengthy baseball article. Denise could tell from the stubborn set of his jaw that he had no intention of venturing farther into the maze of counters with their glittering contents.

Following Mr. Burrow, Denise commented with a chuckle, "It seems that my partner is engrossed in his investigation of the baseball scores. Lead the way."

Mr. Burrow's office was small but tastefully decorated. Design awards lined the walls and flower-filled vases sat on the cherry desk and credenza. Teal leather side chairs invited guests to make themselves comfortable. Photographs of his family occupied a corner of his desk as reminders of his reason for working long hours to satisfy the needs of demanding clients.

Opening a folder on his desk, Mr. Burrow said, "When you phoned, you requested information on the purchaser of a certain bracelet. Unfortunately, I won't be able to help you. We always ask our clients to fill out an address card so that we might send them informational flyers from time to time. However, for this sale, I don't have one. It's not unusual on a cash sale for the buyer to decline, especially if the person is from out of town. Many of our clients are out-of-towners who purchase an item as a memento of their trip to New York."

"Do you think the sales associate would be able to provide me with a sketch of the purchaser?" Denise asked. She was not surprised that the murderer would have preferred to keep his mailing address a secret.

Shaking his head in the negative, Mr. Burrow replied, "I've already asked him, Detective, and he can't be positive about it. You see, we were having a sale that week and were very busy. Considering the foot traffic we had through here, I doubt that he'd remember seeing his own mother. We were just that swamped."

Unwilling to give up, Denise said, "I'd like to speak with him, if that's possible. Maybe he'd remember enough to get me started. I'm visiting another jeweler after I leave you. Perhaps the combined effort will produce a viable sketch."

Rising, Mr. Burrow stated reluctantly, "I'll send Michael Altec to you immediately. Feel free to use my office as long as you'd like."

Alone for a few minutes, Denise thought about the little she knew of the murderer's activities. He had killed a well-known DC-area jeweler and arranged for his apprehension by sending her clues. So far, she had a gold charm bracelet with two unrelated charms that directed her to cities other than DC in which she had yet to learn anything. At this rate, the case would take an eternity to solve.

Michael Altec knocked softly and entered the office, ending Denise's moment of reverie. Taking a seat beside her, the thin older gentleman with graying hair waited patiently for her to begin her questioning. His long fingers interlaced and lay quietly in his navy blue pants-clad lap. He watched with only the slightest curiosity as Denise extracted her sketchbook and pencil.

Flipping to a blank page, Denise said, "Thanks for your time, Mr. Altec. I'd like to ask you a few questions and, hopefully, sketch what you remember of the person who purchased the bracelet."

Clearing his throat, Mr. Altec replied, "I'm only too happy to help, but I'm afraid that I won't be of much assistance to you. It was an incredibly busy day, and I really can't remember the client."

"Perhaps as I ask questions, something will come to you," Denise advised as she studied his tranquil face.

"OK, ask away."

Smiling, Denise asked, "Do you remember the man's height?"

"Average. None of my clients was especially tall or short that day, if I remember correctly," Mr. Altec replied with a look of concentration on his face.

"Age?"

"Average. For this store, that's mid-forties and upward. Definitely not a young person. Young people stand out . . . tourists mostly," Mr. Altec commented absently as he remembered back to that date.

"You don't think he was a tourist?" Denise inquired as she continued to sketch.

Concentrating to hear the man's voice in his memory, Mr. Altec replied, "It's hard to say, but he seemed comfortable in the store. Some people wander, but I remember that he knew where to find the bracelets and charms without any trouble. His accent was not New York . . . more southern but not thick. A soft, slurred southern as if he had lived somewhere else for a while and lost some of it."

"Do you remember the pitch of it? High, deep?" Denise inquired as she jotted notes in the corner of the sketchpad.

"It was high for a man but not womanly. I'd say definitely a tenor voice," Mr. Altec responded, squinting at the memory.

"Can you describe his clothing?" Denise asked as she watched Mr. Altec's face.

"Not really," Mr. Altec replied with a shake of his head. "He didn't wear anything unusual. It's only the tourists who come here in jeans or shorts and T-shirts with funny sayings printed on them. Most other clients are business people, wearing conservative suits and carrying briefcases.

"Mr. Burrow said he paid by cash. Large bills?"

"Not so that I'd be suspicious of their being counterfeit," Mr. Altec stated. "We're always on the look out for counterfeit large denominations. No, he did nothing to arouse suspicion. That's why I can't remember him. He was an ordinary client."

"Did you see anything unusual on his face or hands?" Denise inquired.

"No, nothing," Mr. Altec concluded. "I don't remember

earrings or tattoos. No extreme jewelry. Nothing excessive. He was very ordinary. He blended in with the sales associates and the other clients. I doubt that I'd recognize him if he walked into the store again. Sorry, but that's all I know."

Closing her sketchpad, Denise replied with a big smile, "You've been most helpful. Thanks for your time."

Stopping at the door, Mr. Altec turned and said, "I do remember one thing, however. He walked with a limp, almost dragged his right leg. I hope that helps."

"Thanks. It might come in very handy. If you remember anything else, Mr. Burrow has my card," Denise replied as she followed him from the room and closed the door.

"Well? Was Mr. Altec able to help?" Mr. Burrow asked as he met her in the hall that separated his office from the display floor.

"A little bit. You said it was a busy day," Denise commented as she opened her purse. "I'll leave a few of my cards with you in case anyone remembers anything about that day and client. I'm staying at this hotel if you need to contact me this weekend."

"Very well," Mr. Burrow said as he accepted the cards. "Good luck with your investigation."

Denise smiled her thanks as she slowly turned and walked into the display area. The sparkling jewels seemed to beckon to her as she hurried toward Tom. They still needed to visit the second jeweler before the shops closed for the day.

Closing the magazine, Tom stood and greeted her. "Well?"

"I'll tell you everything I know while we're walking to the next shop," Denise stated as she lightly placed her hand in his and pulled him through the shop's wide doors.

Leaving the gentle music and the perfumed air of the shop behind them, Denise and Tom faded into the sweaty throng for a quick walk to the next shop, located in the garment district. Tom complained loudly about his feet and sulked when Denise would not agree to taking a taxi, claiming that they could make better time than the driver in the almost-

stalled afternoon traffic. He was not impressed by either the
information Denise shared with him or her logic as he pushed
through the thick crowd of Saturday shoppers.

"I'm hungry," Tom whined as they passed yet another
street vendor.

"Later," Denise stated firmly as she pulled him away and
prodded him to continue their journey.

"Isn't there a law against working people without feeding
them?" Tom quipped as they came to a stop in front of the
next shop.

"That law relates to employers. I'm your partner not your
boss," Denise rebutted in a snippy voice.

"Could have fooled me," Tom complained as they
mounted the filthy staircase to the second-floor shop.

"Whatever," Denise stated over her shoulder.

Shaking his head, Tom knew not to argue with Denise
when she was in one of her moods. She was all business and
not in the least interested in being playful. He knew that she
wanted to tie up all the New York pieces of the puzzle before
the play that night. Tomorrow, they would leave for home
with or without the information they needed.

Four

Pushing open the door that read in faded gold letters CHARMING CHARMS . . . LARGEST WHOLESALER OF CHARMS AND PENDANTS, Denise and Tom entered a shop not at all like the one on Fifth Avenue near Central Park. No soft music played in the background. No perfume greeted them at the door. No chandeliers twinkled in synch with the glistening diamonds. Instead, they found a massive box-lined room in which the smell of unwashed bodies permeated the air. A radio somewhere in the clutter played oldies-but-goodies at an earsplitting volume that caused the crowd of shoppers to shout above it. The sales clerks wore faded T-shirts and torn jeans. They chewed gum and munched partially eaten sandwiches that they laid on the filthy counter between bites. They wrote sales receipts on pads of paper rather than keying them into a computer. One man, who Denise later learned was the shopowner, chained-smoked smelly thin cigars and wiped his constantly dripping nose on the back of his hand.

Looking at Tom skeptically, Denise walked toward the counter. Before she could relate her business, a brusque young man stated, "Take a number."

"But I'm here to—"

Cutting off her response, he restated in slow New York–accented tones as if speaking to a recalcitrant child, "Take a number."

Deciding to follow his instructions, Denise stepped over a large wad of bubble gum on the tattered carpet and took a number. The officious young man shook his head and looked at Denise as if she had violated a cardinal law. When the eyes of the other shoppers followed his gaze, Denise stepped back to the safety of Tom's size and scowling face.

"This is a dump," Tom stated in a less than quiet voice.

"Hush, someone will hear you!" Denise ordered quickly, fearing that someone would try to eject them from the store.

"Not hardly," Tom objected without lowering his voice. "I'm having trouble hearing myself. Your murderer certainly gets around. From riches to rags."

"I bet you can get some great bargains at a store like this," Denise commented as she tiptoed to speak into Tom's ear. "If the sign on the door is correct, the killer would have been able to find every kind of charm imaginable here."

"That's not all you can get in here," Tom replied and was on the verge of saying more when the clerk shouted Denise's number.

Stepping forward again and holding out her slip of paper, Denise asked for Mr. Parker. The rude sales clerk looked her over from top to bottom, snatched the paper from her fingers, and then pointed to the man with the smelly cigar. Without notifying the man, the clerk called the next number and left Denise to fend for herself. She was not on Fifth Avenue anymore.

Deciding that the only way to have any success in the crowded, smelly store was to use her muscle, Denise pushed her way toward the man with the stinky, smoldering cigar. As the others glared over their shoulders at her, she reached into her pocket and extracted her shield. Seeing it, they stepped aside, not wanting to become involved in police action.

Not waiting for him to speak first, Denise stated loudly, "Mr. Parker, I'm Detective Dory. I phoned yesterday for an appointment to see you."

"Yeah, I remember. Falla me," the gruff older man replied, waving toward the back of the dirty shop.

Denise looked at Tom, who shook his head and followed

silently. Stepping over boxes dusty with neglect, they picked their way toward a door in the back corner. Mr. Parker unlocked the door with a key that hung from a filthy green spiral coil on his wrinkled wrist, and as he pushed the door open and flicked on the bug-splattered florescent light, hot air rushed into their faces.

Puffing on his cigar, Mr. Parker pushed a stack of papers from each chair, indicated with a grunt that Denise and Tom should sit, and turned on the air conditioner. Rather than providing relief from the oppressive heat, however, the struggling old unit produced a steady cloud of smoke that swirled over their heads and mixed with the cigar smell. Denise coughed none too delicately in the hopes that Mr. Parker would extinguish his stogy, but he paid no attention to her discomfort.

Realizing the futility of evoking civil consideration from Mr. Parker, Denise decided to plunge into the business that had brought her to his shop. The sooner she ended the interview with the greasy man, the quicker she and Tom could leave. After spending time in the cramped, dirty, foul-smelling office, New York City's smog would smell delicious.

"Mr. Parker," Denise began, "as I mentioned on the phone, my partner and I are investigating a murder of a jeweler in the DC area. The killer has sent me a gold bracelet from a renowned New York jeweler and a charm of the Empire State Building from your shop. Further, I've just received another charm, and although the box came without a label, I suspect the charm also came from here. I'm hoping that you will be able to identify the man who made the purchase."

"Let me see 'em," Mr. Parker demanded, sticking out his hand. Dirt caked the nails and ash fell from the cigar as he took the charms into his hand.

Turning the tiny gold pieces over in his grubby hand, he studied them closely for a few minutes. His dirty, ragged nails traced the delicate inscription on each one. Clouds of foul smoke circled his head and often obscured his face from Denise's view. Beads of sweat collected on his bald head as he flipped though the pages of his sales booklets. Without speaking, he returned the charms to Denise.

A lengthy silence filled the small room as Mr. Parker puffed on the last of his cigar. The long nails on his thumb and forefinger conveyed the soggy end of the cigar to his thin, almost nonexistent lips. Sitting back in the tattered, grimy black leather chair, he closed his eyes as if planning to take a nap.

Denise looked at Tom and asked with raised eyebrows if she should speak. Tom shook his head in the negative and folded his hands patiently in his lap. Shrugging her shoulders, Denise pulled out her sketchbook and quickly drew the irascible shop owner. At least her drawing would pass the time until Mr. Parker decided to speak again.

Breaking the silence in a voice too large for the small space, Mr. Parker jarred Denise and Tom from their watchfulness by saying, "Whatta ya want to know?"

"Can you identify the purchaser?" Denise asked as she finished the drawing.

"Yeah," Mr. Parker replied, "but not by name."

"I don't understand," Denise stated as she tried to decipher his code.

Finally stubbing out his cigar, Mr. Parker responded, "About a month ago, someone bought a whole bunch of 'em from me. They're high quality . . . not the stuff I usually sell to the tourist trade. He designed 'em himself; I had my goldsmith make 'em. I made another batch for my upscale customers. All of 'em are 18k gold . . . none of that 10k crap."

"Do you have the man's name?" Denise asked, growing impatient with his slow, plodding manner.

Chuckling grimly, Mr. Parker stated, "Na, I don't keep names. This ain't Bloomies, Detective. I don't send out no sales coupons. This is strictly a cash-and-carry business."

"Can you describe him?" Denise queried as she prepared to sketch.

"Na, too many people come through here in a day. I won't be able to describe you ten minutes after ya leave, and you're one of the best-looking female cops I've ever seen," Mr. Parker replied with a leer that he thought Denise would consider flattering.

"Thanks," Denise managed to reply with difficulty, aware that Tom was holding back the urge to laugh at her discomfort. "Does the sales receipt give details as to the type of charms the man purchased? Might your inventory records be of any help to us?"

Chuckling again at Denise's assumptions, Mr. Parker stated, "Pretty lady, I don't write down stuff like that. He paid $1,000 bucks for a handful of charms. I don't need to keep records for these . . . don't sell enough of 'em. When they run out, I buy more. That's my inventory system. If I was you, I'd keep 'em. They're good. . . . Sell 'em if ya don't want 'em, but don't put 'em in the police evidence file. Someone'll realize that they're good stuff and take 'em, and ya'll never see 'em again."

Rising to go, Denise thanked Mr. Parker for his time and waited for Tom to join her at the door. They had spent thirty minutes in the smelly office and learned nothing. Mr. Parker was as useless as his air conditioner.

"Hey, ya keep callin' the purchaser a 'he.' Why do ya think the person who bought them charms was a man?" Mr. Parker shouted at their backs.

Turning, Denise asked, "What makes you think that it wasn't? You said you couldn't describe him."

Joining her at the front of the store and standing much too close for Denise's comfort, Mr. Parker responded, his foul breath blowing into her face, "Detective, look around. How many men do ya see in this shop? None, zero, zip. That's the usual number of men who come in here. Them that do, well, they're usually with their wives and in a hurry to leave. I'd remember a man who bought a thousand bucks worth of charms. Hell, I would have thought he was runnin' a whore house or something and wanted gifts for his ladies."

"You're suggesting that our murderer was a woman?" Denise queried, ignoring the comment about the bordello.

"Not necessarily. I'm sayin' that the person who purchased those charms was a woman. I made that transaction, and I didn't sell 'em to no man. Maybe your killer had someone else make the deal for him. That's all I'm sayin'," Mr. Parker stated as he bit off the end of another cigar, spat the plug on the floor, twirled the business end of the cigar in the flame of a match, and puffed contentedly to light it.

"Are you sure the person wasn't a man in drag?" Denise asked as she edged closer to the outside door.

Throwing his head back and laughing so loudly that everyone in the store briefly looked in his direction, Mr. Parker stated, "Not hardly. I know when I'm lookin' at the real thing, and that babe had a chest on her. I remember doin' everything I could to keep her in the store, but, when I had filled her shopping list, she paid me and left, takin' with her the best-looking set I've seen in a long time."

Tom turned away to hide the smile that threatened to erupt into a laugh. He was aware of Denise's strong feminist bent and did not want to catch a well-placed elbow in the ribs. He knew she hated that kind of sexist reference to the female anatomy.

Standing regally, with irritation written on her face, Denise asked, "Did she take the list with her? Could you see a name on the paper?"

"Na, she took it with her," Mr. Parker replied as he wiped his drippy nose again. "Funny ya should ask about the paper. It was hotel stationery from the Ritz. Made me wonder if she was a call girl or a chippy for a rich old guy."

Barely able to hold her tongue against the sexist remarks, Denise thanked Mr. Parker by saying, "You've been most helpful. We'll let ourselves out."

Mr. Parker grunted his response and returned to the waiting customers. The circle of smoke continued to surround him as he reached for the pull chain and turned the counter to the next number. As they closed the door, Denise and Tom could hear him shout, "Next!"

The press of humanity continued to clog the sidewalks as

Denise and Tom stepped from the building. Breathing deeply of the smells of New York to clear their lungs, they retraced their steps and walked toward their hotel. Without speaking, they walked back uptown to the Ritz. If they were lucky, they might find someone who would remember the visitor with the interest in charms.

Denise and Tom arrived at the Ritz as a wedding party was departing. They heard the happy laughter of the bride and her family as they entered the stretch limousine that would carry them to the church for the late afternoon affair. The bride's gown filled the car as her father carefully folded the yards of lace around her feet.

Looking at Denise, Tom said fondly, "That'll be you one of these days."

"I'm too busy for all that stuff," Denise sniffed, with a touch of envy in her voice. "Besides, I wouldn't look good in a dress like that. It's too . . . feminine for me. I'm a shift or suit kind of woman."

Chuckling as he followed Denise past the doorman's welcoming bow, Tom said, "You'll change your mind the first time you try on one of those gowns. You're every bit as feminine as that woman, maybe more. You'll look great!"

Walking across the splendid lobby, Denise asked, "And who will marry me? I'm a tough cop, remember? Not many men can deal with me."

The lights from the massive chandeliers sparkled overhead as Tom replied, "What about me? I'm not so bad. We get along great. Our relationship might develop into something special, you never know."

Advancing on the mahogany reception desk, Denise responded pragmatically, "We're further along now than I ever thought we would be. Let's not jinx it by talking about something that might never happen."

"It won't happen if you don't work at it. You're always so busy," Tom rebutted sotto voce.

"I'm not the only one who's too busy. You're always with that dog of yours," Denise hissed between clinched teeth.

"I wouldn't have signed up for that study if you hadn't taken one special assignment after the other and left me alone all the time. A guy needs a partner even if it is a canine," Tom sulked bitterly.

Tapping her foot angrily on the highly polished oak floor, Denise rebutted, "Are you trying to deny me the right to excel at my career? Can I help it if I'm good? Is it my fault if other cities need my expertise and call the chief? You of all people know how much I love being a cop."

Beginning to sputter with irritation and hopelessness, Tom replied, "I'm not trying to deny you anything. I'm just saying—"

Interrupting, Denise continued, "You're saying that our relationship hasn't moved any further because I don't have time for it. You're trying to make me the fall guy."

"I didn't say that," Tom replied with open hands as he tried to remember the cause of the argument.

Snapping with a finality that all but ended the conversation, Denise stated, "Yes, you did. You said that I'm too busy to make our relationship work. You knew what you were getting into when you followed me to DC for the Capitol Hill case. Don't try to lay the weight of this relationship on me."

"Incredible! All I said was that you'd make a lovely bride and now we're at war. Women! Give me a dog anytime," Tom muttered to the back of Denise's head.

"A transfer to the canine corps can be arranged," Denise stated with cold composure.

Without saying another word to each other, Denise and Tom stood on the magnificent oriental rug and waited their turn with visitors who were checking into one of the most famous hotels in the world. They could feel each other seething from hurt feelings but could think of nothing to say that would not cause them to explode into another argument. Therefore, they waited in sullen silence.

Once again, Denise's shield opened doors for them. Flashing her shield, she asked to see the manager. Without a moment's hesitation, the desk clerk showed them into the conference room off the main reception area. Sinking into incredibly comfortable gray leather chairs, they waited silently. Neither one wanted to open the sore wounds of their earlier discussion.

Ms. Walker appeared quickly and introduced herself as the hotel's manager. Joining them at the table, she spoke in a voice that was both professional and supportive.

"I'm at your service, Detective," Ms. Walker said. "How might I be of assistance to you?"

Impressed by the woman's demeanor, Denise quickly cut her eyes at Tom as a mute comment that women can be professionally successful. Then, Denise turned her attention to Ms. Walker. Taking out her sketchbook and pencil, Denise began the questioning session. Tom, understanding that he was in the presence of two strong women, sat quietly.

"Ms. Walker, I'm investigating the murder of a DC-area jeweler. His killer has sent me a charm bracelet and two charms—one of the Empire State Building and the other of a Hawaiian lei. I understand from the manager of the shop from which he purchased the charms that the killer might have stayed here. Rather, I should say that the well-endowed woman who served as the killer's messenger stayed here since she arrived at the shop with a note written on Ritz stationery. I was wondering if anyone might have asked you where to purchase charms about three weeks ago."

Thinking for a few moments, Ms. Walker replied, "So many guests spend their evenings at the Ritz that I find it difficult to be of service on this matter. I vaguely remember a man and his secretary who stayed in one of our suites. He was fairly nondescript, brown hair and eyes, medium height and build, but she was striking—tall, blonde, and very chesty. Perhaps that's the couple."

"Would you be able to find their address or phone number in your files?" Denise asked with a glimmer of hope in her voice. "I'd appreciate anything that would give us a clue to the murderer's identity."

Rising, Ms. Walker responded "I'll ask Miss Clark, one

of the receptionists, to speak with you. They see more of the guests than I do. Someone will join you very shortly while I check the files."

As Ms. Walker left the conference room, the silence once again descended. Denise finished her sketch without speaking to Tom, who sat sullenly at the foot of the long table. Neither wanted to start another argument, especially since neither could figure out the source of the last one.

A discreet knock announced the arrival of the receptionist. Miss Clark wore sensible black shoes that squeaked slightly on the highly polished conference room floor. Her carefully coiffed brown hair barely brushed the shoulders of her maroon jacket on which the elaborate Ritz "R" glistened in gold thread. Her short nails glistened a pail iridescent pink that copied the lip-gloss that sparkled on her small mouth.

Confidently, Miss Clark eased into the chair vacated by Ms. Walker and waited for Denise to begin the questioning. As she waited, she looked from Denise to Tom, perhaps wondering which partner would assume the role of good cop and which would play bad cop. Television programs had told her that law enforcement officers liked to play that game, and she was ready to cooperate fully.

Smiling, Denise introduced herself and Tom and then proceeded with the questioning. Sketching quickly, she asked, "Do you remember anyone in the last few weeks or month asking you for information on a shop that sells charms."

"As a matter of fact, I do," Miss Clark began confidently. "It was about three weeks ago, I think. A woman with a long list in her hand stopped at the desk on her way out to do some shopping. She said that she wanted to purchase a dress from a boutique on Sixth, a charm bracelet from a shop on Fifth Avenue, and some charms for it. I recommended Charming Charms because everyone said it carried charms of incredible workmanship. I've never been there myself since I don't collect them, but that's what I've heard. Anyway, the woman thanked me and left."

"Can you describe her?" Denise asked as she flipped to a clean sheet of paper.

"I remember that she was very blonde . . . too blonde to be real. Her hair looked dyed," Miss Clark confided with a womanly glint in her eyes and a lift of her brows. It was clear that she was enjoying the attention and conversation with another woman.

"Anything else?"

Continuing contentedly, Miss Clark said, "She was tall for a woman, about six feet, I think. She didn't wear much jewelry, only a watch that appeared to be very expensive. Her hands were much bigger than mine and rugged looking. She had an athletic build, not thin and definitely not fat. Oh, and she had big boobs. You know, the kind that men think are great, but women know will sag to the floor with age."

As Denise and Miss Clark chuckled conspiratorially, Tom grunted. He was not enjoying being the brunt of their humor about men. He felt that he should defend the honor of his gender but knew that if he did, they would gang up on him with a vengeance. Deciding to take the careful route, he slumped farther in his chair and pretended disinterest.

"Did you see her again when she returned from shopping?" Denise asked, hoping that the woman had shared her purchases.

Shaking her head, Miss Clark replied, "No, I was probably on break or busy with someone else when she returned. Actually, I don't remember seeing her again."

"Did you ever see anyone with her?" Denise inquired as she closed her sketchbook.

"No, never," Miss Clark replied after a moment's hesitation. "I only spoke with her that one time. I don't think I was at the desk when she arrived or when she checked out. I would have remembered seeing a woman like that. She was so carefully made up that she almost looked like a, well, an older call girl."

"Thanks, Miss Clark, you've been very helpful," Denise commented as a light tap on the door sounded.

At that moment, Ms. Walker returned with a sheet of paper in her hands. Dismissing Miss Clark, she sank into the abandoned chair with a sigh. It was obvious that Ms. Walker had put in a long day and was ready for her evening to begin.

"Well, I've checked our records and can find nothing, not even a credit card imprint," Ms. Walker began slowly. "He must have paid cash for the suite. I have his name as Frank Pain, which sounds made up to me. The handwriting's the same so he must have registered the woman as his secretary under the name of Freda Maze, another contrived identity I'd bet."

Taking the sheet of paper, Denise replied, "Is it unusual for one person to register for the other when they aren't related?"

"No, not if the second party hasn't arrived as yet, which could have been the case," Ms. Walker replied. "Sorry, Detective, but I have nothing that will help you."

Smiling, Denise stated, "You'd be surprised at the help this might turn out to be. With luck, he'll use this name again, and I'll know that I'm tracking the right man."

Rising, Ms. Walker escorted Denise and the still silent Tom to the main lobby. Shaking hands with both of them, she left them to find their way to the front door. Once outside, they walked away from Central Park and toward their hotel.

Five

This time, trudging through the streets of New York, Tom did not complain about hunger, tired feet, or the slow-moving pedestrians. Instead, he walked silently until they arrived at the famous cheesecake restaurant. Denise was so deep in thought that he could think of no way to engage her in conversation. Besides, conversation caused arguments. Once inside, he ordered and returned to his apparent vow of silence.

Maintaining her stubborn silence as well, Denise surveyed the prints on the walls and the clientele, unable to think of any topic that would not lead to a possible argument. The faces of the rich and famous from the world of theater lined the walls, leading Denise to think that every well-known artist eventually ate in the restaurant. Scanning the other patrons, Denise found, to her disappointment, none of them that night. Everyone in the room seemed to be tourists in search of famous faces among the other diners.

As Denise ate the first spoonful of the cream of broccoli soup, she understood the appeal of the restaurant. The prices were reasonable for New York and the food was fabulous. The soup was thick and creamy with a slight hint of sherry and nutmeg. Tom's Manhattan clam chowder looked as appetizing, although she did not ask him and he did not volunteer a comment. However, from the eagerness with which he attacked his bowl, Denise knew that he had not been disappointed by his selection.

Their main courses proved equally delicious. Tom had ordered the porterhouse steak with fried onions and mush-rooms while Denise had wanted to try the chicken with pasta primavera. Both had ordered side salads that arrived on plates still chilled from the refrigerator. Everything was perfect from the hot crusty rolls to the slightly soft butter.

Unfortunately, unlike other couples, Denise and Tom did not share food or compare notes. Each ate in silence, barely casting an eye in the other's direction. Instead, they steadfastly maneuvered their forks and knives with a concentration usually reserved for food judges at the county fair.

It was not until the desserts arrived that Tom broke the silence. The sheer delight of his first forkful of the cheesecake smothered in fresh strawberries caused him to exclaim in complete joy. The expectation had not surpassed the reality.

Smacking his lips, Tom proclaimed, "This is the best damn cheesecake I've ever tasted!"

Placing her spoon on the saucer that accompanied her chocolate mousse, Denise replied coolly, "Did you say something?"

Unable to stand the frost between them any longer, Tom pleaded, "All right, Dory, give it up. I can't stand this silence any longer. We're a team, damn it. Our personal and professional life mesh. You're my partner in every way. I don't know what I said to upset you, but I'm sorry. You have to talk to me. I can't take this any longer."

Smiling, Denise replied, "I was wondering which one of us would break first. You're a tough one. Any other man would have given in long before this. What took you so long?"

Shaking his head, Tom responded, "You're a piece of work, Denise. No wonder we're a team . . . two hard, crusty people attracted to each other."

"Don't go there," Denise advised firmly. "That's what started this whole argument. I'm not that hard and neither are you. Circumstances make us put on this act. I've seen you cry over that dog's hurt broken paw, so don't give me that hard stuff."

Laughing, Tom stated, "Yeah, and I saw you fall apart at

your sister's wedding. If I'm soft inside, so are you. Here, taste this. Good, isn't it?"

Eating the cheesecake from his offered fork, Denise smiled gently into his eyes. Now that they were speaking again, all was right in their world. There was never any doubt that they would have protected each other physically even while not speaking, but it certainly was nice to have Tom's emotional as well as physical presence in her corner.

"It's great. Try this," Denise relied as she spooned some of the mousse into Tom's mouth.

"Rich. That'll go right to those lovely hips of yours," Tom teased with a wink.

"And that cheesecake will settle on your six pack," Denise joked laughingly.

They were glad to have their good humor restored. This was the longest they had ever gone without speaking, and neither of them had enjoyed the silence. They relished their ability to joke with each other, to confide their thoughts and fears without worry, and to allow their new tenderness to pull them closer.

By the time they reached their hotel, Denise and Tom were strolling hand-in-hand. They had forgotten the argument and were eagerly awaiting their evening at the theater. At least, one of them was looking forward to it; the other only hoped he would not snore too loudly.

And the theater did not disappoint. The crowd on the sidewalk almost reverently waited until the doors opened and they could enter. Young people in casual clothing mixed with older folks in evening wear. Stepping into the lobby with its magnificent mahogany paneled walls, sparkling chandeliers, and thick carpets, Denise found herself transported to a world of make-believe in which actors became characters and characters came to life.

The marquee and playbill advertised the play as the oldest running musical on Broadway. Although Denise would have preferred a drama, she knew that Tom would have balked at sitting through anything heavy, thus, she had purchased tickets to this show thinking that, if nothing else, the pretty girls dancing in tights would keep his interest. The music alone would be more than enough to keep her attention glued to the stage.

Denise loved the smell of the theater. She did not know if it was the dust on the curtains, the mixture of patrons' perfumes, or the paint on the sets, but she loved inhaling the aroma of the theater. In college, she had worked as a member of the stage crew and once on the stage in a small part. Denise had been so completely overwhelmed by the theater's magic that, for a few months, she had actually thought of changing from her criminal justice major to drama. However, she decided to follow her original plan in the hopes of some day becoming the chief of a major city police department like her father.

Denise had admired her father tremendously all of her life. He was brave, handsome, courageous, and incredibly tender to his family and friends. She had wanted to follow in his footsteps and almost felt it her duty since her sister had thought police work boring. As a child, she had eagerly listened to his stories after dinner and longed for the excitement and the feeling of commitment that he received from his long days. When he became a chief, Denise had been proud to the point of bursting. She had stood beside him at his swearing in and beamed at the cameras during the photo session immediately after. He had been her hero.

However, he never put any pressure on her to join the force. When Denise had told her father of her choice in majors and her plans for the future, he had been proud and very pleased. Yet he had told her that the decision had to be hers without concern for others. It was her life and her future; she had to be content with the decision. Knowing that a career in law enforcement was more important to her than one in the theater, Denise pushed thoughts of acting from her mind. She never regretted the decision. Watching talented thespians thrilled her beyond description.

Clutching the playbill that the usher had given her, Denise

settled into her third-row aisle seat. Perfectly happy, she breathed deeply and smiled. The theater was home for great names and stunning performances. She knew that night's would be no different and could hardly wait until the musical began.

Tom, however, did not share her enthusiasm. More interested in the chocolate-covered raisins he had purchased from the concession stand than the stage, he munched loudly and barely acknowledged her comments about actors she had enjoyed in other performances and plays that had made her laugh or cry. Watching a good movie with a bag of buttery popcorn was more to Tom's liking. He could not share her rapture at being in the theater.

Fingering the familiar playbill, Denise thought that from one production to the other, the little publication always looked the same. The actors' names changed, but the format remained constant. Scanning her playbill, Denise read the biographies of the players. Many of them she had seen in other productions in New York and as part of road shows that toured DC and played at the Kennedy Center, National Theater, or Warner Theater.

Flipping quickly through the advertisements, Denise arrived at the inside back cover. Startled, she reread the page twice before turning to Tom. Taking his playbill from his lap, she turned quickly to the back, only to discover that it was different. Someone had tampered with her copy.

"Tom, Denise said as she poked him with her elbow and pointed to the two copies on her lap, "look at this."

"OK. What am I supposed to see?" Tom replied as he squinted to see in the low theater lights.

"The pages are different. Look!" Denise insisted as she handed both copies to him.

Holding both so that the light could hit them just right, Tom read the ad for a local car dealer on his playbill. All of the information in the ad dealt with the dealer's good reputation and his fair prices. Next, he looked at the one in his right hand. The picture on Denise's playbill was exactly the same, but the wording was different. Instead of touting the dealer's good qualities, Tom read something completely unrelated.

Whispering over his shoulder, Denise read the message over the photo of the new red car, "Don't worry, Detective Dory, you'll find me. I'm getting tired, making my apprehension easier. You're on the right track. Only a few more days, relatively speaking. Just follow the clues that will lead you to me. The bracelet's a nifty idea, isn't it? I hope you'll enjoy wearing it."

Looking at Denise in disbelief and feeling for his carefully concealed service revolver, Tom stated, "He's here. Your suspect might be watching us at this moment."

"That's right. He must have started watching us as soon as we arrived. I bet he followed us from the train station. He probably saw us at the kiosk and knew that we'd bought tickets for this play. He changed the message on my playbill," Denise commented, looking around the theater for anyone acting out of character.

"Damn!" Tom growled. "I hate feeling like a bug under a microscope. We'd better find this guy in a hurry. I don't like knowing that he knows that we're watching him. We can't see him, but he can see us. This gives me the creeps."

"I'm going to find that usher. Maybe she knows something," Denise said as she rose from her seat.

"I'll go with you," Tom said, rising from his seat. "We have ten minutes before the play starts, and I need some more candy."

Shaking her head at his preoccupation with food, Denise moved against the steady stream of theatergoers descending the aisle to their seats. She made slow progress but eventually reached the doors. Studying the faces of the ushers, she did not find the one who had seated them. Pulling Tom by the hand, she pushed her way into the lobby.

"I'm going to see the manager while you get your refreshments," Denise announced as she left Tom scanning the counter.

"I'll meet you at the seats," Tom replied without looking in her direction. He had set his attention on the concession stand.

Finding the manager's door near the restrooms, Denise knocked and waited. A slightly built, middle aged man opened the door with a smile. Seeing Denise's shield, he quickly invited her into his office.

"What can I do for you, Detective," he asked softly as if he, too, needed to preserve the atmosphere of the theater.

"Take a look at this," Denise instructed as she handed the playbill to the manager. "Someone changed the message in my playbill. From the looks of it, I'd say it's the suspect I'm investigating in a murder case in DC. Any idea how this might have happened?"

"Wow!" the manger exclaimed. "This is a first. Sorry, I can't be of any help on this one. Our printer delivers stacks of them weekly. We don't print too far in advance in case of changes and because of a lack of space to store them. Anyway, we keep them in this closet. The head usher takes the night's stack and places them in convenient spots at the back of the house. The ushers take what they need as they need them. He checks to make sure that plenty of them are always available. There's never been a need for security."

"Can you point out the head usher? Maybe he can tell me if he saw anything unusual tonight," Denise requested as she glanced at the clock on the wall.

Smiling, the manager said, "Sure, he's the guy standing by the center doors. Black pants, white shirt, red tie of head usher, and crew cut."

"Thanks. I'll have a word with him," Denise stated as she left the office.

"Good luck, Detective."

Denise quickly slipped through the crowd that still flowed into the theater. Five minutes remained before the curtain as she made her way toward the head usher. The young man smiled as she approached and handed her a playbill.

"Thanks. I already have one," Denise replied as she showed him her shield. "I'd like to ask you a few questions."

"OK. Why not? What would you like to know?" the young man asked as they stepped away from the door and the crowd.

"Did you see anyone tamper with the playbills tonight?" Denise asked as she showed him her copy.

"No, but I wasn't really looking," the young man replied. "It gets kinda crazy in here when everyone starts arriving. Wow, someone left you a message in yours. That's kinda radical."

"It would be if the person wasn't a killer," Denise conceded. "Where did you leave the stack for the center aisle?"

"On the chair inside the door on the right. That's my usual place. All the ushers know where to find extras that way. I'll show you," the young man volunteered as he pushed his way through the late arrivers.

The lights flashed again as they reached the chair with its remaining copies in clear view. Looking around at the busy ushers, Denise still could not find the one who had seated her. She had a great memory for faces and always remembered waiters, receptionists, and ushers.

"I don't see my usher. Have some of them started to leave already?" Denise asked the head usher.

"No, they're required to stay until after the intermission. If they don't stay, I don't pay," the young man replied.

"Our usher was a female with blond hair pulled into a bun and braces on her top teeth. I don't see her now," Denise commented as she continued to scour the crowd.

Looking at her strangely, the head usher replied, "I don't have anyone like that working for me. None of the women here is blonde, and none of the ladies wears her hair in a bun."

"I never forget a face. She was blonde all right," Denise insisted.

"I have twenty ushers on duty tonight," the young man commented. "Three of them are men. The women all have dark hair to their shoulders or beyond. The men are also brunettes. Sorry, no blondes among them."

"Then, I think my suspect infiltrated your ranks, dressed in your uniform, and delivered my playbill to me without being noticed. He must have hired the blonde to make the switch for him," Denise stated to the very impressed young man.

"Wow, this is better than an Agatha Christie story!" the head usher sighed. He had obviously spent many hours in the theater and lived his life in comparison to the plays he watched daily from the back of the house.

As the lights began to dim, Denise thanked the young man and hurried to her seat. She snuggled against Tom's shoulder as the orchestra played the first strains of the overture. Slipping her hand into Tom's, Denise let the music wash over her and push away thoughts of the killer and his message.

"Any luck?" Tom whispered.

"None," Denise replied. "We'll talk later."

Although Denise knew that the suspect might still be in the theater, she would not allow his proximity to spoil her evening. After all, his selection of charms had brought her to New York City. Now that she was here, Denise would enjoy it to the fullest.

Tom had been good to his word and had slept through part of the second act. However, much to Denise's delight, he had not snored. No one around them had known that he had spent good money for theater tickets only to take a nap through some of the most memorable songs.

From his conversation on their walk to the hotel, Denise wondered if she might have misinterpreted his slumped head and shoulders. She could hardly believe his reaction when he said, "That was the best show I've ever seen. Thanks, Dory."

"Which part did you especially enjoy?" Denise probed skeptically.

"The part when the girls started dancing. That was great," Tom replied as they rode up the elevator to their room.

"Tom, the girls sang and danced almost nonstop. You'll

have to be more specific than that," Denise commented as she continued her interrogation.

"You know the part. Everyone always talks about that part. You know," Tom hedged as he unlocked the door.

"Oh, you mean the most famous song in the show. That part?" Denise asked as she tried to contain the laughter that threatened to erupt at any moment.

"Yeah, that part," Tom replied as he flicked on the bedroom light.

"From the way your head was rolling during the entire play, I thought you had fallen asleep." Denise chuckled as she slipped out of her shoes and headed to the bathroom. She grabbed her overnight case as she went.

Denise spread her few toiletries on the left side of the white and gold vanity, leaving the right for Tom. Opening her case, she extracted the necessary items and her long summer-weight batiste nightgown. Removing her clothes, she adjusted the water temperature and stepped into the shower. The water felt wonderful on her tired shoulders and feet. Walking all over New York had taken its toil despite her sensible-heel shoes.

Raising his voice over the sound of running water, Tom replied, "No, I was awake for that part. I slept through the others."

Denise almost dropped the soap as she laughed at Tom's silliness. He had seen maybe the first scene of the musical but certainly not much else. Unless he had a video camera in his eyelids, he would never know the excitement and fun of the play.

Rubbing the towel briskly over her streaming body, Denise asked, "Why don't you sing a little of your favorite song?"

"You know I have a terrible voice. It's only fit for the shower," Tom replied through the crack in the door. He would have liked to shower with her, but she did not invite him.

Slipping the nightgown over her head and wiggling it down her body, Denise commented, "That's true, but you're always tormenting me with it anyway. The shower's all yours. Sing away, Caruso."

Sputtering, Tom replied, "I do my best vocalizing when I'm alone."

Rinsing the toothpaste from her mouth, Denise turned and responded, "OK. I'm going. I'll be waiting for you. Don't take all night. I'm sleepy, and we have to catch the train early tomorrow morning."

Laughing, Denise closed the door and walked toward the beds. Tom had turned back the spread on both of them. Although they had been dating steadily since the Capitol Hill case ended, they had not yet become physically intimate. They never seemed to have the time to take their relationship to the next step. Either they were working separate cases or they had just finished grueling ones. They had little time to spend on their love life.

Lying down on the bed closest to the bathroom, Denise flipped the pages of her sketchbook while Tom tortured her ears with a pathetic rendition of the show's most famous song. He had heard it early in the first scene and remembered it so that he could prove that he had paid attention to the play. Now that he had made his point, Denise wished that he would shower in silence. The off-key rendition hurt her ears.

Before Denise could turn too many pages, her eyelids became heavy. The combination of the warm shower and the long day made the sketches blur. Sliding under the covers, she quickly fell asleep before Tom could finish his shower and the song.

Freshly showered, Tom entered the bedroom to find Denise lying on her side with her hand resting on her sketchbook. She stirred slightly as he gently pulled it away and kissed her soft cheek. His amorous thoughts would have to wait until later.

Six

When Denise and Tom returned to work on Monday, the squad room was alive with activity. Molly bounded across the room to meet him, displaying uncharacteristic excitement and lack of control. She stood on her hind legs, placed her front paws on his shoulders, and licked his face happily as everyone laughed. The other detectives gathered around to hear all the details of their New York trip.

Everyone had read the report that Denise had faxed to Captain Morton and they were anxious to hear her next plans. She showed them the playbill with the altered last page and the lei charm. Recounting the experience in the Charming Charms shop, Denise and Tom had everyone rolling with laughter, even the captain, who was usually very professional and somewhat somber.

"What's next, Denise? How much further do you plan to stretch my departmental budget?" Captain Morton asked as the laughter subsided.

Seeing that Captain Morton's financial concern was genuine, Denise replied, "From the clues the suspect has given me, I'd say that I'm on my way to Hawaii. I promise that I'll make the trip as short as possible. I'll phone the HPD to request as much help as possible in locating the spot where he says I'll find the next clue. I have a feeling that it's Pearl Harbor since the suspect said that I'd find more at the site of a 'watery grave.' I'll be kind to the budget, I promise."

With a sigh, Captain Morton conceded, "At least air fares

are cheaper now. Try to stay in a reasonably inexpensive hotel, Dory. I'll prepare the chief for the possibility that this case will cost us a bundle. She said that you'd have all of her support and carte blanche for spending. I just wonder if she had any idea of the possible expenses."

Tossing her sketchbook onto her desk, Denise replied, "She should since she runs with that crowd. Don't forget that Mr. Worldly was one of her friends and her jeweler."

Shrugging his shoulders, Captain Morton commented, "There's a big difference between spending her own money on trinkets and using tax payer money to send detectives to distant locations to hunt for clues in a murder case. We'll see what she says. In the meantime, make your arrangements. Let's see if you can solve this one before this guy takes you to Europe."

Removing the chain of paper clips that one of the many office pranksters had left in her coffee cup, Denise responded, "I'll do my best, Captain, but so far the suspect isn't giving me much information. It seems that he hires distinctive looking women to run his errands so that no one will notice him. I hope the trip to Hawaii will produce more than another charm."

Denise cleared her desk of everything except the sketches and charm bracelet with the charms dangling enticingly from it. She had traveled to New York and visited the Empire State Building only to learn from another charm and its accompanying note that she would have to seek information at Pearl Harbor in Hawaii. She knew that the suspect was ingenious and careful in that he hired others to run his errands although he was in view of Denise and her investigation. The suspect knew more about her than she did about him, assuming that the killer was indeed male.

Turning to Tom, who sat hunched over his desk behind her, Denise said, "I've got nothing. The clues are only taking me on trips, not divulging the killer's identity. I need much more than this."

"Maybe Hawaii will tell you more," Tom offered without looking up from his papers.

Lightly tracing her fingers through the mat of hair on Tom's bare arm, Denise said, "I'll check with Ronda, too. Maybe she uncovered something in the deceased social connections that would give me some help."

"Hey, cut that out!" Tom stated in a voice that had grown husky from the tantalizing movement of her fingers. "What are you trying to do . . . distract a fellow officer from the completion of his duties? Go talk to Ronda and leave me alone. I have work to do."

"Be that way," Denise replied with a wink. "In case you're interested, your partner's slobbering on your fresh shoe shine."

Tom immediately looked down to see Molly chewing on a cow's hoof that she had skillfully balanced between her paw and his foot. As a result, saliva ran unnoticed from her cheek onto his shoes. Grabbing the tissue that Denise handed him, he growled his thanks and mopped up the moisture.

Laughing, Denise walked the short distance to Ronda's desk outside the captain's door. Ronda's inquisitive eyes immediately brightened since Denise was one of her office favorites. Denise always gave Ronda plenty of time to complete the jobs she gave her, unlike many of the others who expected her to return the work within a few hours. It was not only the male detectives who piled on work with unrealistic expectations. The women in the department did the same thing. Denise was the only one who realized that Ronda only had two hands.

"How was New York?" Ronda asked as soon as Denise settled in the chair next to her desk.

"Busy and wonderful. The Empire State Building is taller than I expected and Broadway is more congested, but I loved every minute of it," Denise answered with a big smile. "We saw a great musical, although Tom slept through most of it. Did you have a chance to check out those names I gave you?"

"Sure did," Ronda replied as she pulled a folder from her

organizer. "I came in on Saturday for a few hours and ran them through the FBI files. Your contact at the Bureau was very helpful. Unfortunately, all of those people are rich and famous not crooks or murderers."

Scanning the names, none of which was familiar, Denise said, "Thanks for the try. I didn't really think that those people would have records, but I needed to give it a shot."

Fussing with the papers on her desk, Ronda stated, "I didn't know that this area was the home to so many filthy rich people. I knew that Potomac and Bethesda have their share of folks with money, but I didn't know that they were dripping in it. Mr. Worldly's friends certainly never have to worry about a rainy day."

"Maybe not rain," Denise commented, "but murder. If the killer strikes again, he might go after one of them."

Conceding reluctantly, Ronda said, "I hadn't thought of that. Still, it's good to be rich enough to hire bodyguards. If someone were after one of us, we'd have to wait it out."

The squad room had emptied while Denise sat at Ronda's desk. Only Tom and Molly remained of the previous loud gathering of detectives. Sinking into her chair, Denise phoned the Hawaii police department and made arrangements to have a detective's assistance in the arrest if she got lucky. Somehow, as she hung up the phone, Denise had the premonition that the Hawaii trip would not bring her any closer to apprehending the suspect. She would have a nice little vacation but little else.

Turning to Tom's desk behind her, Denise stated, "I'm leaving tonight. Are you interested in going with me?"

"I can't," Tom replied sadly. "I have this report to finish. Some of us work for a living, remember?"

Not wishing to take no for an answer, Denise persisted, "Can't you take leave for a few days? I plan to stay two nights max. That's why I'm leaving tonight. I'll sleep on the plane and be ready to roll as soon as it lands."

"Not this time, Dory," Tom replied with a sad shake of his head. "Joining you in DC while you worked on the Hill case threw me way off schedule. I'd planned to work last weekend, but the New York trip came up. I'm months behind on my work. I can't leave again so soon. Phone me if you need me."

Pouting, Denise whined playfully, "Well, don't say I didn't try. Imagine us lying on the beach covered in suntan lotion with the waves lapping at the shore. Now, instead of taking a mini vacation, I'll have to work the entire time."

"You can lie on the beach without me," Tom stated sadly.

Patting his hand, Denise replied, "But it wouldn't be any fun without you to bury in the sand."

Denise could hear his low chuckle as she returned to her work. She would miss Tom on this trip, but she understood that he could not sacrifice his work for hers. Besides, the suspect might appear if he knew that she was alone. Since he seemed to know the details of her whereabouts, maybe he would join her on the beach.

Surfing the Web, Denise located cheap round-trip fare and hotel accommodations. Booking them on her corporate account, she decided to search for information on Hawaii and Pearl Harbor. Much to her satisfaction, the Internet contained a wealth of information on both. Since she had never visited either, Denise devoured every article she could find on Hawaiian history, colonization, statehood, and current conditions. Her reading of Pearl Harbor information brought tears to her eyes at the thought of so many killed in service to their country.

For whatever reason, the suspect in the murder of Mr. Worldly wanted her to travel to a paradise unlike any in the world. Denise was intrigued as to what she would find. Her imagination had her wearing a muumuu or a grass skirt and dancing a hula while waiting for the server to arrive with another piña colada. Or maybe, the suspect would send a charm to her hotel that would instruct her to take a tiny plane to one of the secondary islands. Following his lead to an exotic location like Hawaii offered incredible opportunities for adventure.

Her research into the fashion industry had told her that

Hawaii offered more than leis, hula skirts, and floral-print shirts. Denise had read about the designers who called Hawaii their home and allowed the stunning vistas to influence their work. Perhaps the suspect planned to strike again there.

However, to her knowledge, the killer had not struck while she was in New York. He had simply provided another clue to his identity. As far as Denise knew, Hawaii might simply be another diversion.

Denise wished that Tom could come with her. The lights of New York had not managed to push their relationship to a new level, but the adventure of Hawaii might if only he could experience it with her. His workload made it impossible for them to explore the endless possibilities for romance that Hawaii offered.

Returning to the work that lay on her desk, Denise pushed all thought of a romantic interlude in Hawaii from her mind. She would have to be content to work her magic at home. Actually, enchanting Tom in the comfort of her own home might be preferable to doing it in an enchanted land. She wanted to know that his reaction was to her and not to the gentle breezes and the hot sun.

By early afternoon, Denise had finished all of the work she needed to do before leaving for Hawaii. Tom and Molly had left the squad room on a case, leaving her alone to clean up her desk, rush home to pack a few things, and take a cab to the airport. She really did not need much, only the old bathing suit that had not been to the beach in years and a change of clothing or two. After feeding her cat, Max, Denise would hail a cab and go.

Denise could tell that Max did not know how to react to her these days. Denise had left him originally with Tom and then with her sister when she went on the Capitol Hill case and alone while she traveled to New York. Now, she would leave him to his own devices again as she rushed to Hawaii.

Turning off the light from the green lamp that she kept on her desk, Denise picked up her bag and left the office. The eerie silence of a room used to activity but now vacant filled her ears as she closed the door and walked down the stairs to the parking lot. Usually when she left on a trip or appointment, Tom wished her well. This time, however, she was alone and she did not like it.

Denise's arrival home was equally as lonely. Max, angry at being left alone so often, refused to greet her. Instead, he remained curled into a ball on the couch. Only the glimmer of the one eye he decided to open told Denise that he had been aware of her return.

After packing a few necessities, Denise phoned a cab and fed the cat. Max sniffed the food and walked away as if his actions would punish her for leaving him. Reaching out to him, Denise cried, "Come, old boy, don't act that way. I'll be back soon."

However, Max was not interested in her attempts. He strolled toward the bedroom without giving Denise another thought. His stubborn independence had kept him alive on the streets of DC. The cat saw no reason to abandon it now for the woman who fed him.

Locking the door, Denise walked down the hall to the elevator. Stepping inside, she thought she heard the ringing of the telephone in her apartment, but she did not have time to check. Having left her cell phone on the table beside her bed, her calls would not automatically follow her. Whoever wanted to speak with her would have to wait until after she returned from Hawaii.

Her heart pounded with a combination of anticipation and fear as the taxi glided through the cars on the beltway. Denise had never been to Hawaii and would never see the enchanted islands if the driver continued to dart in front of other speeding vehicles. Having Tom at her side would have distracted her from the sound of the blaring horns. Alone, she heard everything and sat white knuckled but silent during the ride. She was quite relieved when the cab came to a screeching halt at the airport entrance.

Crowds of people filled the lobby. The low rates had attracted more than the usual number of travelers from BWI

Airport. Rather than check her small overnight bag, Denise decided to stow it in the compartment above her seat. She saw little point in having to wait in the baggage claim areas when she had so little time to spend in Hawaii and so much to do and see.

While waiting for her flight, Denise wandered the airport. She looked into the various shops selling everything from garments to candy. Buying a pack of gum and the latest romance novel, she continued her exploration. She did not want to sit and read for fear of finishing the book and having nothing to do on the long flight. Although she had planned to sleep as much as possible, Denise knew that she would not be able to spend all of her time in slumber. The sheer number of passengers on the plane, the activity of the flight attendants, and the landing in Los Angeles would break into her rest. She would need the book for in-flight entertainment. Traveling alone, she would miss Tom's witty comments and almost constant complaining.

Without Tom at her side, Denise would have no one to keep her company when sleep would not come and the novel had ended. She would need to provide distractions for herself. However, that was not an easy task since she was one of those people who was always active. Being confined to the plane would test her nerves and endurance.

Waiting until the last minute to board the plane, Denise slipped through the relatively empty aisles to her seat in row twenty-four, seat "A." A young man sat in the seat next to the window; the one next to the aisle was still empty. Looking at the seat with a frown, she discovered a package wrapped in white and gold paper and addressed to her resting under the seat belt. Picking it up, she held it under her chin while she stowed her bag and then sat down to open it.

Inside, Denise discovered not only a note but also another paper-wrapped charm. Reading the familiar handwriting, she chuckled to herself. The murderer had become more daring in his latest message, which read, "Now that you're alone without that dog-faced companion of yours, I can hint at the adventure awaiting you. You will find another clue as promised as well as tickets to a show in the Polynesian Village and a luau. I'll be there waiting for you although you might not recognize me. Be sure to read tomorrow's *Post*. You'll find my latest exploits highlighted there."

Turning to the young man in the window seat, Denise asked, "Any chance you saw the person who left this package for me?"

"One of the flight attendants left it. That one with the short red hair," the young man replied as he pointed to the flight attendant coming toward them.

Raising her hand, Denise motioned to the woman, who appeared at her side immediately. Returning the flight attendant's smile, Denise asked, "Excuse me, but did you leave this package in the seat for me?"

"Sure did. How romantic!" the flight attendant gushed. "Your guy must really love you! My fiancé wouldn't think of doing anything like that."

Shaking her head, Denise replied, "I don't have a fiancé. A murder suspect left this package. Can you describe him for me?"

Shrugging her shoulders, the attendant responded with a look of disappointment on her freckled face, "Sorry, but I didn't see him. Security handed me the package after X-raying it. Policy, you know."

Thanking the attendant, Denise slipped the note into her skirt pocket. Feeling her anger rise, Denise wondered about the leak within the police department that allowed the suspect to know her movements. It crossed her mind that the murderer might be a fellow detective with a grudge against the rich and famous of DC. Or maybe one of them had undisclosed funds and ran with that crowd. She quickly pushed away that idea. None of her fellow officers had that kind of money squirreled away. Only the chief was that well connected, and she had not visited the squad room lately. Whoever it was, he was a computer hacker since Denise had bought her tickets on-line and not even told Tom her flight number.

If only Tom were with her. Denise knew that by sharing her thoughts with him, she would at least feel as if she were trying to gain control of the situation. Without him, she could see the case spinning out of control. The suspect was calling all the shots, and she was his pawn.

Only minutes left before take off and the last late passengers were boarding. A woman with a harried husband and two children in tow noisily pushed their way toward the back of the plane. Denise was quite relieved that they would not be sitting near her. Behind them came a man in a rumpled business suit. He did not smile at anyone as he eased into the seat three rows ahead of hers. And still the seat on the aisle across from her remained empty.

Extracting the book and gum from her purse, Denise looked out the window at the terminal. Men in jumpers hurried to load the last of the luggage into the hold. When they finished, the aircraft would taxi to the end of the runway and take off for the West Coast and onward to Hawaii.

Denise felt rather than saw the arrival of the last passenger as a figure loomed beside her and the airflow decreased. She felt the warmth of his body as he searched for a space in the overhead compartments. She heard him grunt as he stretched to stow his bag and then sank into his seat. The fragrance of his cologne was very familiar and made her ache for Tom.

Suddenly, the aircraft lurched and began to move backward. All of the people on the ground scurried away as the craft eased into its taxiing position. The passengers on the Boeing 747 listened to the last announcement to fasten seat belts in preparation for take off as the plane began to vibrate from the revving engines.

At last the great craft was airborne. Denise chewed frantically on the now tasteless gum as the pressure increased in her ears. The book slipped from her lap as she squeezed her nose and swallowed.

"You dropped your book," the voice next to her announced over the hum of the engines. The great craft had reached its cruise altitude and the roar had subsided. Denise's ears no longer popped, but her hearing was far from normal.

"Thanks," Denise said as she extended her hand without looking.

"You're welcome, Dory," replied the man in the aisle seat. Startled and ecstatic, Denise looked toward the voice. "I thought you couldn't get away," she breathed as she looked into the face of the most handsome and desirable man she had ever met.

"I almost didn't. They held the plane for me," Tom replied as he pressed the book into her hand.

Smiling, Denise said, "So you're the reason we're late taking off."

Laughing as his fingers lingered on hers, Tom replied, "One of the few perks of being a cop. In case you're wondering, the captain let me take a little leave to follow you. I'm unofficially working on the case with you if you need me."

"Then I'll put you to work. Read this," Denise stated as she pulled the note from her skirt pocket and handed it to Tom.

"Another love letter? Did he send a charm this time, too?" Tom asked sarcastically as he read the note.

"Oops, I forgot to open it," Denise responded as she unwrapped another small gold charm.

Placing the intricately crafted little charm in the palm of her hand, Denise showed Tom the latest addition to her bracelet. This time the charm did not appear to be symbolic of a location since its shape was that of a tornado, twisting to a gold point at one end. In the center of the thin concentric swirls of gold was a brilliant diamond. Fingering it lightly, Tom raised his eyebrows but said nothing.

As Denise slipped the charm and the note into her bag, Tom turned to the window. He had not liked the idea of a murder suspect sending his partner a bracelet and charms. The thought of the man watching Denise was especially irritating and frightening. However, the diamond inside the little tornado was the last straw. Tom was helpless and futilely angry that another man would send a diamond to his love when he could barely afford to buy her a nice dinner on a cop's salary.

"What do you think it means?" Denise asked as her hearing returned.

"I don't know. Not a clue. I could understand the others but not this one," Tom replied gruffly as he leaned closer to hear Denise's voice over the hum of the aircraft.

Interrupting their attempt at conversation, the elderly woman next to Tom tapped him lightly on the shoulder. Smiling, she asked, "I really don't care about having a window seat. Would your friend like to change seats with me? You could carry on your conversation better that way. It was so sweet of you to arrange for that package to be on her seat when she arrived."

"Thanks. We'd like to sit together, but I didn't leave the package. We're detectives and partners," Tom replied as he stood for the woman to maneuver around him.

The elderly woman gasped and said as she rose, "Police? How exciting! I bet you're on a case. Will anyone be murdered on this plane, like what happened on the Orient Express?"

"No, ma'am," Tom replied as she gathered her belongings. "Nothing that exciting. That only happens in books or the movies."

"Darn!" she said with true disappointment in her voice.

"Where are you going?" Denise asked as he towered over her.

"This nice lady is changing seats with you. Get your stuff," Tom instructed.

As the elderly lady stepped forward, Tom eased into her seat and Denise eased into his. Leaning over the aisle, she thanked the woman, who replied with a gush, "I'm curious. If he didn't leave that package for you, who did? A secret admirer? I just love a good romance, don't you?"

Laughing, Denise responded, "I'd like to know, too."

Although Tom's sullen attitude quickly turned to a soft snore, Denise was thrilled that he had joined her. She would never have insisted after he said that he had too much work to do. She would never have wanted him to think that she considered her cases more important than his. However, she had not looked forward to traveling the distance to Hawaii and working the case without him. She needed him to watch her back.

As Tom slept, Denise opened her bag and extracted the box containing the charm bracelet. Carefully, she snapped the newest addition into place. Three charms, two representing places and the third a natural phenomenon. Try as hard as she could, Denise could not make the connection between them. The only thought that came to mind was that the suspect was the twirling winds that blew her, the diamond, from one city to the other in search of his identity. Perhaps the article in the next day's *Washington Post* might help make the association clearer. She would have to wait and see.

The flight was so smooth and uneventful that Denise almost forgot her dislike for air travel. She found being confined to a relatively small space with no escape claustrophobic. However, with Tom sleeping beside her and a good book in her hands, Denise managed to ignore the long hours and almost enjoy the peace and quiet created by the constant and reassuring hum of the engines. Only the occasional cry of a child managed to disturb the flight.

Landing in Los Angeles for a one-hour refueling stopover gave them a chance to leave the plane. Walking around the airport, Denise enjoyed the opportunity to stretch the confinement from her legs. Tom, however, complained about having to interrupt his slumber. Unlike many of the passengers, they did not purchase items in the shops that beckoned. The outrageously high prices did nothing to make Denise want to open her wallet.

Returning to her seat, Denise could feel fatigue seep into her bones. Although it was still afternoon in California, her body thought that it was time for bed. Declining the beverage and only picking at her salad, Denise began to tune out the conversations around her and the engine's hum as she readied herself for sleep.

Tom, for once, had trouble falling asleep. His nap on the fight from the East to the West Coast had been so satisfying that he felt remarkably refreshed. Watching his sleeping partner, he smiled and wondered if other people in relationships enjoyed looking at each other as much as he enjoyed gazing at Denise. Seeing her filled him with a profound happiness.

The slight curve of her lips as she slept made him want to kiss her and feel the warmth of her mouth under his. Resisting, Tom watched Denise as gentle puffs of breath escaped from the delicately parted lips. He observed the slight rising of her lush bosom with each sleeping breath. She was a delight for the eyes when awake and a wonder of creation when sleeping. Some day he would try to find the words to describe his feelings to her.

Instead of waking her, Tom slipped her little hand into his. The size of his hand almost dwarfed hers as he closed his fingers around her delicate ones. Resting his head on the seat near hers, he watched her until his eyes became heavy and closed.

As they neared Hawaii, Denise awakened at the light touch of the flight attendant. "We're landing soon. Check your seat belt and tray table, please."

Groggily, Denise obeyed and then gazed at Tom. His smile was warm and lightly touched with sleep. The nap had done both of them good and helped protect their bodies from the agony of the time change. Although it was very early morning to their bodies, they would be ready for the possibilities that awaited them.

Hawaii . . . a paradise island of beautiful people, stunning vistas, and shimmering waters awaited them in the morning. Neither Denise nor Tom had ever visited the islands, and both were looking forward to the mini working vacation. If they were lucky, they might be able to steal a little beach time.

Knowing that the suspect expected only Denise to emerge from the plane, Tom waited until the last person had disembarked before leaving. They had decided to meet at the hotel, rather than taking the same taxi. Denise hoped that the suspect would focus on her and not notice Tom's presence. Under the cover of the massive crowds, they might be able to avoid the watchful eye of the killer.

Although she had booked a room in a fairly modest hotel on Oahu, light fabrics, swaying palms, and stunning vistas thrilled Denise and satisfied her expectations of paradise. Showing her shield to the night manager, she explained the need for a change in accommodations and for absolute secrecy. He understood and discreetly made the switch himself.

"Detective, there's a letter for you. I hope you'll enjoy your stay on our lovely island," the manager smiled as he handed her the note.

"Thank you. By the way, what's the best time to visit the Pearl Harbor Memorial?" Denise inquired as she held the familiar velum in her fingers.

"I'd suggest 10 A.M.," the manager replied, handing her a pamphlet on the places to visit on Oahu. "Families will not have arrived and the day's heat will be at its minimum. It's not a place that you want to visit with a lot of kids . . . too solemn and reverent. However, the Park Service employees really do a good job of keeping the kids in control. It's a memorial to sailors who died for this country not a playground. I've never experienced rudeness or noise."

"Thanks," Denise replied as she walked toward the elevator, scanning the pamphlet.

Before pressing the elevator button, Denise opened the envelope to find the now familiar handwriting. She was not surprised to discover that the man she was hunting knew the identity of the hotel at which she was staying. If he could know the flight number and time of departure, information that she had not even shared with Tom, then he could easily hack into her computer or pay off an informant within the department and discover where she would stay.

Holding the single sheet to the light, Denise scanned the looping script that read simply, "Welcome to Hawaii! I'll see you at the Polynesian Village tonight. I'll be the one in the lei."

Shaking her head at the killer's attempt at humor, Denise slipped the note into her bag. That one, along with all the others, would eventually find its way into the evidence folder safely locked in her desk. Perhaps whatever clues the suspect would leave at Pearl Harbor and at the Center would add much needed information to the case.

Once in her third-floor room, Denise gravitated toward the window in the darkness and gazed into the view. Lights twinkled in the distance and up the sides of Diamond Head. Torches dotted the creamy sands that lay just below her window. Stepping onto the balcony, she listened to the whispered voice of the ocean as it lapped against the shore.

Unable to pull herself from the aroma of the sea, Denise breathed deeply of the sweet, salt air. Under the flickering torchlight, she watched the surf pound on the shore and lovers stroll along the sandy beach. She could envision the hungry gulls overhead as they flapped their wings and called to her to feed them. If she had time after visiting Pearl Harbor and the Polynesian Village, she would join them for a swim in the warm, inviting water before returning home. Maryland beaches were wonderful, but they could not compare with those of a tropical island.

The sound of Tom entering the darkened room and throwing his suitcase on the second bed just barely penetrated the calm created by the water's voice. Even his angry mutterings as he banged his foot against a chair could not disturb the tranquillity. Denise could feel the trip-induced fatigue slipping from her shoulders as Tom joined her on the veranda.

"No, Tom, get back. We don't want anyone to see you," Denise ordered as she pushed him inside.

"What? I'm a prisoner?" Tom bellowed as he watched Denise close the door and draw the heavy drapes.

Turning on the lights, Denise replied, "No, but you shouldn't stand on the veranda. We don't know if we're being watched."

"I'm in Hawaii, but I can't look at the surf," Tom sputtered angrily as he sank onto his bed. "You don't think this means that I'm in prison?"

"No," Denise stated as she placed her hands on his rigid shoulders, "it means that we have to be careful until after the visit to the Polynesian Village tonight. That's when our killer said that he'd contact me."

"This is getting old fast," Tom complained as he angrily stuffed his clothes into the drawers on the left side of the dresser. "Why do we have to hide from him? We're the good guys, remember."

"We're not hiding. I just want to see if he'll appear at the luau tonight," Denise replied in a soothing tone. She would rather have Tom calm and focused than angry and impetuous.

"Will we have to eat in separate restaurants all day? And tour Pearl Harbor separately?" Tom asked with continued irritation at the inconvenience.

"I hadn't thought about that, but I guess we will. If he's watching and sees us together, he might not show himself tonight," Denise replied thoughtfully.

"Or, he might be so angry that he'll confront you," Tom suggested as he angrily pulled open the dresser drawer that contained the only pair of pajamas he owned since he slept in the nude when not sharing a room with Denise.

Yawning and stretching, Denise replied, "Let's think about that when we're not so tired. Maybe there is an advantage to calling his hand. If he sees us together, he'll know that we're prepared to confront him. It would certainly save money on taxi fares. Besides, I'm glad you decided to join me. The trip will be so much more fun with someone else along."

Stomping to the bathroom in his bare feet with his pajama bottoms in one hand and his toiletry case in the other, Tom commented, "If anyone should be lurking in the dark and taking circuitous routes, it's the perpetrator. He should be hiding from us, not the other way round. I'm going to brush my teeth and get ready for bed."

Smiling, Denise realized that Tom's mood had changed to a more malleable one. She quietly turned back the beds and pulled her long nightshirt from her overnight bag. Even if she had not been too sleepy for a night of romance, Denise knew that Tom would be asleep and snoring before she could return from the bathroom.

The gulls calling at her window woke Denise early. Tom, an early riser, had already showered and dressed. He stood on the veranda drinking complimentary freshly perked coffee from the little bar in the entertainment center. Denise could tell from the set of his shoulders that he had decided that lurking in the shadows did not suit him. He stood boldly at the veranda's railing tossing bits of crackers to the waiting gulls.

Denise did not join him until after her shower. Part of her was a little angry with Tom for exposing their cover and not waiting for her to decide their course of action. However, the other part was glad that the charade was over before it could become more than irritating. She wanted to track the killer and experience Hawaii with Tom at her side, and hiding from an unknown observer would not accomplish her goals.

Opening the complimentary newspaper that lay on the dresser, Denise quickly discovered that her attempt at subterfuge had accomplished nothing. Written in familiar handwriting over the *Washington Post* banner headline, Denise found a message that read, "I didn't want you to miss the article at the bottom of the front page. The time change might have confused you. I hope you and Tom enjoy your day. I'll see you tonight at the Polynesian Village."

Sighing in frustration at her inability to escape the watchful eye of the perpetrator, Denise walked toward the window as she flipped over the paper. Under her right thumb, she found the article to which he had made reference. Their killer had struck again.

"Tom, look at this," Denise instructed as she stepped onto the veranda without giving the birds or the surf a second thought.

Turning to face her, Tom replied, "Good morning to you, too. I see you haven't had your coffee yet. What do you want me to read?"

"You're right, I haven't. Here, read the note at the top of the page, then take a look at that article," Denise instructed as she hurried inside for her first cup of Tom's thick, strong coffee.

Folding the paper like a commuter so that only the top was visible, Tom commented, "So, our little game of hide-and-seek was for nothing. He knows that I'm here. Good, I decided while taking my shower this morning that I wasn't going to play that game anymore."

Calling from inside, Denise instructed, "Now read the article . . . bottom right."

Rearranging the paper as the gulls abandoned their futile attempt to convince him to toss them any more food, Tom read the headline that stated in semibold letters, MANHATTAN FASHION DESIGNER FOUND DEAD. Their suspect had promised that the morning paper would contain news of his latest exploits and he was right.

"He's been a busy little man, hasn't he?" Tom proclaimed sarcastically as he sat on the foot of the bed. "He hacked into your computer to uncover your plans, planted a present in your airline seat, and discovered that I had accompanied you and that we'd changed rooms. On top of that, he murdered another fashion industry great. He must have committed the crime before following you to the airport."

Leaning over his shoulder, Denise commented, "I'm sure he did. Either that or he arranged to have someone do it for him. At any rate, he knew that the paper would carry the story this morning. Are there any details?"

"None. . . . Typical information. Byron Cummings was

the man's name. Seems he was a big name in clothing design. Says that he had worked with renowned jewelers like Worldly. They might as well have printed the specifics of his death. With the killer able to hack into computers, it's a waste of time to try to keep information from a man who's orchestrating all of our actions. Maybe you should phone the captain," Tom suggested as he returned the paper to the table.

Looking at her watch and deciding that Captain Morton would probably still be in his office, Denise stated snidely, "Won't he be thrilled to hear from me? He's paying all this money for me to follow clues to one murder, and the perpetrator commits another while I'm still in the airport. So much for my reputation."

Rising to her defense, Tom replied, "It's not your fault that there's a leak in the squad room. Besides, you didn't really think that he'd stop with one murder."

Dialing the familiar number, Denise responded, "That's true, but I never thought he'd commit a murder after luring me to the city to catch him. I didn't think he'd do anything immediately after I had left either. Looks like he would have worried about the NYPD being on the lookout. I guess I expected that he'd already made his move and was ready to change locations. He obviously has a great deal of contempt for the law."

"You'll catch him yet. There's plenty of time," Tom stated blandly. He had moved to a place somewhere between anger and fury. The suspect was now trying to make Denise look incompetent. It was one thing to stalk her and know her every move, but it was another all together and much more alarming to try to discredit her ability to solve a case. To impugn her authority and skill would make her a target for every killer and thief in the Washington area. Tom felt an overwhelming need to protect Denise from the perpetrator and defend her from the press. He knew that reporters loved a hero but would quickly turn on anyone who did not live up to their expectations.

Raising her finger to indicate that she wanted silence,

Denise announced, "Captain, hi, it's Denise. I saw the article in the *Post*. Actually, the perp informed me that I'd find an article about him in the paper this morning. Any more information than what I see here?"

She listened quietly and then replied, "Yes, we'll return in a few days. I'm heading for Pearl Harbor now and then I need to check out a lead at the Polynesian Village. Right. I understand. Yes, another friend of the chief's. We'll be back soon. Yes, we'll do our best. Good-bye."

Ending the conversation, Denise turned to Tom and relayed the information that the captain had given her, saying, "The victim is another one of the chief's society friends. It seems that this fashion designer is only slightly less famous than the one murdered a few years ago. He's one of the biggest names in New York, Paris, and Rome. Our suspect certainly runs with the rich crowd. I don't know what he uses, but this guy died of fever and convulsions, too. It must be a very strong and rare poison."

Grabbing his jacket and preparing to leave the room, Tom said, "He'd have to be very rich considering the money he's paying to lure you to different parts of the country. First, he kills a jeweler in DC, then a fashion designer in New York. What will he do this time when you leave? He certainly wants to get your attention."

"He has it," Denise replied tartly as she slipped from the room as the door eased shut.

They rode silently to the lobby. Both were deep in thought and happy to be the only passengers in the elevator. Neither wanted to have to make small talk with strangers who might be the killer.

On their way out, the desk clerk gave Denise a thin envelope with her name in the all-too-familiar script. Reaching inside, she extracted two tickets to the luau and the customary note, which read, "It would be a shame for Tom to have to eat alone. See you there." After showing it to Tom, she slipped the tickets into her purse and followed him into the bright sun at his usual hurried pace.

Slipping her arm through Tom's, Denise walked silently. She was so deep in thought that she barely noticed the signs for mahimahi sandwiches, coconut punch, and potted orchids to take home. The killer was watching, that she knew for certain. One day, they would come face-to-face. Denise would be ready.

Seven

Although the day was comfortably warm, the strength of the sun hinted that the mercury would soon top out at ninety. A gentle breeze helped to evaporate the perspiration that collected on Denise's forehead as the result of her effort to keep up with Tom's long strides. Unlike New York, the streets of Oahu were not packed with tourists, making it easy for them to travel at Tom's usual breakneck pace. They stopped only long enough to hail a cab, and then the views of the shopping centers were speeding past them.

Arriving at Pearl Harbor, Denise could feel the change in the surroundings. People whispered and did not laugh out loud. They walked more slowly as they boarded the launch that would take them to the memorial to the dead sailors of the Japanese attack. They sat in hushed silence as the transport carried them into the harbor. Men removed their caps as they stood in front of the wall bearing the names of the dead. Men and women wiped tears as they looked at the remains of the sunken ship with the bodies of the men entombed. Pearl Harbor was an experience unlike any that Denise had ever had.

The always stoic and unflappable Tom was also moved. He read the names in silence and lingered at the rail overlooking the turret. His eyes misted as he thought of the black sailors restricted to mess duty who served and died for their country. He remembered the one who had received a medal for his bravery yet been denied the highest honor because of his skin color. Although they came to Hawaii and Pearl Harbor in search of a clue that would lead them to a killer, Denise and Tom found so much more at the memorial to the brave dead.

However, unlike the other visitors, they had business to conduct. Denise and Tom worked as unobtrusively as possible as they looked under the few benches that dotted the memorial for an envelope from their suspect. Finding nothing, they hunted down the Park Service officer in charge of the memorial. With his help, they searched the launches but, again, came up empty-handed.

Thinking that the perpetrator was laughing at them for Tom's presence, Denise was almost ready to give up when she noticed a small box wrapped in white and gold paper taped to one of the strategically located trashcans. Walking toward it, Denise smiled and shook her head in recognition of the killer's bold attitude. He had left his clue attached to a trashcan without concern that someone would dispose of it. He held the game and Denise in such contempt that it did not matter to him if his information did not reach the detective on his case.

Breaking the seal of heavily applied shipping tape, Denise immediately recognized the looping style of the suspect's handwriting. She opened the package as Tom joined her and peered over her shoulder. Inside, along with the usual note, Denise discovered another charm.

Holding the note steady against the stiff breeze, Denise read the difficult handwriting with ease. She had learned to decipher the curling letters and the swooping style from the earlier notes and barely gave the extravagant style any notice. As always, the rich velum felt good between her fingers.

Sharing the information with Tom, Denise read the note aloud saying, "From Polynesian Village's lush green hills, travel east to the gorges, buttes, and ravines where thunderstorms drop rain on the arid terrain but fail to nourish it. From sea level to 8,200 feet above, from green to buff and red. More later."

"Now where's he taking you?" Tom asked with a scowl of disgust.

"It sounds like the Grand Canyon to me. Let's see if the charm's any help," Denise replied as she unwrapped the little treasure.

The sun immediately glinted brightly off the shinny surface of the tiny animal. Shading it with her hand, Denise saw that the charm was in the shape of a donkey or burrow. Its tiny ears and tail were almost lifelike.

Begrudgingly. Denise stated, "I've got to give him this much . . . he's certainly imaginative. He must have spent a fortune at Charming Charms in New York."

Wiping the sweat from his brow, Tom asked, "What's the significance of a donkey? I might understand a chunk of rock but not a donkey."

Chuckling at the memory, Denise answered, "When I was a kid, my parents took us to the Grand Canyon. Mother wouldn't go with us, but Daddy took us on a donkey ride from the south rim to the interior. Mother said that nothing would make her ride on one of those temperamental beasts. Anyway, we had a great time. We stayed overnight at a campsite and went out scorpion watching. That was one of the best vacations I've ever had."

"You're a sick chick if you think scorpion watching is fun," Tom replied as he snapped the tiny donkey to the offered charm bracelet. It seemed content next to the lei.

"Not sick, just adventurous." Denise defended her childhood memory. "Anyway, I was young. I don't think I'd do that now that I know better. I didn't even think about the possibility that the donkey might misstep and fall or deliberately throw me down the canyon."

Returning the bracelet to its box and Denise's bag, Tom commented, "So, you're going to the Grand Canyon next. By the time you apprehend this perpetrator, you'll have traveled more than on any of the other cases that have taken you away from the office."

"That's if the captain will agree," Denise stated. "I need

to phone the office anyway to see if Ronda learned anything about Mr. Worldly's family, his kids in particular. Maybe she'll know something about a family feud by now."

Walking more slowly than usual, Tom added, "I guess that means that I'll fly home alone. I'm feeling like a fifth wheel."

Denise offered hopefully, "Why don't you advance some more leave? The captain will probably let you. I'd love to have you with me. I feel safe with you at my back."

Teasing, Tom asked, "What makes you think that I want to use all of my vacation following you around the country? I might have other plans."

"Like what . . . picking fleas off that mangy partner of yours?" Denise rebutted happily.

Pretending to be offended, Tom replied, "Molly's not mangy. She has the best coat of any other canine in the corps. I brush her two or three times every day. She's a great partner. You could do worse."

"I have," Denise commented with a chuckle. "My first partner drooled and looked like Frankenstein. Molly's a doll compared to him."

Slipping his arm around Denise's shoulders as they strolled toward their hotel, Tom asked again playfully, "Would you really like for me to stay? I haven't confirmed my passage on the Good Ship Lollypop as yet. I'm at your service."

"I'd love to have your company, but who will take care of Molly," Denise asked as she smiled into his habitually serious face.

Laughing, Tom replied, "The same person who's watching her now . . . your sister. She was the only person I could find on such short notice who would take that mean cat of yours and Molly."

"My sister!" Denise exclaimed. "She hardly has time to breathe with all those kids and a catering business."

Stopping to buy two cans of soda, Tom replied, "She's OK with it and the kids love Molly. I'm not too sure what they think about your cat, however."

"What about the captain? Will he give you more leave?" Denise asked as she drained the can.

"No problem," Tom stated with confidence. "He told me when I left the squad room that he wants me to offer you as much help as you need. This case is not only high profile, it's dangerous. While you're on the killer's trail, he's following you. Not a good combination."

Sighing deeply, Denise said, "Let's return to the hotel. I want to give Ronda a call to see if she can shed some light on the suspect's identity. Maybe he's one of Mr. Worldly's kids."

"Or maybe just a guy with a grudge against people in the fashion industry," Tom suggested as he tossed the cans into the curbside trashcan.

"Possible," Denise conceded. "I haven't ruled out anything. He hasn't given me enough clues. The newspaper said that the designer died as the result of severe convulsions just like Mr. Worldly. If pathology determines that the same poison, microbe, or virus killed both of them, then we'll know that we're tracking the same man . . . a dangerous man who uses biomedical weapons rather than guns. Until we know something more concrete, we'll have to be open to anything."

Reaching their hotel, they quickly entered to escape the heat and burning sun. Despite the off-shore breeze, the burning rays of the sun penetrated their clothing and scorched their skin. Although Denise had worn a baseball cap to protect her face and covered her ears with sunscreen, she could still feel them tingling.

"Detective Dory," the manager called as she entered. "There's a call for you. You can take it on the phone by the elevators."

Nodding her thanks, Denise walked to the bank of elevators and row of phones. Scowling, she picked up the receiver. Ronda's voice almost assaulted her ears as she shouted into the phone, "Hi, Denise!"

"You don't have to shout. I can hear you just fine," Denise replied in a normal voice.

"Oh, I thought the connection might be bad across the ocean and all," Ronda said as she brought her voice down a few notches.

"That's old technology. These days, the phone company uses satellites. What's up?" Denise asked as she grinned at Tom who had stuck his fingers in his ears against the shrill of Ronda's voice.

"The captain told me to call you with the pathology results on both bodies," Ronda replied in a voice still too loud for Denise's comfort.

"Great," Denise agreed. "I was planning to call you. That's why I returned to the hotel. What do you have for me?"

Reading slowly, Ronda replied, "The tests show that both designers died from the same kind of illness that causes severe cramping, fever, convulsions, and death. However, that pathologist doesn't know the source yet. Oh, and the captain says for you and Tom to be careful. The chief wants this case solved, but she doesn't want you two killed in the process."

Quickly jotting a note in her sketchbook, Denise responded, "We're being careful. Don't worry about us. By the way, did you find out anything about Worldly's family? Any chance the suspect might be one of them?"

"I learned a whole lot of nothing," Ronda replied, "They're clean . . . all of them. Not even a parking ticket among them. You won't find your killer in that family. They're a close group. No arguments among them."

"Thanks. The killer wants me to follow him to the Grand Canyon next. I'll phone you from there. Tell the captain that we'll probably leave for Arizona some time tomorrow. It all depends on what I learn tonight at the luau," Denise stated as she closed her sketchbook.

"I'll tell him. When might you return from this little vacation? Luaus, touring, you're certainly living the life," Ronda asked, jokingly.

"Soon, I hope. I really don't like living out of my suitcase," Denise replied. "This guy can't keep his guard up forever. He'll slip sooner or later."

Taking the phone from Denise, Tom said, "Ronda, tell the captain that I'm staying on the case for a while longer."

"I'll tell him," Ronda stated. "He said for me to tell you that he's not charging you leave time for this. As far as he's concerned, you're on official business as Denise's backup."

"Ask him to phone ahead so that the police in the vicinity of the Canyon know that we're coming," Denise instructed after reclaiming the phone. "We might need extra help."

"Leave it to me," Ronda stated. "Anything else?"

"Nothing, thanks. We'll see you in a few days," Denise replied and ended the conversation.

Turning to Tom, Denise felt a strange sense of confidence spread over her body. Suddenly, she knew, just as she did on the Capitol Hill case, that everything would turn out right. The perpetrator would eventually expose himself. When he did, she would be there to apprehend him. It was simply a matter of time. With Tom at her side, Denise felt ready for anything.

As they rode up the elevator, Denise asked, "How about a swim? That water looks so inviting. Let's do it. We don't know when we'll ever return."

"I bet I can change faster than you can," Tom replied as an answer.

Like two kids on vacation, they quickly changed into their suits, one in the bathroom and the other out of sight near the nightstands. Grabbing the special yellow towels the hotel provided for beach use, they rushed down the back stairs to the waiting chairs and pounding surf. The allure of the Hawaiian sky was too great for them to resist.

"Put lotion on my back, please," Denise requested as she handed Tom the bottle.

She stood clothed in a very dignified and concealing black tank. However, to Tom, Denise looked like Venus. Her arms and legs were much longer and more muscular than he had supposed from seeing her in her clothing. Even the running shorts and T-shirt that she wore on weekends failed to do her lithe frame justice. She was stunning, and Tom was more smitten than ever.

"This stuff is sticky," Tom muttered in a husky voice as he spread the lotion on her back and shoulders.

"Take off your T-shirt and let me do your back," Denise ordered as she filled her hands with the cool, white lotion.

"That's OK," Tom hesitated. "I don't really need any. I don't burn."

"Doctors say that everyone should use suntan lotion against the drying effects of the sun. You don't have a choice. Turn around," Denise repeated.

Obediently Tom stripped off the T-shirt that concealed the thick muscles of his chest and back. Denise almost gasped at the sight of the ripples that played along the brown expanse of flesh. Standing in front of her, Tom looked like a candidate in the Mr. World contest.

"It's cold," Tom complained, nervous at standing before his partner dressed in so little.

"Don't be silly. Your skin's just hot, that's all. The lotion is cooling," Denise replied as her hand slowly eased along the thickly muscled back. She had often touched Tom's muscular arm, but she had never realized through his clothing that he looked this buff. He always wore baggy, too big shorts and T-shirts when they jogged together.

"Done yet?" Tom asked impatiently.

"Almost. Just a little more on the top of your shoulders and ears. When did you build up your muscles like this?" Denise asked as she capped the lotion bottle, hoping that her voice sounded steadier than his.

"I've been working out more lately. Molly needs a strong hand. Besides, you're always too busy working on a case to go running with me. I've got to do something to keep in shape," Tom replied. He was glad that he wore the longer leg, loose-fitting swim trunks. He had never liked the tiny bikinis that some men enjoyed, not wanting to attract too much attention. If he had been wearing less, Denise would have noticed his reaction to the touch of her hand on his skin.

Afraid that Denise would notice his intense interest in her through the draped fabric, Tom shouted, "Last one in buys breakfast."

"That's not fair! You had a head start!" Denise complained as she charged after the incredibly sexy figure darting toward the waves. After the heat created by their bodies, the warm water would feel cool. Denise made a mental note to be as careful around Tom as she was in tracking killers. Their relationship was moving slowly; she did not want passion to push it into uncharted territory too soon.

While playing in the water like children, Denise discovered a different, less stern side of Tom. He had quickly lured her into water up to her neck and relished in dipping under and swimming away from her. The stillness of the ocean, as compared to the Atlantic, was a joy. Without the heavy waves and the undertow, Denise felt almost liberated.

Not being a confident swimmer, she would bob and tiptoe after him. When she could not find him, she would push against the sandy bottom and wade to shore. However, before she could reach the shallow water, he would reappear and pull her out again.

His laughter was infectious. Denise found that she could not become angry with him for dunking her because he was having such great fun. She responded not with scolding but with giggles, and Tom loved it. Making her cling to his neck, he gave her rides around the water that was much too deep for her limited swimming ability. She clung to him and roared with laughter as she surfed lying on her stomach using Tom as her board.

Denise had never felt so relaxed and so totally safe. Despite playing in water that could have drowned her, she was completely at peace, knowing that Tom would take care of her. She clung to him, allowed him to dive with her on his back, and raved about the shells he brought from the depths for her.

She had not enjoyed herself this much since she was a small girl and her father had taken the family to the beach.

The waves had felt harder then, either because she was a little girl or because it was the Atlantic Ocean. Either way, she had cried when the first one had knocked her down until her father had picked her up and carried her on his shoulders. He could not swim at all, but his love of the water and his strength quickly allayed her fears. She had felt completely safe in his arms, just as she did in Tom's.

Returning to the shore, they toweled some of the water from their streaming bodies and stretched out on the beach chairs. The sun and the breeze quickly turned the remaining moisture into salty spots that dotted their bodies. The rays warmed their skin and lulled them to sleep.

Suddenly, Denise felt someone standing over her. Quickly, she awakened and instinctively reached for the service revolver she kept under her pillow. Then she remembered that she was not in her apartment but on the beach in Hawaii, so she shaded her eyes from the sun and squinted to see the face of the person towering above her. As hard as she tired, Denise could not make out the features of the shadowed face, although she knew that it was not Tom from the narrowness of the physique. However, she could not tell if the intruder were male or female. The amorphous form could have belonged to either.

The figure did not speak. Instead, Denise felt something fall onto her stomach before the figure turned and blended with the crowd. Even in silhouette, she could not determine the figure's gender. The chest and buttocks were flat like a young boy's, and the gait in the shifting sands could have belonged to either.

"Tom, Tom, wake up! You're supposed to be watching my back," Denise called as she turned toward him. Sitting up quickly, she found that his chair was empty.

Shading her eyes again, she saw Tom lumbering across the sand with two dripping ice cream cones in his hands. His passion for the sweet confection had been a nuisance in DC while they worked the Capitol Hill case and looked as if it might interfere in his duties on this one. If he had been

by her side, he might have been able to apprehend the unin-
vited visitor.

"Ice cream," Tom announced the obvious as he handed
her a dripping strawberry cone. "You'd better eat it fast."

"What do I care about ice cream?" Denise asked sarcastically, waving the envelope at him. "I've been visited by the
perp and all you can talk about is ice cream."

"What?" Tom asked as he sat on his beach chair and stared
at Denise's shocked expression.

Exasperated, Denise replied, "He walked up and dropped
this envelope on my stomach. At least, I think it was a guy.
He was so thin and flat that I really couldn't tell. You're
supposed to watch my back, be my backup, but you were
off buying ice cream."

Unruffled, Tom licked his treat before answering, "If I'd
been here, I would have been asleep. I still wouldn't have
seen him. Be thankful that he only dropped an envelope."

"That's what I'm saying. He could have shot me," Denise
puffed with anger.

"But you're not dead, Dory. Open the envelope. Besides,
our killer doesn't use a gun, remember," Tom directed with
a seeming lack of interest in his carefully controlled voice.
His red tongue quickly caught another drip of chocolate ice
cream.

Raking him with her angry eyes, Denise commented
through clinched teeth, "If I didn't know that the tightening
of your jaw meant that you're angry, I'd think that you didn't
care about me. However, knowing that you're fuming inside
because the perp is watching and stalking us, I'll let you
slide."

"What does it say this time?" Tom asked directing her
attention away from him and to the note. As he watched
Denise read the familiar handwriting, he absently licked the
ice cream. She was right; he was furious. She could have
been killed. He would not leave her alone again.

"Now that I have your attention, I'll read it to you," Denise
replied snidely with the remnants of her anger. "Let's see,

he writes 'Dear Dory: Wear the bracelet tonight. I want to hear it jingle as you dance the hula. It's all arranged. The emcee will call you to the stage. I'll be one of the other members of the audience on stage with you. See if you can find me. If you can't, we'll meet again tomorrow.' Sick! He's using my nickname now."

"Did he enclose a charm?" Tom asked, holding his irritation in check.

"Of course," Denise stated as she unwrapped the little package. "It's a rainbow. I was right. The donkey did mean the Grand Canyon after all. The rainbow charm confirms it. I wonder if he's using a tour book or if he has visited all these places."

"What's so important about rainbows in the Grand Canyon?" Tom asked as he studied her face. Something in the glow of her eyes said that Denise was enjoying the game of wits with the perpetrator.

Dreamily, Denise replied, "They're simply the most stunningly beautiful in the United States and maybe even better than the ones in Ireland. They stretch over the entire expanse of the Canyon. The colors are breathtaking . . . like nothing you've ever seen. The rainbows seem to grow out of the rocks and absorb all of their vibrancy. The Grand Canyon and the Mediterranean Sea definitely prove that a Creator or Divine force exists."

"I remember the summer I went with a bunch of my buddies. We had made a little money that summer before our freshman year in college and were anxious to spend it. We decided on the Canyon since a few of us had never been there. I'm glad we did. We stayed at a little inn on the cliff of the South Rim. I remember sitting on the veranda and watching the colors change on the Canyon walls. It was great."

Feeling a spark of jealously at the tone in her voice and the look of sweet memory on her face, Tom asked, "What else happened on that trip? Did you go with all girls?"

Laughing at the expression on his face, Denise replied, "No, it was a mixed group. I fell in love that summer and had my first kiss. I was standing on one of the observation decks looking down at the Canyon floor. He put his arms around me from the back and gave me a big hug. When I turned around to speak to him, he kissed me. Soft, tender, a nice first kiss."

"Umphf," Tom grunted his displeasure.

"Don't you remember your first kiss?" Denise asked with sincerity.

"No! Guys don't remember stuff like that," Tom responded firmly.

"I bet you do. You don't forget anything. Tell me about it. You owe me that for leaving me alone and unprotected," Denise insisted as she finished the last of her waffle cone.

Shrugging his shoulders, Tom replied flatly, "She was a friend of my sister's and always at the house. One day, I kissed her. I guess I had wanted to know what the big deal was about kissing, so I did it. Nothing spectacular. We didn't date or anything. She was just a girl in the right place at the right time."

"Very romantic!" Denise commented sarcastically. "Hardly anything to record in your diary."

"I told you that kind of stuff isn't important to me," Tom grumbled as he pulled his T-shirt onto his sticky body and collected their towels.

"What is important to you, Tom?" Denise asked as she joined him for the short walk to the hotel's back door.

Turning to look her full in the face, Tom replied with more conviction in his voice than she had ever heard, "Now, this moment because it might be our last. We don't know which one it'll be. In this line of work, you've got to enjoy all of them to the fullest."

Following him to the elevator along a path made by other sandy feet, Denise thought about his comment and decided that Tom was right. They did not know which moment would be their last. The suspect could have killed her instead of simply dropping an envelope on her stomach. She decided that she would seize the moment that night when they returned from the luau. They had been careful in their relationship long enough.

After her shower, Denise slipped into a short, spaghetti-strap, floral print dress that seemed to be appropriate for a luau. Its white background made her tan look even darker and the bright colors accentuated her slim figure. Knowing that she would be in view that evening, she was glad that she had packed the cute high-heeled sandals that made her legs look fabulous.

Slipping the charm bracelet on her right wrist, Denise surveyed her reflection in the mirror. She needed no makeup to brighten her suntanned skin. Her hair had picked up a slightly coppery glow that looked great with her new tan. Her eyes glinted with anticipation. With luck, she would come closer to catching a killer and her partner that evening.

Nodding his approval, Tom stated simply, "You look good."

"Thanks," Denise replied, knowing that this was the best she would ever hear from him.

Tom usually did not notice what she wore or how she looked and seemed surprised when other men mentioned her beauty to him. He did not take her for granted. It was just that Denise always looked and smelled great. He did not see any reason to compliment her on the obvious every day.

"You look pretty delicious yourself in that white knit shirt and slacks," Denise added playfully. "All the women will swoon when they see you. That outfit really shows off your skin color and muscles."

"Do I look too conspicuous?" Tom asked as he took the first and only look at himself in the mirror.

Teasing but meaning every word, Denise stated, "I wouldn't exactly say that, but you will definitely not escape notice. I'd better hold on tight if I'm to keep you at my side tonight."

"I'll change. I don't want anything getting in the way of our work. I need to keep my eyes on you and the killer," Tom replied as he started to unbutton his shirt. He was so literal that he had missed the overt hint of things to come in Denise's voice.

Grabbing his hands, Denise said, "No, don't do that. You're fine. Let's go. I always forget that you can be so literal when you want to be. Loosen up a bit."

Shrugging, Tom replied as he followed Denise to the door, "I thought I was loose."

Denise decided on the ride to the lobby that she would make him relax when they returned from the Polynesian Village. Even if it took a private and provocative hula, she would make sure that Tom did not misunderstand the nuances of her meaning. As soon as they were off duty, she would cast a little Hawaiian magic of her own.

Eight

The Polynesian Village occupied a seeming remote location on the other side of the island. Thick groves of palm trees and banana plants lined the road interspersed here and there with pineapple fields. Everywhere she looked, Denise saw massed hibiscus flowers, so prolific that they would make gardeners at home envious. Their huge blooms fluttered gracefully in the breeze.

While Denise gazed out the taxi window in amazement, Tom slept. The sight of the island's flora only held his attention for a few moments, and then he drifted off to sleep, lulled by the warmth and the motion of the car. Try as she might, Denise could not interest him in more of the island's natural resources.

However, Tom awoke quickly when they arrived at the Village. With all the people in attendance, he needed to be alert for a killer whose identity they did not know. Greeters laden with leis welcomed the visitors, as tourists milled everywhere. Some were wearing the garish commercial Hawaiian shirts, while others looked more circumspect in casual clothing. Each one received a lei and a warm smile. Regardless of their attire, they looked ready for a pleasant evening and delicious meal.

The Polynesian Village was more than a pleasant restaurant; it was an exposition of Polynesian culture. People from each of the islands that comprised the Polynesian chain worked a booth or display. They exhibited their wares, demonstrated native handicrafts, and offered ceremonial songs. After an evening at the Village, attentive tourists would have gained a fair knowledge of the traditions and culture of the islands. Of course, the central shopping area offered visitors the opportunity to purchase memorabilia of every description. From expensive coral and pearl jewelry to T-shirts, tourists could find ways to spend a few extra dollars.

While Denise and Tom mingled with the crowd, they kept on the alert for anyone who might be watching them rather than the demonstrations. Except for the women who overtly ogled Tom and the men who smiled their approval at Denise, no one seemed threatening. As a matter of fact, if it had not been for the redhead who almost fell into Tom's arms, they would not have had contact with anyone.

As they approached the Samoan exhibit, a tall redheaded woman wearing ridiculously high heels snagged her heel on a slightly raised section of the walkway. Trying to catch her balance, she staggered against Tom's strong chest and threw her arms around his neck. Instinctively, his arms encircled her. Her body pressed urgently against his as she struggled to regain her balance. Her hair brushed his face as she righted herself and her lips just barely missed colliding with his.

"I'm so sorry!" the redhead gushed as she untangled herself from Tom's arms.

"Are you OK?" Tom asked as he watched her smooth her hair and rearrange her shirt.

"I'm fine. I shouldn't have worn these shoes. It was silly of me to wear new shoes to an outdoor affair," she cooed at Tom, ignoring Denise completely.

"Well, be careful. Good-bye," Tom replied as he started to walk away.

"You saved me from a nasty fall. May I buy you a drink or an ice cream?" she asked, standing provocatively close with her hand on her right hip.

"No, thanks. Enjoy your evening," Tom responded, gazing helplessly at Denise for the assistance that never came.

"I'm staying at the Hilton, if you'd like something stronger than these tropical fruit drinks. I'd really like to repay your chivalry more personally," the redhead smiled seductively as she stroked the bulging muscles in Tom's arm.

Stepping slightly away, Tom replied, "Not necessary. Good evening."

"Well, if you change your mind . . ." the woman said to his retreating back.

Denise struggled between the desire to laugh uproariously at Tom's discomfort and the need to smack the woman. If Tom's reaction had been different or if he had appeared to enjoy the woman's advances, she would have stepped up to defend her turf. However, his obvious discomfort at the nearness of the woman and the spectacle she was making of them caused her to remain silent.

But now that Tom was free of the redhead's clutches, Denise laughed so hard and so silently that tears welled in her eyes and threatened to spill onto her cheeks. Even Tom's angry glare could not stop the spasms of laughter that tore through her body. The sight of her touch-me-not partner in the embrace of that effusive redhead almost caused her to split her sides.

"What's so funny? I kept the woman from breaking her neck. Is that funny?" Tom demanded angrily after Denise had regained her composure.

"For a grown man, you're so innocent," Denise chuckled as she wiped the last of the tears from her eyes.

"I am not," Tom declared, defending himself and then added, "What do you mean?"

Still chuckling, Denise replied, "I told you that outfit would get you in trouble. That woman didn't trip, she deliberately fell into your arms."

"She did not. She tripped because of her shoes. You heard her say that her heels were too high and she didn't know how to walk in them," Tom rebutted angrily at Denise's suggestion.

Looking at him skeptically, Denise commented, "The shoes were not new. While she was draped all over you, I could see the bottoms. They weren't old, but they had definitely seen wear. She knew what she was doing. I warned you about the effect of that shirt and your muscles on women."

"Dory, you're one twisted sister, you know that. That woman tripped. She did not throw herself at me. My shirt does not turn women into sex fiends," Tom insisted angrily as they continued their stroll through the Village.

"I suppose her offer of a drink later was nothing either," Denise commented, looking into his face from under her brows.

"She was grateful, that's all," Tom declared firmly. "Besides, why would a woman fall into my arms like that?"

Wanting to have a clear view of Tom's face, Denise stepped into a little opening away from the foot traffic. Turning to Tom, she stated, "You're handsome and sexy, that's why."

As the anger faded from his face, Tom asked, "Do you really believe that, or are you just saying it because of that woman?"

"I know it," Denise replied softly. "Why do you think I warned you about that shirt? I don't want other women noticing my partner."

"You've never said anything before," Tom responded hesitantly. He was still not sure if Denise, the major prankster in the office, was serious or teasing him.

In her usual straightforward manner, Denise stated, "I haven't seen you half naked on a Hawaiian beach before. Believe me, you're quite an eyeful."

"You're speaking only as my partner?" Tom asked as he studied her face. Their relationship had progressed nicely since the Capitol Hill case, but he was still not on solid footing. Denise was often distracted and mercurial. He never knew exactly where he stood with her.

"I'm speaking as your partner, a woman, and your . . . friend," Denise replied as she hunted for the right word. She was neither a girl nor his significant other nor his lover. Other than his partner and friend, she did not know how to classify herself in relationship to him.

"Oh, my friend," Tom responded. The disappointment was obvious in his voice and on his face.

"You know how I feel about that 'girlfriend' title. I'm not a kid. You get my general meaning," Denise replied, trying to soothe his hurt feelings.

"Just this once, so that we're on the same page, can you please use it? I need to know that we're together . . . an item . . . a couple," Tom asked plaintively.

Studying his face for only seconds, Denise felt incredibly warm. It was not the effect of the Polynesian night that made her feel tingly all over. It was the knowledge that the man who had never demanded anything of her and took their relationship as it came to him had made himself vulnerable. He needed to hear that Denise felt that their relationship had validity and substance.

"All right. Until we can find a better title, I'm your girlfriend," Denise replied softly.

Immediately, Tom's strong arms encircled her body and pulled her against him. Unconscious of the smiles that greeted them, he placed his lips on hers in a sweet, warm kiss that spoke all the terms of endearment that he could not say. As she melted into him, Denise knew that regardless of the nomenclature, she belonged to Tom. The direction of their relationship was still unclear, but it was definitely on the move to something other than friendship.

Pushing back to look into his face, Denise smiled and said, "We're on duty, remember. That redhead in your arms already called attention to you. Kissing a brunette a minute later only adds to your charms. I think you've achieved enough notoriety for one evening."

Grinning from one ear to the other, Tom replied, "Just remember if someone asks you, you're my girl."

Holding hands and easing into the crowd, Denise and Tom continued toward the dining pavilion along the torch-lit path. The security of his hand on hers made the Village seem brighter and calmer. The crush of people seemed less oppressive with Tom's strong arm near hers. Denise wondered if, after all this time of being Tom's partner and best friend, this might be love. She certainly felt deeply about him and could not imagine life without him. He had her back *and* her heart. They had never spoken of the next step in their relationship. They spoke of moving to it if they could ever manage the demands of work, but neither had ever defined it. Perhaps the relationship had defined itself.

Glancing quickly up at Tom, Denise could tell that he was also deep in thought. Emotion darted across his usually unlined blank face. She wondered if he were sorting out the same thoughts and reactions. The kiss had been so uncharacteristic of the reserved, controlled man that she'd known all these years. Perhaps he regretted doing it and wished that they could return to the life of silence they had lived until that moment of unexpected passion. Yet the kiss had not been passionate. Instead, it had contained an incredible sweetness and a sense of eternity. She wondered if he was as confused as she was by the change in their relationship. When the demands of work did not press against them, Denise would have to explore his thoughts.

The flickering torches gave way to the glow of hundreds of candles as they stepped from the path into the dining area. Every table held a multibranched candelabra that twinkled in unison with the candles in the overhead chandeliers. White flowers, both hibiscus and orchids, floated on water in crystal bowls resting on mirrors that reflected the light. The fragrance of their blooms mixed with the aroma of the luau's menu to produce an exotic effect.

Joining a table for eight, Denise and Tom introduced themselves to the others who were there to eat and make merry. The diners sipped greedily on the spiked fruity punch and munched the salad already at their places. Only Denise and Tom requested the nonalcoholic version, but the others did not seem to notice.

As the waitress cleared the table between courses, Denise surveyed the room. A small stage stood at the back, the entrances to the kitchen to the left and right of it, and the exits on the sides and to the rear near the stage. The wait staff all wore Hawaiian garb with the women in hula skirts and the men in knee-length loincloths. All of them wore the traditional lei.

Although most of the dancers were Polynesian, the group contained many races. One of the tall, blond waitresses looked vaguely familiar. However, despite her excellent memory for faces, Denise could not recall where she had seen the woman.

Although she did not find anything suspicious, Denise could almost feel someone watching her. Dismissing the thought as the effect of having the waitress always at her elbow, she tried to relax and enjoy the meal. However, knowing that the killer would soon join her on the small stage detracted from the evening.

Not even having Tom at her side could relieve the tension. Since entering the dining room, she had become instantly ill at ease. All of the warmth of his kiss had evaporated and the need to be vigilant and on guard replaced it. The delicious aroma and taste of the meal ranked second to the feeling of suspense in the air. From the stiffness of Tom's posture, Denise could tell that he felt the negative energy also.

Yet the other diners did not seem to be aware of it. They attacked their meal with gusto and drank copious amounts of the punch, spiked or plain. They did not have a care in the world. A murderer was not watching them.

Denise placed her fork and knife on the barely sampled plate of food. Immediately, the waitress appeared and asked, "You've hardly eaten anything. Would you like something different? The chef is always willing to make substitutions."

Smiling graciously, Denise replied, "No, the food was delicious. I'm still adjusting to the heat and change in water. I'm fine."

Nodding sympathetically, the waitress replied, "The dessert might be more to your liking. It's mango sherbet and quite delicious. It'll help to settle your stomach."

Leaning toward her, Tom commented, "You're certainly a

skillful liar. I wouldn't have been able to think of something that fast. Have you seen anyone suspicious?"

Without stopping her surveillance, Denise replied, "I'll take that as a compliment. It comes from years of eating alone and being badgered by unwanted male attention. No, I haven't seen anyone. I'm beginning to think that he's not here."

"He's here all right. I can feel him watching us. I just wish I could catch him in the act," Tom commented as he clinched his teeth.

"If you're right, he'll soon take center stage," Denise added, reminding him of the killer's earlier note.

Tom growled, "Yes, with you on the stage with him. He has an unfair advantage."

The dessert arrived and was as pleasing as the waitress had indicated. The cool sherbet helped to ease some of the heat-induced tension that had gripped Denise's shoulders and back in a merciless vice. The waiting was definitely getting on her nerves.

As soon as the noise of silver on crystal subsided, a spotlight illuminated the stage. A gentleman dressed in an incongruous tuxedo appeared from the wings with a microphone in his hands. Introducing himself as the emcee for the evening, he proceeded to recognize groups of people enjoying the dinner.

Denise and Tom applauded with the others as newlyweds stood to acknowledge their unions, people celebrating birthdays waved their thanks, and tour groups on vacation shouted their existence. Thinking that the people at her table from Washington state were the last that the emcee would recognize, Denise turned her chair for a better view of the stage.

To her surprise, the emcee consulted his list one more time. Laughing amiably, he stated, "Here's a first. In all my years as the emcee at the Polynesian Village, no one has ever asked me to introduce this kind of couple, but here goes. At table number fifteen at the back of the house, let's welcome Detectives Dory and Phyfer from the Montgomery County Maryland Police Department. I understand that they are in

Hawaii investigating a murder case. Let's hear it for the detectives."

As the spotlight landed on them, Denise would have liked to have crawled under the table. Never had so much attention come her way. Instinctively, she knew that this was only the beginning of the pranks the killer had in store for them.

Turning to Tom, who sat rigid with anger, Denise mouthed, "Smile and wave."

Obediently, his face broke into the most frightening forced smile she had ever seen. Instead of looking pleasant, he succeeded in appearing to be the model for a Halloween jack o'lantern, complete with grimace and flashing white teeth. She hoped that her feigned happiness would appear more convincing.

As the reserved applause died down, the emcee announced the first act. Much to Denise's delight, the hula dance instruction that the suspect had promised did not open the show. Instead, jugglers in loincloths mesmerized the audience with incredible feats of balance and dexterity.

Not daring to look at Tom, Denise glued her eyes to the stage. She could feel the heat emanating from his rigid body. She knew that Tom seethed from the embarrassment of being made a spectacle in front of the crowd of people and having the suspect blow his cover. To have said anything to him might have made matters worse. She hoped that others with grudges against law enforcement officers were not in the house and packing concealed weapons.

Denise always tried not to dwell on the very real possibility that one day someone would shoot at her. As a rookie, she had been involved in shootouts, but the perpetrator had not been deliberately shooting at her; she had been simply a member of a group at which he directed his anger. However, now that she was on this case and chasing a killer across the country, she had become a target for personal attack. The public exposure further compounded her problem. Tom's inability to laugh off the attention made them a more ideal target for someone with a grudge.

Although she applauded vigorously, Denise did not enjoy the jugglers or the bicycle act that followed. She was waiting for the dancers. Nothing would be able to provide her with any relief until after the dance act. If the killer did not contact her by then, she would be safe.

Denise and Tom did not have long to wait. The troop of hula dancers took the stage following the sword swallower. Their grass skirts rustled intriguingly as they formed two rows of swaying hips that undulated to the exotic sound of the ukulele. Expressive fingers cut the air as they told the story of loves forgotten. Most of them were stylishly thin, but not emaciated, although one seemed a little stockier than the others and a bit familiar, too. However, they all looked stunning as they swished and swayed.

At the end of their number, men carrying long poles joined the women on the stage. With the women surrounding them, the men began to dance, placing their feet between the rhythmically colliding poles that quickened dangerously. Each step contained an intricate pattern that required concentration, balance, and skill. Everyone waited breathlessly for one of the men to have his foot slammed between the poles as the tempo reached a furious pace.

When the dance ended, the crowd went wild. The performers responded with bows and an encore first by the women and then the men. This time, a tribal drum set the pace for the swaying hips and the dancing feet.

The drumbeat continued as the dancers walked into the audience. Quickly, the men and women selected diners who would join them on stage for a hula lesson. Pulling the stuffed diners to their feet, the dancers led them onto the stage.

Denise was on the verge of taking a deep breath when she felt a hand on her shoulder. Looking up, she saw a handsome Hawaiian dancer smiling down at her. He reached into Denise's lap for her hand, pulling her to her feet and propelling her forward so she could join the eight others on the stage.

The dancers tied hula skirts around the waists of the four men and four women while the emcee told the audience that normally men would not wear the skirts. However, the skirt facilitated the learning process. Standing side by side with instructors directly behind them, the students learned to sway and swirl their inexperienced hips.

The sight of instructors directing the awkward movements of their stiff students must have been hilarious because the audience howled its approval. Glancing to the left and the right, Denise saw that she was not the most uncoordinated in the group, although she would still need many more lessons before she could perform the hula in public. At least she was able to follow the hand motions while the instructor continued to direct the sway of her hips.

With her concentration completely on the dance, Denise forgot about the murderer. She had examined the faces of the dance instructors and the students and found none of them particularly menacing. Since she did not possess a description of the murderer, she could not take any precautions. Knowing that Tom sat in the audience would have to be enough.

Once the dance lesson began, all of the participants looked equally ill at ease on the stage. As for the instructors, they all wore heavy stage make-up to give them the healthy island glow. She could tell that many of them were not native-born Hawaiians and needed the warmth of the darker makeup to give them the richness of the tropical complexions.

As they moved into the final minutes of the act, Denise heard a change in her instructor's voice. Throughout the lesson, he had offered suggestions for improvement as the others had done. He had told her to shift her weight for the maximum swirl of her hips, to extend her fingers for more expressive movement, and to relax her spine for better rotation. At one point, he had stepped back to allow her to exhibit her mastery of the new steps along with the others for their fledgling dance.

However, her instructor had returned to his position behind her when it was time for him to introduce a new dance step. Yet his hands had not felt the same. He pressed his fingers into her flesh, pushing rather than guiding her.

Before she could object to his new attitude, a voice behind her hissed, "Don't think of calling to your partner, Detective Dory. It wouldn't do any good anyway. One of my helpers would stop him before he could rise from his seat. A blow to the head with a juggling pin would stop even a big man like your partner. I wish he hadn't followed you, but that's to be expected considering the depth of your relationship with him. I had wanted you all to myself. You didn't eat much of your dinner. Nervous about our first dance?"

Unable to see to the back of the room because of the bright stage lights, Denise said nothing. Her heart pounded in her ears. Her throat constricted. Denise doubted that she would have been able to call for help from Tom even if he were not in danger.

When she nodded almost imperceptibly, the voice continued, "No need to break your concentration, Detective. Relax. I can feel the stiffening of your muscles. I guess you're wondering about my motives behind the murders. Greed, that's the most important one. The men I killed were my competitors. They stood between me and ultimate fame and success. Any other motive is insignificant. I want to be the premier jewelry and fashion designer in the country and, eventually, the world.

"Why did I select you to be the detective on the case, you ask? Well, that's simple. You're the best at what you do and I'm the best at my profession. I thought it would be more fitting for you to track me than a simple, flat-foot, no-name detective.

"I can hear your mind ticking away. You're doing quite well on the dance, by the way. Your attention to details under duress is impressive. I bet you want to know where and when I'll strike next, don't you? Well, I won't tell you. You'll have to do a little research for that one. Suffice it to say that I haven't finished. I still have a competitor or two to eradicate before I can stand alone as the best designer bar none. Remember, my world is not only jewelry but clothing as well.

"My time is up. It's been fun dancing with you. Look

under your chair when you return to your table. I've left a little trinket for you. By the way, thanks for wearing the bracelet. I have such good taste. I made the charms and ordered that fool at Charming Charms to purchase them especially for me from a friend who agreed to be my front. I told him that soon all the rich and famous would flock to his pathetic little establishment. Out of greed, he agreed to stock them. One of my helpers made the purchases to keep nosey detectives from being able to trace them to me. That Charming Charms fellow was all too happy to pocket the profits. You'd be surprised at the steps I've taken to ensure my anonymity. Sometimes, however, I wonder if I'd be more famous if you caught me. All the greatest artists have been more famous in death. Good-bye, Detective."

The pressure on her waist immediately stopped and so did the music. Turning around quickly, Denise saw no one, only empty space where the instructors had stood. The audience applauded the students wildly as they returned to their seats.

Tom sat with the seven others at the table. No one hovered behind him. No one threatened his life. As a matter of fact, he did not even look as if he had been aware of being in danger. The familiar blank expression covered his face and made his emotions unreadable.

Shaken but able to follow the directions and look under her chair, Denise pulled out another envelope. Sinking into her seat as the house light came up, she reached for a glass of water. Her hands shook noticeably as she raised it to her lips.

"You're shaking. What happened, Dory?" Tom asked. "I didn't see anything from here."

Taking a deep breath to compose her nerves, Denise replied, "My last dance instructor was the murderer. A fairly androgynous voice said for me not to call for help or his assistant would knock you out or maybe kill you. I don't think I've ever felt more like a victim in my life. I was helpless to do anything. I could only dance."

As anger filled his voice and turned his face hard, Tom said, "He didn't hurt you, did he?"

"No, he squeezed my sides a bit, but nothing else," Denise responded, feeling much more composed now that she was safely away from the stage. "I couldn't see you because of the lights. I didn't know if someone had already hurt you or if anyone was even standing near you. It's a terrible feeling not knowing what's happening to your partner."

In the emotion of the moment, Tom heard but did not respond to Denise's declaration of affection for him. Too many things were happening at once for him to focus on any one thing for long. He needed to learn as much from her as possible while the memories were still fresh.

"Did he say anything else," Tom inquired as he gently held Denise's hand in his.

"Oh, yes, he was very talkative," Denise exclaimed. "He feels a real need to remove all of his fashion industry competition from the face of the earth. He wants to be the number one fashion and jewelry designer. He said that a few people still stood between him and that title. He even complimented himself on his good taste when he saw me wearing the bracelet. He made all of the charms. Quite a fanatic for details."

"He sounds like someone I'd rather not have to tangle with," Tom commented. "His attention to detail will make him even harder to apprehend."

"I know," Denise agreed, "but he'll slip up one day. When he does, I'll be there. Actually, he even said that he might want me to catch him. He thinks he might become more famous that way. Sick."

Tom did not like the hard glint in Denise's eyes. Never had any of their cases ever affected her as this one had. She had not taken any of them personally; they had simply been part of the job. This time, she appeared to have lost her impartiality. He wondered if the threat to his life had contributed to the change in her.

Deciding to delve further into this idea once they returned to the hotel, if nothing distracted them, Tom asked, "What's in the envelope?"

A carefully wrapped little package tumbled onto the table

as Denise extracted the note. She read the familiar handwriting, "Book tickets home. After Arizona, the adventure turns nostalgic. Add this charm to your bracelet. See you soon."

"Home after Arizona," Denise repeated. "I guess Mr. Worldly wasn't the only successful designer in the Washington metro area. It would seem that our killer is set on removing a few more from the Washington area."

Pulling the charm from the paper, Denise fingered an incredibly detailed miniature of the Lincoln Memorial. She could see the wrinkles in Lincoln's knuckles recreated in the little gold charm. The craftsman had drawn the tiny dome to perfect scale.

Turning to Tom, Denise said, "Let's go back to the hotel. We need to sort out the clues. Somewhere in this collection of charms and notes, we'll find the identity of the killer."

Slipping his arm around Denise's shoulders, Tom led her into the Village. Most of the tourists had disappeared and the booths stood empty. As they made their way toward the exit, Denise picked up a flyer for the night's performance. Stuffing it into her bag, she decided that it might come in handy. At the very least, it would serve as a souvenir of the evening.

Denise's mind covered much ground on the ride back to the hotel. She knew that the killer did not use a traditional murder weapon, preferring to poison his victims through some form of biological element that the pathology department had not been able to identify. After eliminating all of the usual poisonous substances, the pathologist was still at a loss to identify the agent. While she waited, Denise would continue to follow the suspect's clues and try to learn his identity. Maybe in Arizona he would provide her with a clue to the poison.

Fingering the charm bracelet that glittered in the streetlight, Denise contemplated the meaning of the little hurricane with the diamond. She had thought that the killer had meant symbolically that he was the hurricane and she was the diamond caught in it. Although that was still possible, she wondered if the little charm carried still more meaning.

"What are you thinking, Dory," Tom questioned as he interrupted her musings.

"That sleaze at Charming Charms lied to me," Denise stated in a matter-of-fact voice. "He said that he designed the charms."

"Didn't he?"

"Not according to our killer," Denise replied. "He said that he made them and arranged for Charming Charms to stock them so that he could purchase them through a middleman. Quite an elaborate scheme."

"Did the killer say that he used a woman as an accomplice?" Tom asked. "Remember the guy at Charming Charms said that he sold them to a woman."

"He didn't say, and I wasn't in a position to ask any questions," Denise replied with a shake of her head.

"Maybe next time he'll let you ask questions," Tom suggested.

"We'll see. I just hope my next encounter with him isn't while hanging over a cliff," Denise commented sarcastically.

"I'll do a better job of protecting you this time," Tom added with anger. "That guy won't get that close to you again."

Patting his hand, Denise replied, "Don't blame yourself. You had no way of knowing that he'd be that deceptive."

"Just the same, I'm taking more precautions this time," Tom stated in a matter-of-fact manner.

Changing the subject, Denise asked as she laid the little hurricane in her palm, "By the way, have you noticed that all of the charms except this one have a place connected to them?"

"So?" Tom asked, not quite understanding her point.

Furrowing her brow, Denise mused, "Don't you wonder why this one is different? This one doesn't match the others. The others, the Empire State Building, a lei, a rainbow, a donkey, and a replica of the Lincoln Memorial, all make sense. I can attach a place to each one of them, but I can't do that with the little hurricane with the diamond. I wonder what that one means."

Shrugging his shoulders, Tom replied, "Maybe he just liked that one and wanted you to have it. Let's face it, the man's not right mentally. He's a killer who likes to gift the police following him. None of this makes sense to me."

"I guess you're right," Denise agreed reluctantly as they entered the hotel lobby.

"Well, at least we got a nice vacation out of this trip," Tom commented, trying to look on the bright side.

"And it's not over yet," Denise reminded him with a smile.

Grinning like a little boy, Tom stated, "That's right. Tomorrow, we leave for the Grand Canyon. Not bad at all. Lots of travel on someone else's dime, good food, and great company."

"Who's the good company?" Denise teased as she waited for the night manager to check for messages.

"You are. You don't think I'm talking about that psychopath we're following, do you?" Tom responded with a quick frown.

"Ah, a compliment. It must be the Hawaiian sun that's softening your gruff exterior," Denise joked while she skimmed the call-back sheet.

"Anything important?" Tom asked, peeking over her shoulder.

"Yeah, the captain wants us to call him . . . anytime, day or night," Denise replied, following him to the elevator.

"Must be important for him to want us to wake him," Tom remarked dryly. They had worked for the captain long enough to know that he never wanted to hear from any of his detectives during his off-duty hours.

Captain Morton believed that work should stay on the job as much as possible. His policy was that he spent twelve hours in the office so that anyone who needed him could contact him there. No one should have a reason for calling him at home.

Denise speculated as Tom unlocked the door, "Maybe pathology has isolated the virus that killed both victims. That would certainly give us more than the nothing we have now."

Flipping on the lights, Tom replied, "You don't have much of a case, do you, Dory? You know that the man's a designer, a prominent and ambitious designer. Maybe you should interview all of Worldly's circle of friends and enemies."

Dialing the captain's number, Denise replied, "I'm a step ahead of you on that one. While you were in the shower I asked Ronda to make the appointments for me. I phoned her this morning, not knowing that the killer planned to take us home after the trip to the Canyon."

The phone rang only twice before Ronda picked up. Her usually cheerful voice quickly assumed a serious tone when she heard Denise's voice. In a matter of minutes, she had transferred the call to the chief's office.

Covering the receiver, Denise whispered, "This doesn't look good. The captain's in the chiefs office."

Tom sat on the bed and waited while Denise stood with the phone at her ear. Periodically, she would make a sound of affirmation, but she did not control the conversation. The expression on her face was very serious and her tone crisp when she spoke.

"Yes, ma'am, I'll tell him. Thanks for your continued support, Chief," Denise said as she hung up the phone.

"Well?"

"I hardly spoke with the captain at all," Denise reported as she slipped off her shoes and began turning back the beds. "The chief did most of the talking. Another one of her designer friends died last night Washington time of this mysterious fever and convulsions. This one was a specialist in wedding attire. I hadn't heard the name but, apparently, Clive Fields's designs were very popular with the moneyed set. He's the wedding gown designer of choice this year. That's three designers dead."

Ticking off the deceased on his fingers, Tom stated, "A famous jewelry designer, a high fashion designer, and now a wedding specialist. I wonder who's next."

"I don't know, but we'll soon find out in Arizona," Denise stated as she grabbed her purse and headed toward the door.

"Don't forget that our killer plans to remove yet another obstacle to his success on this trip. I just wish I could figure out how he's doing it."

"Where are you going? It's almost 1 A.M.," Tom exclaimed as he stretched.

"Downstairs," Denise replied with her hand on the knob. "I need to buy some fashion magazines. I should have done this sooner. I'm not up on this stuff. When do I ever wear anything fancy or expensive? Even if I had the occasion, I couldn't afford the stuff that Worldly makes. I need some background information on the industry and its heavy hitters. I got caught up in the mystery of the charms. The charms only show me where the murders will take place not who will be the victims. Whoever is next on the killer's list should be sufficiently famous to have a picture or two in a magazine."

"Dory, the shop has closed! Buy them in the morning. It's time for bed," Tom objected, holding a pillow in his hands.

"Don't wait up for me," Denise instructed. "I have homework to do. The night manager will open it for me."

"I'll help you," Tom offered as he pushed his feet back into his shoes.

"No, this is a one-woman job," Denise replied waving off his offer. "You can't help me because I don't know what I'm looking for. The clues are under my nose, but I can't see them. Maybe something in the magazines will help, but I won't know until I try. Good night."

As the door closed, Tom sighed deeply. All thoughts of a romantic end to the evening vanished with the click of the lock. Slowly, he trudged to the bathroom to brush his teeth before turning in for the night. He knew Denise too well. There was no point in waiting for her to return. When she devoted herself to study, nothing could stop her.

Riding to the first floor, Denise briefly thought of the evening with Tom that she had planned . . . the seduction, the erotic hula, the gentle lovemaking, and the romantic drinks on the veranda. All of that would have to wait. Now that she had recovered from the shock of being held victim while a group of people watched without knowledge, she could not allow anything to distract her from the job of finding and stopping the killer. For her sake and that of the potential victims, she needed to forget the pull of her social life and concentrate on solving the murders.

Nine

Denise's eyes were badly bloodshot from a night of reading in the lobby. From experience, Tom knew not to speak with her as she mumbled to herself while packing her things, barely touched breakfast, and sat slumped in the cab on the ride to the airport. She was grumpy from lack of sleep as they boarded the plane to Arizona. He was actually relieved when she fell asleep twenty minutes into the flight.

While she slept, Tom flipped through the pile of expensive fashion magazines on her tray table. He had never seen so many skinny models, who looked more like boys than women, in expensive clothing that hugged their nonexistent curves. He found nothing sexy about their bony frames, their thin hair, and their pasty complexions. To his horror, he discovered that the black models looked just as dreadfully undernourished as their white counterparts. These models and the clothes they wore did not appeal to him at all.

Tom liked women with meat on their bones, not fat women but phat women. He wanted to hug something other than a carcass to his chest when he made love to a woman, and he liked to feel curves under his hands not rigid angles and jutting hip bones when he kissed her. In Tom's mind, a woman should be soft and rounded, not hard and boyish. The boy look turned him off. Androgynous women were not for him.

Looking at one of the pages that Denise had dog-eared, Tom read the article with a total lack of interest. The reporter had raved about the latest fashions while the photographer

had captured the thinnest woman he had ever seen in a pose
that was supposed to be provocative. With a look of disgust
on his face, he turned the page. There in a full-color adver-
tisement was Joseph Worldly draped over the shoulder of
two waifish women adorned in gold necklaces that weighed
heavily on their thin necks and bracelets that tugged at their
skeletal arms. The caption read, WORLDLY GOLD DESIGNS . . .
THE WAY TO EVERY WOMAN'S HEART.

Reaching for a magazine with brides on the cover, Tom
flipped the pages to find an article about the fashion industry's premier wedding designer. Clive Fields's name appeared
in every paragraph and under each photograph of wedding
gowns, mother-of-the-bride dresses, and bridesmaid gowns.
Some of the gowns were so outrageously risqué that Tom
wondered about the kind of woman who would appear at her
own wedding wearing a piece of sheer fabric that barely concealed her nipples. Others were so extremely fashioned as
to resemble costumes in a Hollywood movie or Broadway
show. Turning more pages, he looked for fashions that real
women like Denise would find interesting. Finding none, he
tossed the magazine onto the growing pile on his tray table.

The next magazine's promise of normal-looking clothing
quickly evaporated as he turned the pages. After passing the
ads for perfume, watches, and ready-to-wear outfits, he discovered the high-fashion section, haute couture in all its glory.
Again, emaciated women modeled outlandish outfits that the
captions said all women would die to own. In the middle of
the spread, Tom saw a group of models leaning in uncomfortable poses on the shoulders of the designer Byron Cummings.

Checking the date on the front cover, Tom found that the
magazine was current. Cummings had probably celebrated
his good fortune at being included in the magazine's featured
articles only weeks before his death. A centerfold photo opportunity would probably have been good for business. Little
did he know that the exposure would cause his death.

Although Tom tried to connect the victims to their elusive
killer, he could see nothing concrete other than the obvious

fact that they were all designers. He wondered if their new-found notoriety had been the cause. Perhaps the killer had been jealous that his colleagues had earned the recognition of the centerfold spot and he had not. However, many successful designers did not appear in the glossy magazines and were still successful in their professions. The killer must not be the type who could accept being on the second-string team.

Picking up yet another glossy, Tom found his answer. Printed on page fifteen was a list of the top ten designers in the United States. Denise had circled in red ink the names of the jewelry, haute couture, and wedding designers who were among those selected for the honor. Beside each name the publisher had printed the hometown address. Since most of them operated large design studios and welcomed the publicity, anyone would be able to find them with little difficulty . . . even the murderer.

Joseph Worldly of Bethesda, Maryland, had ranked in the tenth position, Byron Cummings of Manhattan had sat in position nine, and Clive Fields of Washington, DC, had occupied number eight. The killer was either not on the list and was trying to remove all obstacles in the way of his making it next time or was near the top and hoping to prevent anyone from eliminating him from his position. Either way, Denise had discovered the names of the next victims and their hometowns.

Running his finger up the column, Tom found Anne Desoto of Tucson, Arizona, in the seventh position and Paul Settles of Baltimore, Maryland, in position number six. The killer had instructed them to go to the Grand Canyon although the murder would actually take place in Tucson, miles away. By the time they returned home, the murder of the Baltimore designer might have already taken place.

Without hesitation, Tom nudged Denise awake. Stretching, she rubbed her swollen eyes and turned toward him. Even with this new information and urgency about the case burning in his mind, Tom still found her the most stunning woman he had ever known. Looking at Denise, he did not know how any man could find those models attractive. None was as beautiful as his partner.

Instantly awake, Denise asked, "What's happening?"

"Did you phone the Tucson police about this? What about the folks in Baltimore? Did you notify them?" Tom demanded as he pointed to the magazine article.

Nodding, Denise replied, "Sure did, first thing this morning. Heard some choice words, too. I forgot about the time differences. Good thing I've worked on cases with most of them."

"Then you've solved the case," Tom declared with confidence.

"Not really," Denise answered straightening her mussed hair. "Look at that magazine and the next one. Each one has a list of the greats and near greats in the fashion industry. It's all so subjective."

Tom opened the next magazine in the pile to the page Denise had dog-eared. Reading the list, he discovered that Joseph Worldly had not ranked at all on that one and Anne Desoto had the number two spot. The next glossy ranked designers by specialty, putting Clive Fields at the bottom of the wedding designer list, Byron Cummings in the middle of his specialty, and Anne Desoto an honorable mention for her area of expertise.

"We have nothing," Tom stated dejectedly.

"That's right," Denise replied with a yawn.

"Then why did you phone Tucson and Baltimore?" Tom asked.

"I'd rather be safe than sorry," Denise replied without emotion. "Besides, a couple of them appeared on both lists. I have a composite list in my sketchbook. Until the murderer strikes a few more times, we have nothing. If he decides that we're too close and stops, we have nothing. I couldn't even give my colleagues a description of the murder weapon or the killer. I'm going on speculation and fairy dust. If pathology had identified the murder weapon, we'd have something, but . . . we have nothing."

Frowning, Tom commented as he placed his large hand over her small one, "I don't think I've ever seen you like this."

"That's right because I've never felt like this," Denise replied slowly. "I realized last night on that dance floor that we can't prevent another murder. You and all the others watched as the murderer whispered in my ear, yet you saw nothing out of the ordinary. He's smart. We ate a pleasant meal and saw nothing suspicious although he was in the room with us. We watched the jugglers and didn't suspect that they might have been connected with the killer. We have a trail littered with shards of information that might, one day, come together to form an image. Right now, we've got nothing."

"You're exhausted or else you wouldn't talk like this," Tom commented as he pulled Denise's head to his shoulder.

"You're right; I am," Denise replied with a yawn. "I sat in that lobby all night going through every fashion magazine I could find in the hotel and the all-night pharmacy down the street. You've seen the results. Bits and pieces of stuff but nothing definitive. As soon as we get home, I'm going to sit down with the pathologist and go through every possible theory and every drug or substance known to science that might cause high fever and convulsions."

"Why didn't you ask me to help you?" Tom asked as he lightly kissed her forehead.

Sighing, Denise replied, "Partly because I didn't see the answer until early this morning and partly because I have to do this myself."

"I don't understand. We're a team," Tom said as he smoothed her hair.

"It's payback time," Denise responded, looking Tom wearily in the face. "The killer held me at the tip of his fingers last night. He told me that he could get to me at any time, but I was helpless to find him. I have to do this alone. You can't help me. No one can. You might as well go home. You can start the substance investigation, if you'd like, but even that I need to supervise. I'm going on hunches and nothing else."

With disappointment in his voice, Tom responded, "I guess this means that I won't visit the Grind Canyon."

Looking at his unhappy face, Denise said, "Not this time. We'll take a vacation there after this case ends. Right now, you're a very pleasant distraction. I need my wits about me to solve this case. With you around, my mind's in a jumble of emotions."

Smiling like a kid who had just received a bag of candy, Tom nodded and said, "Glad to hear it. I thought I was the only one who couldn't think straight. You're right, you do need your time alone. I'll see you when you come home."

"Hey, not so fast! We still have a few hours left on this flight. Let's snuggle," Denise replied with a laugh.

Denise had dreaded telling Tom that they would have to split up. She had worried that he would not understand and think that she had changed her mind about him. Snuggling against his strong chest as his muscular arms enfolded her, she knew that she need not have worried. Tom was first and foremost a cop. He understood the need to go solo on some cases even while teamed with a compatible partner.

She had only told him a partial truth about her late-night work. Denise had spent part of the evening trying to figure out a way to break the news of their separation to him. That task had weighed more heavily on her shoulders than the need to uncover the murderer's identity and the murder weapon.

Along with the realization of her own vulnerability, Denise had discovered that she loved Tom. She had not remained silent for her benefit while the murderer whispered in her ear, but for Tom's. She had not been willing to take the chance with his safety. If she had been alone, she would have swung around and tried to overpower the man. Now, because of her need to protect her partner—her love—she had blown the opportunity to apprehend the murderer. Because of her, another designer would die.

Although Denise rested with her head on Tom's shoulder for the remainder of the flight, she did not sleep. She had notified Tucson and Baltimore police departments of the possibility of the murderer striking in their jurisdictions, but she had not been able to provide a description of the killer or his method. Stifled laughs had greeted her explanation of his motives. Her colleagues found it difficult to believe that anyone would kill for rankings in fashion magazines.

Maybe they were right. Doubt and indecision lurked in the back of her mind even as Denise tried to convince the detectives that they should notify the designers on the list of the possibility that they might be in danger. Her voice had sounded hollow and unsure. If she had been on their end of the telephone, she would have laughed, too. She also found the assumptions difficult to believe.

Yet, these shards of information were all she had. The Capitol Hill case followed a pattern and had a clearly defined motive. This one did not. Even Denise had difficulty that anyone would murder for a place on a popularity list.

She had decided during that night that having Tom on the scene had dulled her instincts with the glow of love. The nearness of him had reduced her usually sharp senses to fluff. She had been so busy thinking of the joy of being with him, of experiencing him, and of sharing everything with him that she had neglected her duty. As soon as he returned to their squad room, her edge would return.

But she would miss him terribly. Denise loved to share meals with him, walk with her hand in his, and touch his shoulder for reassurance. Her evenings would be lonely without him at her side. She even loved the sound of his snoring from the other bed. However, if she worked quickly, Denise would soon be with him again.

By putting Tom and everything else pleasurable from her mind, Denise would be able to solve the case. If she badgered the pathologist enough, between the two of them they would be able to discover the identity of the poisoning. At any rate, she would try.

After an uneventful flight, they parted at the airport—Tom to catch the next flight to Reagan National Airport and a taxi

to the precinct and Denise for the inn on the South Rim of
the Grand Canyon. They both knew that the separation was
necessary if they were to apprehend the murderer. However,
neither looked forward to the time apart.

Smiling bravely into his blank expression, Denise stood
on her tiptoes and planted a light kiss on her partner's cheek.
Quickly slipping his arms around her, Tom drew her close
and pressed his lips against hers. With memories of the previous night dancing in her head, Denise melted against him.
The embrace was all the sweeter knowing that it would have
to last until she reached home again. With luck, she would
spend only a few nights in Arizona. That is, if the murderer
cooperated and the case began to jell.

To Denise's surprise, a driver awaited her in the departure
area. With the taste of Tom's kiss on her lips and the fragrance of his cologne on her clothing, she had walked past
a man in a green chauffeur outfit who held a sign bearing
her name. Retracing her steps, Denise returned to find that
the manager of the inn where she was staying had sent him
to meet her. Taking her one bag into his strong hands, he led
the way to the van in which other guests waited.

Taking her seat and holding her bag on her lap, Denise
relaxed and looked out the window. The scenery was breathtaking as they drove through heavily forested areas on the
way to the South Rim. She could hardly wait to see the Canyon itself. It must be spectacular if the show along the road-
side was this phenomenal.

And spectacular it was. Denise only vaguely remembered
the trip to the Canyon as a child with her parents. She remembered being struck by the beauty of the surroundings,
but she could not remember any of the specifics. Now, as an
adult seeing it with mature eyes, Denise saw the hand of God
in every corner, in every rock, and in every cloud. The Divine
Himself painted the rainbow that stretched across the length
of the Canyon. No human being could have imagined the
breath of colors that spanned the spectrum. The Grand Canyon was truly the product of God's creation.

The Canyon itself with its pinks, reds, blues, browns, and violets filled the eye with wonder. To live so close to such perfection must be a blessing, yet the people who lived on its fringe did not appear to notice it. Like any other natural wonder, they had become inured to its beauty. However, for Denise, the Canyon held riches to explore.

Standing at the security rail and looking down toward the Colorado River that wound through the Canyon, Denise wished that Tom were at her side to share the view. She longed to watch the eagles soar and dive as they hunted for food or played on the currents. She wanted to have someone with whom to share the glory of the Canyon, the sight of the rabbit hopping among the scrub trees, and the insects skittering along the ridge. Denise knew from their visit to the Empire State Building that Tom was nervous about heights, but she felt that he would still be able to enjoy the tremendous views.

Shouldering her bag, Denise tore herself away from the Canyon's ever-changing face and entered the inn. She found the interior comfortable and uncluttered. The owners had paneled the walls in a rich, dark pine that contrasted greatly with the bright sun and colors of the Canyon. They had grouped heavy comfortable chairs sat in inviting clusters in front of the fireplace, which must have been a great source of enjoyment after a winter's walk on the Rim. A small but complete store sold upscale gifts and memorabilia, representative of the Native American tribes that once populated the area.

Families lingered in the lobby, waiting for their bags to arrive from the van. Denise quickly checked in and walked up the one flight to her room. The view from her window beckoned her to come outside and enjoy the Canyon; however, inside, the warm reds and browns lured her to take a much-needed nap.

Putting the pleasures of exploring the Canyon on hold, Denise searched her room for any communication from the killer. Despite opening every drawer, the closet doors, and the medicine cabinet, and turning back the covers of her bed, she found nothing. This time he had not left a note or tried to make contact. Wistfully, she hoped that he had decided to give up his rampage. Although it had only been a few hours since she had seen him, Denise missed Tom and home.

Stripping off her clothing and slipping between the sheets, Denise fell instantly asleep. Numbers and columns of names plagued her dreams. Faces and places swirled around her. Constant reminders of the night in the Polynesian Village and the feel of the suspect's hands on her waist invaded the darkness. She could not shake the feeling of being watched.

Feeling no more refreshed than she did before taking the nap, Denise arose and took a quick shower. The sun was lower now and the heat of the day had begun to subside. She wanted to watch the changing patterns of color as they marched across the Canyon walls.

Entering the lobby, Denise joined the line of people registering for the evening donkey ride into the Canyon. Lightly touching the little charm, she wondered if the suspect would make his presence known that evening. She hoped that her next encounter with him would be less threatening than the first.

Turning from the concierge's desk, Denise wandered into the bar for a soda. As she waited, she watched the cable news that played as background noise for the steady stream of conversation over drinks and munchies. Leaning forward, she strained to hear as the headline flashed on the set.

"Turn up the T.V., please," Denise asked as the bartender brought her drink.

"Sure," he replied. "They're talking about the fashion designer murders again. Seems there's been another one."

Absently sipping the cold soda, Denise listened as the commentators's voice sounded behind the captioned photograph of Miller Franklin. According to the reporter, Franklin, a native of Tucson, Arizona, had been a nationally acclaimed designer of men's clothing who threatened to dethrone the leading haute couture kingpin. He had died earlier that day of fever and convulsions caused by an unidentified virus.

The loud slurping noise of Denise's straw as it hit the bottom of the cup pulled her back to the moment. Another murder had occurred under her nose. She had followed the suspect's direction and come to Arizona but had been unable to stop another murder. She hated being a pawn in his chess game for power.

"Another?" the bartender asked.

"What? Oh, no thanks," Denise replied absently.

"Terrible, isn't it," the bartender commented as he wiped the moisture from the bar's surface. "Who would have thought that designers would ever be in danger from a killer. They dress people. How much more benign can you get?"

Studying his face, Denise responded in a voice laced with frustration, "Yeah, it's terrible all right. Thanks for the drink."

Blending into the other guests of the inn, Denise walked into the bright afternoon sun. Despite the grandeur of the Canyon, Denise saw nothing. Her mind was running through the few facts she had managed to cull on this case.

Stepping to the railing, Denise pulled out her sketchpad. Instead of capturing the changing face of the Canyon, she added Miller Franklin's name to the list of dead designers. Consulting the rankings she had compiled from the assorted sources, she found that his name had not been among them. Looking further, Denise saw that he had been a tenth-place entry on only one list.

"Damn!" Denise muttered to herself. "I missed this one."

Rushing into the inn, Denise found the bank of pay telephones near the restaurant. Remembering that the captain had said that he welcomed calls from her at any time of day or night, she dialed his number. The ever-efficient Ronda answered on the first ring.

"Ronda, it's Denise. Is he there?"

In a voice tinged with sarcasm, Ronda replied, "Where else would he be with the chief breathing down his neck about this case? Wait a minute."

"OK, Denise, let's have it," Captain Morton responded, omitting the usual chitchat.

"I've compiled a master list of possible targets," Denise replied swiftly sensing his no nonsense mood. "I missed Franklin because he appeared on only one list. I've rechecked and think I've identified everyone."

"OK . . . so?"

"We need to notify the local police department that the killer might come to their area. We have to tell the people on the list that they're in danger," Denise replied, hoping that she sounded more convincing than she felt.

"Detective," Captain Morton stated firmly, "if we do that, we'll upset a whole lot of people and bring a whole lot of attention to our force. If you're right, it'll be good attention, but if you're wrong, the chief will not be happy."

"But, Captain, if we don't warn these people, they'll be sitting ducks," Denise stressed strongly.

Objecting firmly, the captain rebutted, "And what will we tell them? How can the other jurisdictions protect them? You know they won't stay inside to be safe. Can you give them a description of the killer or the weapon?"

"No. Are you saying that it's hopeless?" Denise asked dejectedly.

"Until you can trap the killer or pathology can isolate the cause of death, I'm afraid it is," Tom replied with finality.

Denise stood thinking in painful silence. Realizing her frustration, the captain added, "I'll phone the jurisdictions and put them on notice. However, if I were in their shoes, I'd take a wait-and-see posture."

"I understand," Denise conceded reluctantly. "I'll have to apprehend him to stop him."

"That's basically the answer, Detective," Captain Morton replied in a softer tone. "Some cases are like that."

In a voice tinged with resignation and futility, Denise stated, "I'll see you in a few days, Captain. Maybe pathology will know something definitive by the time I return."

Offering salve for Denise's hurt feelings, the captain commented, "You're good at turning hunches into reality. Maybe when you return, you'll try your hand at identifying the cause of death. Pathology needs all the help it can get."

"I'll give it some thought, sir," Denise replied.

"By the way, how's Tom?"

"He's not here. I sent him back to help pathology."

"You're alone?" the captain exclaimed. "I didn't want you to work alone on this one, Denise. This guy's too crafty and too dangerous."

"I'll be OK," Denise replied with a confidence she did not feel. "I'm following up one of his notes and should return home in a day or two. If I need backup, I'll ask the local police or the park service for help."

"Be careful," the captain stated and hung up.

As the line went dead, Denise thought about her dance partner and shuddered. It would certainly be difficult to be careful around a suspect she could not identify and a murder weapon she could not see. At least, he had not tried to remove her from his path to fame and glory. On the contrary, the suspect appeared to enjoy the game of cat-and-mouse they were playing.

The sun was setting red on the Canyon as Denise joined the others for the donkey ride from the observation area to the rest area at the midpoint. She had not ridden a horse let alone a donkey since she was in college, and even then she had been afraid of the large size of the animals in comparison to their small brains. Now, looking at the rather unintelligent expression on the donkey's face, Denise almost wished she had not decided to follow the charm's clue.

Denise watched as the children in the group practically jumped onto the back of their extremely docile mounts. They had simply grabbed the reins and mane, swung their legs over, and pulled their way onto the beast's back. They had made it look much easier than it was.

From the very beginning, Denise had difficulty. First, she could not swing her leg over the saddle on the animal's back. She tried standing on her tiptoes, but she still could not get the lift and the bounce she needed to propel herself up and

over. Next, despite the fact that the donkey was shorter than
a horse, she could not put her foot in the stirrup while standing on the ground. After several attempts, the animal turned
its large head and looked at her with a mixture of annoyance
and sympathy in its huge eyes.

Taking heart from watching more mature women, Denise
guided her mount to a nearby rock, stepped onto it with her
right foot, slipped her left into the stirrup, and swung the
right over the beast's back while holding the rein and its
mane. To her surprise and that of the donkey, Denise found
herself in the saddle. After adjusting the stirrups to the proper
length, she encouraged the cooperative beast into the line
that would descend to the Canyon surface.

However, another problem occurred as soon as the donkey's hoofs reached the trail . . . Denise became paralyzed
with fear. The drop was incredibly steep and the path was
infinitesimally narrow. From the safety of the observation
decks, the Canyon had appeared to slope gently. Despite
hearing the ranger say that many visitors plunged to their
deaths every year as a result of not respecting the dangers
at the Canyon, Denise had not believed that the descent
would be almost straight down. To compound her fear,
Denise peered beyond the animal's head to see that the path
was only wide enough for one beast at a time to traverse it.
One wrong step and the animal would plummet down the
slope with Denise on its back.

Tom! In her mind, Denise screamed for Tom to come and
rescue her from the back of this smelly animal that at any
time could decide that it did not want to continue carrying
her and dump her over the side. She clung to the animal's
mane and neglected the reins that lay limply in her hand. If
the donkey decided to throw her, she would cling to him and
probably take him with her. She took small consolation in
the fact that the beast would die for its troubles.

In her panic, Denise knew that Tom never would have
taken this ride to the station on the ledge of the Canyon. He
never would have mounted the smelly little beast that trod

so calmly down the steep narrow path despite her panic and death-grip on its mane. Tom would have taken one look down the Canyon wall and returned to the inn. The colors, the birds, and the desire for discovery never would have lured him to put his life in the hands of a big-eared cousin of the horse. She should have exhibited the same common sense. The thought that she was risking her life on the insane ride to catch a murderer almost made her sick to her stomach.

Denise was so afraid that she did not see the flowers clinging tenaciously to the cliff or rabbits hiding among the rocks. She did not see the assorted hunting birds swoop from the sky to catch invisible lizards for their supper. Staring straight ahead and praying constantly, she did not see the wonder of life on the arid plane. Denise could finally understand her mother's reaction to the Canyon and wondered what had ever possessed her father to take two little girls on this suicidal ride.

By the time they reached the way station, sweat had drenched Denise's blouse and jeans. Her fingers had seized in her grip on the animal's mane. Her mouth had dried of all saliva from the constantly muttered prayer. Her backside hurt from the friction of the saddle. Her calves ached from gripping the beast's wide middle. She was so frightened that she would not release her grip. One of the station assistants had to assist her from her mount.

Once on firm ground again, Denise surveyed her surrounding and tried to relax. The temperature was hot and the air was still. Their shoes kicked up little clouds of dust with each step. The reds and blues were even more vivid without the sun's haze to distort them. And, the sky overhead was tremendously blue and clear.

Feeling a bit stronger, Denise joined the others in sipping the offered sodas. When she tired to open her mouth to speak, her teeth still chattered fiercely. Looking up the Canyon wall, she wondered how they had ever made the descent. From where she stood at the way station, she could not see the path they had just traveled. It had vanished into the red dust of the Canyon.

The ranger herded them into a small auditorium and began a lecture on the topography and wildlife of the Canyon. His carefully chosen slides provided a closeup view of the terrain and the inhabitants of the Canyon, especially the South Rim on which the owners had built the inn.

Denise carefully examined the faces of the other adventurers. Most of them were in family groups with only a few couples and even fewer singles. One couple, obviously newlyweds, was far more interested in each other's hands and eyes than in the history lesson. Denise thought that they should have stayed in their room rather than risking their lives for a lecture they did not hear.

Not seeing anyone that even vaguely reminded her of anyone she had ever met, Denise allowed herself to think of Tom. Professionally, she wondered if he would be able to uncover any clues as to the identity of the substance causing the convulsions and fever. Personally, she wondered if he missed her as much as she missed him. She would have liked to have been able to whisper comments into someone's ear during the lecture. Her hand would have fit so nicely in his while watching the slide presentation. However, the truth was that he would not have been in the way station with her anyway; he would have waited in the bar for her return.

As soon as the lecture and show ended, the ranger took them for a walk along the flat part of the ridge. It seemed that they had reached an area that for ages had been used as a resting spot. The way station stood halfway between the floor of the Canyon with the Colorado River bisecting it and the South Rim many feet above. Denise heeded the warning about not touching the plants and the animals. She admired their beauty from a safe distance. She had no desire to be stung or bitten.

A tall buxom blonde dressed in skin-tight stretch jeans and a form-hugging tube top with a white blouse over it stepped closer to Denise as they followed the ranger. Denise had noticed her earlier and knew that the woman was also alone. The woman was vaguely familiar, but Denise could not place her. Denise in her sensible jogging shoes and the woman in heeled clogs made an unusual looking pair as they picked their way along the rocky path.

"Exciting, isn't it?" the blonde cooed in a voice that was incongruously delicate for her stature.

"If you're referring to that ride down the cliff, I'd say frightening," Denise replied, trying to put on a brave face in light of too-fresh memories.

"That was kinda scary but wonderful at the same time," she gushed this time.

"I certainly hope the return trip won't be quiet as exhilarating," Denise replied, trying not to stare at the woman's overly made-up face and full wig.

"My name is Freda Maze, by the way," the woman introduced herself and extended her large gloved hand. "My friends told me that I simply had to take this little excursion. They said that it's to die for."

"Denise Dory. My friends warned me not to do this. As you can see, I didn't listen," Denise commented as her hand vanished inside Freda's. The name rang a distant bell.

Freda Maze was a large woman. She was not the largest Denise had ever seen, but she was certainly in the running for the title. Her hands and feet were the size of a man's and her head under the big-hair wig was tremendous. She was not unattractive, just over done. She was a caricature of women, having an ample chest, thick false eyelashes, abundant hips, and a killer walk. Denise felt diminutive beside this Amazon.

Denise remembered a girl at her college who was almost as large as Freda. She had played field hockey with the gusto of a man, knocking slower, smaller teammates from her path as she tried to win every point. She had actually been a very gentle person, only large. Freda was probably the same way.

The longer Denise talked with Freda, the more she knew that she had seen her before. The familiarity of the name plagued her, too. It was not that they had been friends, but they had been in the same place at the same time.

Denise was so absorbed in her thoughts that she stubbed her toe and toppled headlong toward the rocks. If it had not been for Freda's quick reflexes and strong arm, Denise would have taken a very bad spill. However, Freda's quick thinking had saved her before she could even touch the ground.

Suddenly, Denise knew that she had heard of Freda or someone exactly like her. Checking out her companion quickly, Denise thought that Freda might have been the blonde who purchased the charms at Charming Charms. She certainly matched the description. She could have been the hula dancer at the Polynesian Village, considering the ample proportions of her body.

Yet, there was something more. The hands were familiar. As Freda's arm went around her waist, Denise recognized the hands. They were so similar to the ones that had held her waist. The way they dug into her flesh had been the same. The spread of the fingers had been the same.

However, the voices definitely did not match. The voice on the stage at the Polynesian Village had been soft and husky and definitely male. Freda's had that breathless quality of 1950s actresses. Freda's was that of a woman.

Like the owner of Charming Charms, Denise could tell a woman when she saw one or, at least she thought she could. She had once arrested a female impersonator for theft who could make any woman look frumpy.

"Thanks," Denise said with a shaky smile. "That would have been a nasty fall."

"No problem," Freda replied gently. "Let's catch up with the others. It's almost time to leave."

"Let's hope the ride back is more comfortable than the ride down," Denise commented as she rubbed her sore bottom.

"At least you won't have to sit on the sore part. You'll have to lean forward for most of this trip or else slide backward and land on the ground," Freda counseled expertly.

"How do you know the fine points of riding up hill?" Denise asked as she tried not to stare at Freda's excess makeup.

"I grew up on a farm. Riding's second nature to me," Freda replied with a grin.

Denise was all too happy to immerse herself in the small talk about farm life and later the ranger's departure instructions. She wanted to put the nagging thought that she had seen or spoken with Freda at another time from her mind until she reached the rim. Her first priority was surviving the return trip on the smelly little animal's back. She would pursue her suspicions once she was safe from rocks, dust, and scorpions.

Ten

The trip up the Canyon's steep wall was almost as harrowing as the one that brought her to the way station had been. As Freda had said, Denise spent the entire ride leaning toward the donkey's ears. Every time she tried to stretch her painful back by sitting properly, she would start to slide off the saddle. The incline was so steep that she had no choice but to focus on the path ahead and ignore the pain in her back.

Sandwiched between the ranger leading the group and Freda, Denise at least felt safer than she had on the descent. Last time, she and a ranger had brought up the rear, giving her ample time to contemplate the disasters awaiting her. This time, she was among the first to reach the top. The climb did not seem as long with only one rider in front of her.

However, her bottom was just as sore and her hands equally raw this time. The blisters she had worn in the palm of her hands by the tight grip on the reins and the mane on the way down the hill had popped on the trip back up. Her thighs and calves felt rubbed raw from brushing against the animal's sides. She smelled both of sweat and donkey and was in desperate need of a shower.

Despite Denise's discomfort when they reached the top, Freda appeared ready to go again. She wanted to take a helicopter ride over the Canyon to see night descend and the colors darken. Denise begged off, stating that she would watch from the front porch with the others and a glass of sherry. Freda had giggled and walked away with the eyes of all the men on her swaying hips as the women frowned in disapproval.

Returning to her room, Denise immediately shed the smelly sweaty clothes and turned on the shower. Easing under the refreshingly cool flow, she could feel not only the sweat but also the worries wash away. After the horrible initial stinging, even the blisters responded to the cleansing effect of the water. Not since her days of playing the wing position on her college field hockey team had a cool shower felt so relaxing. She usually liked to boil her tired body under hot water. However, after a day in the heat of the Canyon, only cool would do.

Wrapping herself in one of the hotel's huge bath towels, Denise returned to her bedroom. The sky had darkened considerably since her return from the way station and night was definitely arriving. Standing at her window, Denise could see the last of the hunting birds circling overhead in search of a branch on which to perch for the night. Looking down on the front porch, she spotted the others enjoying drinks before dinner as the sky changed from red to a dark red and blue mixture, to blue and a black overlay, and, finally, to black.

Not wanting to eat alone, Denise slipped into a pair of slacks and sleeveless shirt. Easing her feet into strappy sandals, she turned out the light and left the room. She had almost phoned Tom but decided to wait until after dinner. Eating alone after all she had experienced the last few days did not appeal to her.

Freda hailed Denise as she entered the dining room. No longer dressed in such clinging clothing, Freda appeared less worldly. She had brushed her hair until it was hanging straight rather than standing like a yellow helmet. At least Denise thought she had brushed it. In fact, Freda might have changed wigs. At any rate, she wore demure slacks and a T-shirt.

Her hands, however, had not changed. No longer encased in gloves, they sparkled with rings on each long finger. Freda did not seem self-conscious about her size and used her hands expressively, almost like the hula dancers, as she spoke.

"You should have come with me. You really missed great views of the Canyon," Freda gushed in her usual breathless manner as soon as Denise slipped into the vacant seat beside her.

"That's OK. I've seen enough views for one day," Denise responded as she consulted the menu. She decided to order the Cornish hen with raspberry, cranberry, and nut stuffing rather than the filet mignon that Freda selected.

"There's nothing like swooping into the darkness in a helicopter," Freda gushed as she attacked her salad.

"Maybe not, but I really enjoyed my shower," Denise replied, eating with relish. She had neglected to eat lunch and was starving.

"Not the same thing at all," Freda insisted, sipping her wine.

"As my grandmother used to say 'If God had wanted me to be a bird, he would have made a feather duster grow from my butt,' " Denise replied before adding, "I'm used to staying on the ground, and I've done entirely too much flying these last few days."

"Oh, what do you do for a living?" Freda asked. Denise could not tell if she really wanted to know or if she were simply being polite.

"I'm a police detective in Maryland," Denise responded, "What about you?"

"Nothing as interesting as that," Freda hedged as the waitress appeared with her rare filet mignon with mushrooms and onions.

"I'm sure your job is interesting. What is it?" Denise pressed as she sliced into the juicy hen.

"I'm a female impersonator," Freda replied as she studied Denise's reaction. "When I'm not on stage in the Big Apple, I hire myself out for parties and such."

Looking her over critically, Denise almost laughed. Freda, with the wig, breathy speech, giggle, and oversized frame, certainly fit the part. She had been wondering about Freda's size and now she knew. Freda was in fact a man.

"That beats being a cop for originality," Denise replied, buttering a roll.

"Are you surprised?" Freda asked as she continued to study Denise's reaction.

"No. Actually, it explains a lot. You know, the hair, the eyelashes," Denise responded honestly.

"I thought today when I stopped you from falling that you had guessed," Freda stated in her usual gushy voice.

"You're right," Denise agreed with a smile. "Your hands are much too strong for a woman's. Thanks again for saving me from a bad fall. I could have broken something."

The effects of the wine had removed Freda's reserve and she said, "You're welcome. You know, my life's not as exciting as you'd think. I've been hired for some strange gigs. One man hired me to wear a plunging neckline and buy charms for a charm bracelet. He sent me to a hole-in-the-wall joint that reeked of cigarettes, cigars, and dirty bodies. It was terrible."

"Where did you buy the charms?" Denise asked, no longer interested in the Cornish hen.

"From a place called Charming Charms in New York," Freda replied with a flourish of her long hands. "It's a dump. You don't ever want to go there without taking a man with you. The people who work there are tough and the customers are worse."

Pouring a little more wine for Freda, Denise asked, "Can you describe the man who hired you?"

"Oh, sure," Freda replied after a large sip. "I've worked for him dozens of times and not always to go shopping either. Once he hired me to pretend to be the personal secretary of a wealthy but eccentric businessman. When I checked us into a hotel, I could tell from the expression on the desk manager's face that he thought I was the man's lady friend, if you get my meaning."

Pushing aside her plate, Denise asked, "After dinner, do

you think you could describe the man who hired you for me? I'd like to sketch him and you."

Flattered at the attention, Freda replied, "Why are you so interested?"

Folding her hands on her lap, Denise responded, "I'm investigating a murder case. Your employer might be connected with it. Your description might come in handy."

Smiling, Freda stated, "In that case, I'd be happy to help. I've worked for him so many times that I know every cranny in his face. I've even done magazine layouts for him. I don't especially like doing them because I have the feeling that I'm the butt of a tasteless joke, but I need the money for personal reasons."

"I'm going to get my sketchpad and pencils. I'll meet you in the lounge in a few minutes," Denise stated as she rose from the table and nodded to the others.

Looking at Denise's almost full plate, Freda said, "Aren't you going to finish your dinner? You haven't had dessert either. You eat like a little bird."

"There'll be more than enough time to eat once I finish the sketch. I'll order a sandwich in the bar if I get hungry," Denise replied as she waved good-bye.

Rushing to her room, Denise thought of all the questions she would ask Freda as she sketched. Unlocking the door, she flicked on the light and entered quickly. She stopped short of the desk and her sketchpad when she spotted the envelope on her pillow. Strangely, she was not surprised to find another message from the suspect. She was, however, tired of being watched without being able to make some observations of her own.

Tearing it open, Denise read, "Detective: Have you figured out the significance of the hurricane yet? Here's a clue: You're not in Kansas anymore, Dory. If that doesn't help, look to the center of the country for inspiration. The Bible might help, too. Enjoy the charm."

Denise was deep in thought as she unhooked the bracelet in preparation for adding another charm to the links. Unwrapping the little package, she uncovered a tiny replica of the Washington National Cathedral complete with spires and arches. Slipping it onto the links, she wondered what connection the Episcopal church might have on the case and knew that she would find out sooner than she wanted to know. In the meantime, she was keeping Freda waiting.

Freda was sitting in the bar patiently sipping a soda when Denise arrived. Looking up, she asked, "Are you ready? I've never sat for a portrait before."

"It's not a portrait, Freda, it's a simple set of sketches. I'm not that good," Denise replied as she began to work.

"I don't care what you call it. This is wonderful attention. I want one of them, you know," Freda stated as she pulled her legs under her on the large leather chair.

"First, I'll need your help on the case. Describe the man who hired you to buy the charms from Charming Charms," Denise demanded as she sketched Freda's gift.

"Well, he was about my height and age with balding, thin, but nicely styled brown hair. Oh, yes, it had a little gray at the temples," Freda began, lapping up the attention. "His eyes were a fairly unspectacular brown. His clothes were the most impressive part. They were exquisite. I don't think I've ever seen such lovely fabric. Have you finished yet? Let me see the sketch."

"I haven't finished. Keep talking," Denise replied without looking up from her paper. On one sheet of paper she sketched the reclining Freda and on the other she jotted a description of the suspect.

"His suit appeared to be a silk and wool blend," Freda continued concentrating deeply. "At least, it felt like that when I touched his arm. The shirt was handkerchief linen; I'm sure of that. Everything was carefully coordinated and matched perfectly. The shirt picked up the light gray lines in the suit and the tie's stripe pulled it all together and added just a splash of gold. Wonderful. And he wore black Bally loafers that caressed his feet. I'm sure his socks were silk, too. They looked like it."

Looking up, Denise saw that Freda had closed her eyes and appeared to be experiencing some form of rapture over the man's clothing. Not being especially impressed by clothing, Denise wished that she would return to the more substantive information that she needed. Putting the finishing touches on the sketch of Freda, she quickly began the sketch of the man.

"For your troubles," Denise stated as she handed Freda a signed copy of her sketch.

"That's wonderful!" Freda gushed. "You've captured my essence perfectly."

Prodding Freda for more, Denise stated, "Let's return to your description of your employer. I need more specifics. Describe the shape of his face and eyes. Tell me the direction of his part. I need details."

Sitting up and becoming very professional, Freda replied, "His face was oval with a fading widow's peak. He combed his remaining hair backward and slightly to the right. The gray around his temples and ears was more noticeable on the left, but he was more bald on the right. You know what I mean . . . more forehead than when he was younger. That deep 'M' look to the hairline. His right ear was pierced, and he wore a small diamond stud . . . good quality because it sparkled like mad."

"Now this is what I needed," Denise interrupted Freda's trance-like recitation. "Continue, please, by describing his nose."

Preening her hair, Freda continued, "Well, it wasn't a beak, but it wasn't small either. Functional at best. Definitely not his best feature. I think it rounded a little at the end and was a little like Karl Malden's, you know, like a little buttocks, but not as pronounced as the actor's. It definitely wasn't as cute as Brad Pitts' or as masculine as Denzel Washington's."

"And his eyebrows and eyes," Denise prompted as Freda tried to stray from the subject.

Contorting her face into all sorts of expressions, Freda replied, "The brows were the same color as his hair but without the gray. One of them had a slight feathery arch almost as if he had penciled it in for effect. His eyes were dark and expressionless except for the wrinkles at the corners. I'd say that they were laugh or sun lines, but I never saw him smile. He squinted a lot, though. I remember now, he wore reading glasses when he did close-up work. Otherwise, I never saw him in glasses."

Sketching busily, Denise asked, "Tell me about his mouth. Smile lines, smoker's wrinkles?"

"First, let me tell you about his face and then I'll talk about his mouth," Freda directed as Denise sat patiently watching her enjoyment of the spotlight.

As she sketched, Denise periodically looked up to watch Freda's expression. At all times, she saw an honesty that Denise did not think Freda was faking. She really seemed to be seeing the man's face in her memory.

"His cheeks hollowed under the high cheekbones. His chin had a slight dimple and the beginnings of jowls. If he had been a heavier man, he would have looked like an old hound dog," Freda laughed at her funny description, clapping her hands together.

Seeing that Denise was not laughing, she continued, "His mouth was kinda bowed, not like the old movie stars, more subtle than that. It was gently rounded and a little pouting. I know many women who would die for that look, if you'll excuse the tasteless pun."

Meeting Denise's stern face, Freda commented, "A girl's gotta try to inject a little humor. You're so serious. Lighten up, Denise baby."

Smiling, Denise ignored the attempt at humor and replied, "Tell me about his ears. I'm almost ready to show you the composite."

Scratching her head and readjusting her wig, Freda replied, "There's not much to tell about them. They weren't large or misshapen, just ears. They were the kind that hug the head rather than protruding. The lobes were attached, if I remember correctly. I noticed that when I saw the earring. A lot of people have the other kind like yours."

Making the last lines on the sketch, Denise turned the book so that Freda could see the composite. Squealing with delight, she gushed, "That's him! That's the man. He looks so lifelike that I expect him to talk to me. You're a regular Michelangelo."

"You gave a very good description. Now, I'd like to get a description of his walk," Denise suggested as Freda sipped another rum and soda.

Holding the sketch at arm's length while she listened, Denise noticed the resemblance between Freda and the suspect. The high cheekbones were the same. Freda's bowed mouth was similar but more pronounced, perhaps as the result of carefully applied lipstick. She had said that people envied and copied the look. Freda's cheek hollows were deeper but similar, almost as if she were trying to camouflage excess weight. The wig covered her natural hairline and her ears since she had loosened the ponytail and arranged the curls to flatter her face. The similarity was striking. Denise certainly hoped that Freda had not described herself in an effort to hold her attention.

Turning her attention to Freda, Denise listened carefully as she described the suspect's walk. "He saunters as if proud of himself. You know the walk . . . head high, hips tucked under, and shoulders square. Since I'm a lady and have never seen him without his clothes, I can only say that he looks like a Wall Street baron."

Denise suppressed a chuckle at Freda's description, wondering when or if she had ever seen a baron, Wall Street or otherwise. The interview had gone exceedingly well with Freda providing helpful information, if it were truthful. If not, Denise had certainly learned a lot about the person the suspect had hired to be his go-between. Freda certainly had a vivid imagination and an interesting way of involving the listener in her discussion.

"How did you meet him?" Denise asked as she sipped her soda.

"That's easy. He came to my show. You might not know it,

but I'm a well-known female impersonator. Lots of important people come to see my show in SoHo," Freda replied proudly.

"Did he hire you to come on this trip, too?" Denise inquired leaning slightly forward to catch every word.

Laughing, Freda replied, "Of course, he did, but he called it a vacation for services well done. I was in Hawaii, too. Didn't you see me?"

"Hawaii?" Denise repeated incredulously. "What were you doing there?"

Proudly, Freda replied, "I was one of the hula dancers . . . one of the blondes, as a matter of fact. I'm surprised you didn't recognize me. I expected you to remember me from New York."

Remembering the woman at the hotel manager's desk and the hula dancer, Denise had confirmation of her suspicions. She had thought the woman looked familiar but could not quite place her. Freda's admission had given confirmation to her thoughts.

"I thought you looked familiar, but I wasn't sure. I had a memory but nothing firm," Denise replied with a smile as she fingered the bracelet.

"Is that the one he gave you? Look at those charms! They really are pretty. I couldn't see them very well in that dark, nasty Charming Charms," Freda stated as she leaned closer for a better view.

"Yes, and here's the newest one, as if you didn't know," Denise replied with a knowing smile.

"What does that mean?" Freda asked with an incredulous expression.

"You're the one who delivered it, aren't you?" Denise asked with a wry smile.

"You found me out!" Freda laughed heartily. "I arranged for the maid to deliver it to your room. I knew we'd be at dinner together, and I wouldn't be able to do it."

Turning very serious, Denise advised, "If I were you, I wouldn't have anything more to do with this man. You might become more than a messenger if you stick around too much longer."

"What do you mean?" Freda asked with genuine alarm written on her face.

"I mean that he's a killer," Denise replied in a straightforward manner.

"No!" Freda exclaimed in disbelief. "He couldn't be. He's not the type. He's a businessman not a killer. He wouldn't want to get his clothes dirty or his hair mussed."

"Not all killers use their hands or a gun, Freda," Denise replied with a crooked grin.

"Then how does he do it?" Freda inquired, placing her third drink on the table and giving Denise her undivided attention.

"He uses some kind of germ or virus that causes fevers and convulsions," Denise responded with open hands that showed her frustration at not being able to identify the product more fully. "You really should stay far away from him."

"How does he administer it?" Freda asked with a mixture of interest and skepticism.

"That's what I don't know," Denise answered. "Pathology hasn't identified the substance yet, so we don't know the application method. That makes him even more dangerous. He isn't even around when it works. Be careful."

"Oh, I will. You can count on that. You won't see me in his company ever again," Freda replied as she drained her drink and ordered another. Responding to Denise's scowl, she said, "I need one more to steady my nerves."

Paying their bar tab, most of which was Freda's, Denise said, "Thanks for helping me with the composite and for the company. I'm beat and I'm going to bed. Good luck with your show. I'll have to come to see you in New York one day soon. Maybe my partner would like to come with me."

Laughing and lifting her last drink in salute, Freda replied, "You're welcome, and thanks for the drinks and the sketch. From what I saw of your partner while we were in Hawaii, he's not the type who would like my show. He doesn't look like the type who'd enjoy a drag queen's act. Good luck with your investigation."

Frowning and then breaking into a laugh, Denise replied, "That's right. You saw Tom at the Polynesian Village. You might be right at that. Good night."

Denise yawned as she entered her room. It had been a long, tiring day, but, if Freda had not been lying, it had been a profitable one. She had a sketch and description of the killer, more than she had had before the trip to the Grand Canyon. Further, the information had come from someone who had worked with him closely.

She wondered what Tom would think of Freda. He would probably find her information as potentially unreliable as she did. However, at the moment, it was all she had. Freda had shared the information without hesitation. If she were lying, she was certainly good at it. She never hesitated to give the descriptions. Remembering the similarity in Freda's appearance and that of the man she described, Denise again wondered if she had simply described herself. Denise would have to wait until after she apprehended the murderer to know for certain if Freda had been a reliable source.

As she prepared for bed, Denise remembered that she had to catch an early flight the next morning. Knowing that she hated to rush and pack before leaving, she tossed all but the clothes she needed for the trip and her toiletries into her bag. The outfit she had worn on the donkey ride still smelled of the beast and her sweat. Not wanting to ruin her other clothes, Denise slipped the smelly ones into one of the hotel's paper laundry bags. It would add a little cushion of protection between her clean outfits and the donkey's unique essence.

The maid had left a chocolate on Denise's pillow, but she was too tired to eat it. Tossing it onto the dresser beside the bracelet and the note, she slipped into bed. She usually reviewed the day's activities as a way to relax and bring closure to her work before going to sleep every night. However, she was too tired to do it and fell asleep immediately.

Eleven

When Denise arrived in the squad room, she found the familiar high energy level and pandemonium. The smell of slightly burned coffee filled the air. Tom sat hunched over his papers with the usual cup of stiff brew at his side. Molly slept at his feet with her big head resting lovingly on his foot. Nothing had changed.

Everything looked the same until she reached the bulletin board on which they posted newspaper articles associated with their cases. Instead of a success story, Denise read headlines for each of the murders her suspect had committed since her assignment to the case. She did not need the reminder that her batting average had taken a dive to the basement. She knew that her reputation had suffered a great blow, and she was determined to do something about it. Now that she no longer had to follow the suspect's clues out of town, she could concentrate all of her energy on finding him.

"Hey, Dory, you're back!" Tom exclaimed, forgetting that he was usually very staid and stoic in the presence of other officers. "Why didn't you call me? I'd have picked you up at the airport."

"Glad to see me, huh?" Denise beamed happily. "I took a cab. I didn't see any reason to bother you. Any new developments?"

"None that you don't already know," Tom replied as he worked to regain his composure. They had not been separated long, but he had missed her. The companionship of his

canine partner was no longer enough. His concern for
Denise's safety had pushed Molly's presence to the background.

"Pathology hasn't isolated the substance yet?" Denise
asked without expecting to receive a positive response.

Shaking his head, Tom replied, "No, nothing. I've asked
our contact at the FBI to take a private look at the report.
Maybe he'll come up with something. Anything new on your
end?"

"Yeah, take a look," Denise responded as she showed Tom
the latest addition to her charm bracelet.

"The Washington Cathedral? What does that have to do
with this case?" Tom echoing Denise's first reaction to the
charm.

"I didn't understand either until I read this. Take a look,"
Denise responded as she thrust a passage copied from the
Bible at Tom.

"I still don't get it," Tom replied, returning the paper and
looking at Denise skeptically.

Placing the paper inside her sketchbook, Denise replied,
"I'm not saying that I've completely made the connection
either. I'm planning to go to the library today as soon as I
sort through my notes. However, I think the Midwest reference in the note and the Bible passage about winnowing out
the weak has something to do with the case. At least I hope
it does. Other than Freda's description, we don't have anything else to go on."

"Who's Freda?" Tom frowned. "I'm feeling very much
out of the loop right now, Dory. Bring me up to speed and
fast."

Replying quickly, Denise said, "Freda's a woman I met
on the donkey ride down the wall of the Grand Canyon. You
would have hated it, by the way. Hot, smelly, horrible. Scary,
too. The donkey had hardly any path at all to walk on. You
would have turned back after the first few feet."

"You're right," Tom agreed. "I wouldn't have gone at all.

I don't like donkeys and heights. Now start at the beginning.
I'm still confused."

"OK, but let me get a cup of coffee first. Did you make
it?" Denise asked as she walked toward the table.

"Who else would come in here early to do it?" Tom complained with good humor. "Those slobs drink it like water,
but they never make a single pot. Bums every one of them!"

Stirring the thick, strong coffee, Denise replied, "I've
missed this stuff. None of the hotels could quite duplicate
it. NYPD came close but not exactly."

"You're damn right!" Tom responded with pride.

His coffee was indeed the talk of the entire police department. Many had tired to duplicate his recipe, but they had
all failed miserably. Some thought it was the fact that he
never washed the pot that added the flavor. Others said he
overmeasured and that was what made it thick and rich. Still
others insisted that he left the pot on the heat so long that
the brew thickened without any help from him. Many had
begged Denise to tell them Tom's secret, but she did not
know either. Tom refused to give anyone the satisfaction of
duplicating his trademark coffee.

"OK, this is what happened after we split up at the airport," Denise began as she sipped her coffee. "I went on the
donkey ride down the Grand Canyon as the killer suggested.
The view was fabulous, but the conveyance smelled, literally.
My butt is still sore from the rocking motion of the beast.
Anyway, we finally arrived at the way station where we saw
a film, heard a lecture, and rested. While there, I met Freda,
actually, she saved me from falling over a rock. Are you
following me so far?"

"No problem here. You met Freda who saved you from
falling," Tom repeated as he scratched Molly's head.

"Right," Denise continued with a frown at the slobbering
dog. "After dinner, I found out that Freda had worked for
the suspect. She provided me with this great composite and
a general description of the man."

"That's great!" Tom interrupted. "Finally some hard evidence. I was beginning to think we'd never have any."

"Not so fast," Denise cautioned. "Freda's a transvestite, a star in a drag queen show. The man she described looks remarkably like her."

"What!" Tom exclaimed, reaching for the composite.

"Turn to the back of the book," Denise instructed. "I made a sketch of her as a gift to thank her for her help. And I made one for us."

On the last page of the sketchbook, Denise had made a drawing of Freda as she chatted about the killer. Freda had not noticed since she thought Denise was jotting down notes of her experiences with the killer. Now, comparing the two sketches, the similarities were overwhelming.

"It looks like the same person," Tom replied as he held the two sheets at arm's length.

"To me, too," Denise agreed. "Freda told me that she was the big blonde who made the charm purchase from Charming Charms. She was one of the hula dancers, too, you know, the big one that looked a little out of place. The most striking difference is the eye color. Freda's are a gold and hazel mixture and his are a piercing brown."

"Let's get the NYPD to arrest her on suspicion of murder," Tom suggested, reaching for his pad of paper and writing himself a note.

"With what as evidence?" Denise queried in frustration. "Until we know the nature of the substance, we're sunk. We can't arrest her anymore than we can stop further killings."

"OK, so what's next?" Tom asked, returning the pad to his messy desk. "You have a composite of the possible suspect that looks strikingly like the person who described him to you. You know that the murder weapon is a virus or a germ, but you can't isolate its source."

"I'm going to the library and then to church," Denise stated as she drained the last of the thick brew from the cup. "There's a connection here that I can't make out. I need some books."

"Do you need any help? I've almost finished my work here," Tom asked not wanting to be separated from her again.

"Can your girl friend spare you? She looks awfully needy," Denise replied, looking at the expression of contentment on Molly's face.

"She'll be OK for a while," Tom chuckled as he cleared the clutter from his desk. Sputtering, he added, "You've only been here a few minutes, and my paperclips are already a mess. How did you manage that, Dory?"

"Have you ever thought that I might not be the only one who does this to you? Besides, I just walked in the door. How could I have done it?" Denise asked as she trotted behind him. As usual, she was bringing up the rear . . . happily.

"No one else has that much nerve," Tom replied as they started down the street at his usual fast pace.

Tom was right. Denise had made a chain from his paperclips. She was the one who did it all the time. She kept an extra clip caddy in her desk, one that matched his exactly. Whenever he was distracted, she would exchange that one for the original. Tom had never been able to prove that she did it, although he was almost positive. While he had been studying the composite and the sketch of Freda, Denise had switched the two caddies. If only solving the mystery were as easy as getting on Tom's nerves, it would be a piece of cake.

However, this case was not easy to solve. Everywhere they turned, they ran into a brick wall. Denise hoped that being at home again would provide her with leads. She was becoming tired of the bumps on her head.

"Did you miss me?" Denise asked as they reached the intersection. For a moment, they stood side-by-side with nowhere to go until the light turned green.

"Why do you ask me that?" Tom growled. As always, he hated the mushy love stuff and hardly ever showed his emotions. The kiss at the Polynesian Village was a completely unexpected treat.

"Because I want to know. A woman likes to hear those things," Denise insisted, slipping her arm through his.

"Come on, Dory, we're on duty. We can't talk about stuff like this when we're on duty," Tom insisted as he placed his hand lightly on hers.

"Why not? You kissed me while we were on duty," Denise persisted as they crossed the street at a more leisurely but still quick pace.

"That was different. The tropical sun had cooked my brain," Tom snarled as a smile played on his lips. "OK, yes, I missed you. I thought that was obvious from my big smile and stupid outburst."

He had noticed the expression on their colleagues faces and knew that everyone would soon be talking about his uncharacteristic display of affection toward his partner. Tom was a very private man who kept his thoughts to himself. He hated it that the entire squad knew that he had missed Denise and that he cared for her.

"Good, I'm glad you missed me. I was very unhappy without you. Now, why did you miss me?" Denise teased, knowing that Tom objected to personal discussions almost as much as public displays of affection.

"Here's why," Tom replied as he grabbed Denise by the shoulders and pulled her against him. He did not seem to notice the stares of the pedestrians as they walked around them.

The sun shone brightly on them as he pressed his lips to hers and gave her the second most wonderful kiss of her life. She clung to him tightly and did not want to let go for fear of falling to the sidewalk. When Tom showed his affection, a woman really knew that he cared.

Lifting her sunglasses and looking tenderly into her eyes, Tom demanded, "Satisfied? I love you, Denise, and I missed you more than I'd miss my favorite pair of socks. You mean the world to me. OK?"

"I get the idea. You don't have to drop a safe on my head," Denise laughed as she playfully kissed his chin and cheeks.

For the first time in their working relationship, Denise and Tom were the object of stares from passersby, and they did not care. Wrapping their arms around each other again, they embraced once more. Not as hard and fast as before, but sweetly and lingeringly. In a world in which people killed their competitors for the sake of national ranking, their public display of affection appeared to be an expression of sanity.

Looking away shyly, Tom said, "As much as I'd like to continue this pleasurable reaction to your return, I think we're drawing too many stares. If the entire squad hasn't walked by here yet, it will soon. Let's go."

Linking her arm happily in his, Denise replied, "All right, but don't forget that you owe me a few more kisses. I'm feeling quite deprived."

Pressing her arm tightly against his ribs, Tom commented, "I intend to make good as long and as often as you do. From now on, we'll be inseparable."

Reaching the library door, Denise turned and said, "That might become a little inconvenient if either of us has a nature call."

Shaking his head, Tom quipped, "Now who's being literal? You know what I mean."

"Sure do," Denise replied over her shoulder teasingly. "You mean that I'm your girl and you're my fella."

" 'Fella?' Is that what going west does to you? 'Fella?' " Tom repeated.

"It's no more offensive than calling a grown woman a 'girl,' " Denise replied as they advanced toward the reference section of the library.

"It's all in perspective. Besides, we agreed to find a better term. Now that I've heard 'fella,' I'll work harder at it," Tom agreed as they pulled a few volumes from the shelf.

"I thought you would," Denise commented almost distractedly.

"Exactly why aren't we using the computer for this?" Tom asked, carrying the heavy tomes to the table. "We could have searched the Web for whatever it is that you want without leaving the office."

"I know, but the hacker would have been able to trace everything I found," Denise replied running her finger down the index. "I don't want him to know that we're on to him."

"We are?" Tom rejoined with a chuckle. "That's news to me."

"Good. I like keeping you slightly off balance," Denise laughed softly, not wanting to incur the wrath of the librarian.

"I thought I was the one who was keeping you off balance. You were certainly off your feet when I kissed you," Tom teased lightly.

"Don't worry. I'll get used to it. It's just new to me. After you've done it a few hundred times, I won't even notice," Denise retorted with a laugh that caused the librarian to look in their direction.

"Sush!" Tom hissed. "She'll throw us out."

"What a shame! We'd have to play hooky," Denise whispered with a tease in her voice as she pressed her shoulder against his so that Tom could not miss her meaning.

"Not a bad idea. Let's go. Besides, I promise that it won't get boring," Tom stated as he pretended to rise while holding his place in the book Denise had passed to him.

"Hold your horses. We'll have plenty of time for that later," Denise replied as she gently pulled him into his seat.

"One of these days, Dory, you're going to have to make good on your innuendoes," Tom stated with a low chuckle.

"One of these days, I will," Denise replied with a wink.

Chuckling softly, Tom returned to scanning the pages Denise had shared with him. Although he was not quite sure why she wanted him to read about the Salem Witch Trials of 1692, he did it willing. All she had whispered was that he needed to look for descriptions of the illnesses that plagued the people during that time.

"I think I found something," Tom stated as he leaned his shoulder against hers.

"What . . . a way to show your affection in public or information on the people?" Denise asked as she leaned toward him. They had pressed their shoulders so closely together that not even a sheet of rice paper could pass between them.

"You have a one track mind, woman," Tom growled softly with a smile playing at the corner of his lips.

"So do you or else you wouldn't have understood my meaning so fast," Denise chided with an impish grin.

"Do you want to see what I've found or are you only interested in me for my body?" Tom asked pretending that Denise had hurt his feelings.

"Normally, I'd say only your body, but I've found some good information, too. Let's see if there's somewhere that we can sit and talk," Denise replied as she walked toward the reserve librarian's desk.

The woman greeted Denise with a cheerful smile. "What might I do for you," she asked.

Flashing her shield, Denise stated, "My partner and I are doing research on a murder case. We need to discuss our findings. Do you have a room that we could use?"

"Of course," the librarian responded. "We have a lovely little conference room that hardly anyone uses. As a matter of fact, we use it mostly as a lunch room. Collect your books and follow me."

Denise motioned to Tom for him to follow her. She almost split her sides trying to contain the laughter as he tried to collect all ten of the massive tomes, balance them, and walk at the same time. Pressing her lips tightly closed to keep the sound from escaping, Denise rushed to help him. An expression of relief and annoyance played across his face as she took the top four volumes into her arms, leaving him with the heaviest and largest.

"Thanks," Tom muttered. "I was wondering if you'd realize that I'm not your beast of burden."

"What happened to the days of chivalry when women didn't have to lift a finger?" Denise commented in a whisper as they followed the librarian to the back of the building past the book binding room.

"Haven't you heard? They liberated the slave and women. We're equals now. How's about you carrying one of these heavy ones, too," Tom responded in a mocking tone.

"Not on your life, partner," Denise replied with a chuckle. "I'm selective in the way I spend my calories. Besides, you don't want me to be too tired tonight, do you?"

"Another soon to be unfulfilled promise," Tom muttered as they entered the little room that the librarian had called a conference room.

"Is this OK?" the librarian asked eagerly with an expression that stated her desire to be of assistance.

"It'll be just fine. Thanks," Denise replied with a smile that seemed to make the woman very happy.

"I'll reserve the room for you so that no one will come in. The facilities are just a few doors down the hall if you need a rest room or a copier," the librarian added as she closed the door and left them to work.

The large table with its twelve chairs badly dwarfed the small room. A computer sat in one small corner and a microfiche in the other. A vividly colored screen saver played on the monitor, providing the only color in the gray room.

Denise could not imagine that anyone ever used this small space for meetings. It would never have served a large group. The dust at her end on the table confirmed her suspicions although the other end showed that someone regularly used the room and the computer. The crumbs validated the librarian's lunch room story.

"It's good that I'm not allergic to mites and dust," Tom stated as he opened the book to the section on the Salem Witch Trials.

"Really. This room needs a good cleaning. We'll have to work fast or perish," Denise replied as she settled into the very hard, cold metal seat.

"There's no falling asleep in here," Tom commented as he sank into the very uninviting chair.

"OK. What did you find on the Salem Witch hunts that

relates to this case?" Denise asked as she opened her sketch-book to take notes.

Relaying the material he had read, Tom stated, "At first the girls, to relieve boredom I guess, asked a slave for information on witchcraft, but after they got caught dancing in the woods, they blamed, who else, the black woman for con-juring with the devil. The events quickly changed from a fairly harmless fascination with something different from their usual boring lives to a witch hunt. Even though the slave confessed to having dealings with the devil, the girls weren't satisfied and started blaming women they didn't like of casting spells on them. They started having convulsions and seeing things that didn't exist. Many people, including John Proctor, stated that the girls were only being malicious, especially Abigail with whom he had had a brief affair. After he ended it, she still wanted him. He told the court that jeal-ousy and hatred of his wife caused Abigail's behavior and that she wasn't bewitched at all. According to this article, nineteen people were hanged for witchcraft that year based on the evidence presented before a court by those girls."

"I remember reading Arthur Miller's play on the Salem Witch Trials. I still don't quite see how the behavior of the girls relates to our case. I was hoping for a connection or a mention of drugs or a potion," Denise said as she shifted in the uncomfortable seat.

"Just wait a minute, I'm getting to the point," Tom advised with a wave of his hand. "Anyway, a psychologist recently noticed that the behavior of the girls—the fever, convulsions and speech disorders, and diarrhea—might not have been an act. The psychologist thinks a fungus might have caused their behavior. If the girls' testimony were true, then it's possible that they might have suffered from a disease caused called convulsive ergotism."

"Ergotism? I just read about that. Here, look. I thought it was something that kids got in the old days. Strange that we'd both find information about it. Kismet, karma, or just plain luck. Whatever the reason, it must relate to our case,"

Denise insisted, trying to remember something in Miller's play that would connect to their investigation.

"This article says that it's caused by eating grain that's been infested with the ergot fungus," Tom replied, pulling the article away from Denise and running his finger down the length of the column to find the specifics. "The fungus thrives in hot, humid, wet conditions and causes the grain to develop a cloudy, sticky substance. Rye is especially susceptible to it, but wheat and barley can develop it, too. Eventually, the contaminated parts of the grain turn black."

"Cooking doesn't kill the fungus?" Denise asked as she scanned the page that contained photographs of the tainted grain.

"No, it remains active even with heat. The only way to control it is to eliminate the fungus from the seed," Tom stated expertly.

"Why don't we hear about it today?" Denise asked as she turned the page to search for her answer.

"I guess farmers work harder to rotate their crops, plant the seed deeper, and employ improved sanitation standards. The article said that commercially controlled seed and grain doesn't contain the fungus. Today, it mostly affects farm animals that eat infested grasses in the pasture. People hardly get it," Tom replied as he finished his mini lecture.

"But it's possible that people could contract convulsive ergot if the farmers weren't careful," Denise stated as she sorted through the information in the article she had been reading.

"That's right. However, I don't think that anyone would take that chance with their livelihood," Tom commented, turning his attention to the books open in front of Denise.

Nodding in agreement, Denise replied, "You're probably right, but an individual with a grudge might be willing to spend the time creating the marshy environment in which to grow the infested grain."

"Are you saying that the suspect grew or purchased tainted

grain and made cereal from it that he fed to his competition?"
Tom asked with a skeptical expression.

Shaking her head, Denise responded, "No, of course, he
didn't do that. He would have needed to work with a cereal
company to pull off something like that. His colleagues
would have noticed a change in the cereal's appearance if he
had simply inserted his contaminated grain. It's not possible
that a flour producer would have become involved in this
sick scheme either."

"Then what?" Tom asked. The articles had provided information that, so far, appeared interesting but useless unless
they found an application for it.

Denise spoke slowly as she worked out the possibilities.
"He might have grown the contaminated grain himself,
ground it himself on one of those home machines, and baked
desserts or bread with it. He then could have invited his
colleagues, or should I say victims, to dinner and served it
to them. They never would have suspected or known."

"Wouldn't the doctors or the pathology lab have been able
to isolate the presence of ergot in the victim's stomachs?"
Tom asked as he began to follow her thoughts.

"No, I don't think so," Denise replied shaking her head.
"Doctors hardly ever see it since it's not a problem anymore.
According to that article, people take a derivative of ergot
for migraines since it works on the blood vessels in the head.
Some of our parents' friends probably took a derivative during their hippie days . . . LSD. No one would notice ergot
in the contents of the stomach."

Rubbing his eyes, Tom commented, "No wonder so many
people took bad trips. The article makes it sound as if the
ergot fungus is potent stuff."

"That's my point," Denise stated, "It wouldn't take much
to make the competition sicken and die. If people could get
the ergot fungus in the 1960's and 1970's and make LSD
from it, someone today could use it to taint baked goods."

"I saw a payphone near the bathrooms. I'll call our FBI
contact and ask him to run the stomach contents through

their lab to look for ergot fungus," Tom stated as he massaged his stiff back. Because he was a tall big man, the metal seats did not provide his back with any support.

"I'll be here if I can gain access to the Internet from that computer," Denise stated, pointing to the monitor with the wild screen saver. "I want to search the databanks for celebrity parties and interesting recipes that incorporated wheat, rye, and barley flowers."

Navigating the maze of chair legs, Denise made her way to the back of the room. Crumbs on the table's surface confirmed that someone had lately eaten a sandwich in the conference room. Brushing them aside and spreading her copies of old fashion magazines on the table, Denise began her on-line search of the Washington Post.com archives. She knew that somewhere in the files she would find the answer to her questions. Now that she had a possible murder weapon, she needed the method.

Reading articles about fashion celebrities, parties attended by patrons of the arts, the debut of spring and fall lines of fashion houses, and the personalities behind the designs, Denise learned more than she ever wanted to know about the industry. The number of possibilities for infiltration by an unscrupulous and jealous individual was mind-boggling. Any one of the major players could have become driven by ambition and greed and killed the others.

In addition to haute couture and ready-to-wear, celebrity lines existed as extensions either of established houses or of the Hollywood film industry. Celebrities who had made their name as television stars endorsed women's fashions sold in discount stores. Knowledgeable television hostesses peddled outfits for the fashion conscious hostess. Sports personalities paraded apparel for the athletic. All of these subcategories modified their designs from those of the main fashion houses. Each one of them had designers who sat at the computer or the grafting table and turned out the fashions that would soon find their way into the closet of working men and women, housewives, businessmen, sports enthusiasts, and retirees.

Deciding to focus on the haute couture industry, Denise pulled her magazines closer so that she could compare the names in the newspaper articles with those in the rankings. With luck, between the *Washington Post* and the *New York Times* she would be able to isolate a list of people who traveled in the same circles within the fashion industry. From that list, she hoped to isolate the suspect.

Having exhausted the archives of both on-line newspapers, Denise turned to the microfiche. The on-line files only contained the more recent articles. She would have to pay a fee for older ones. However, with access to the microfiche at her disposal, Denise saw no reason to incur the expense. The fiche made difficult reading, but she had already isolated the general topic and could proceed directly to it in her search.

Following a hunch and squinting at the reader, Denise scrolled through the fiche for two years earlier until she found the first article relating to a reception following a fashion show. Reading it quickly, she discovered that the designer had entertained in his home following the debut of his new line of women's clothing. The next day, he fell ill with diarrhea, fever, and convulsions. He had died of unknown causes two days after his party. His wife had assumed control of the company but had sold it within a few months to one of his competitors who absorbed the lines into his own.

Looking forward to the summer of that year, Denise discovered that another designer of men's ready-to-wear had thrown a party following the highly acclaimed premier of his fall fashions. His friends and colleagues had dined on only the most exquisite of seafood, fowl, and pastries. The next morning, the host lay in bed shivering with a high fever. By the time he had arrived at the hospital, he was beginning to suffer from convulsions. He died later that night of convulsions and dehydration, leaving no heirs. His business partner continued to oversee the operation of the business.

The holiday season of the same year, several designers

hosted a private soiree to celebrate their successful year. According to the newspaper article, all but one of them ate the chocolate mousse cake; the designer allergic to chocolate refrained. The next day, all of the others felt varying degrees of illness with the one who had consumed all of her cake being the most ill. The others stayed in bed for a week with fever and an upset stomach, but the unfortunate woman with the sweet tooth lay in the hospital, during which times she suffered from hallucinations. She died of an undetermined virus without regaining consciousness. The doctors were at a loss to find the cause.

Pushing away from the fiche, Denise flipped the pages of the magazines until she found photographs of the deceased. In a few cases, they had been with friends or family, none of whom was present in another photograph. They looked perfectly healthy in the photographs but had died as the result of an unidentified virus.

Tom appeared while Denise was comparing the guest list from each party. Only one person had appeared on both lists, the lady with the sweet tooth. Denise realized that she would need to broaden her search. She needed to find the guest list from every party attended by a designer for the last two years. She knew that only then would she be able to find the killer. If they would have any possibility of success, she would need Tom's help to undertake that monumental task. She would have to rely on the memory of many people to help compile the list.

Denise began scrolling to the beginning of the next year and found information on a pre-spring season fashion gala hosted by a consortium of fashion designers. From the article, Denise could tell that all had gone well. However, after the party the group had assembled at the home of one of its members for a little post-party celebration. From the coroner's report, it appeared they had eaten a special chocolate cake and consumed vast quantities of champagne. The next day, the host, who had consumed the least amount, only suffered from a headache while the others required hospitalization. The result was that the host's business partner died. The grieving host decided to continue the business alone.

"You won't believe what I've found," Denise said as she tore herself from the fiche.

Holding up his hands to avoid what he knew would be long diatribe, Tom stated, "Before you tell me what you've discovered, our friend at the Bureau was most helpful. He immediately called his contact at the CDC for help. Unfortunately, they no longer had the stomach contents and couldn't conduct further tests. However, the scientist stated that your theory was plausible. The downside of this is that we'll have to wait until the next victim dies before he can test your theory."

"He won't have to wait long if my hunch is correct," Denise interjected when Tom stopped for a breath.

"Why not? Have you identified the murderer?" Tom asked as he drew up a chair beside Denise and sat down.

Shrugging, Denise replied, "No, not yet, but I've found an incredible number of deaths in the fashion industry due to mysterious unidentified viruses. I'm surprised that no one tried to connect the deaths to one person before now."

"Have you found a likely suspect?" Tom asked, scanning the microfiche articles that Denise had printed.

"Not yet," Denise replied slowly. "There're still too many variables. I haven't been able to compile a single list from which to delete names, but I'll get there. I'm feeling more confident about the task than I was before we arrived."

Leaning back in the uncomfortable chair, Tom invited Denise to share the knowledge she had gained with him. Folding his hands over his stomach, he listened attentively as she told him about the parties, the illnesses, and the deaths. The name of the killer was the only thing Denise had not learned.

"When do you think he'll strike again?" Tom asked as they gathered the copies and prepared to leave.

Pointing to the Style section of the paper, Denise replied, "According to today's paper, a group of internationally renowned designers will meet in DC this week. We'll have to keep our eyes open for a party and invite ourselves."

"Oh, I forgot to give you this," Tom replied as he pulled a very familiar looking envelope from his jacket pocket.

"Not another one! I guess he didn't vanish. When did this arrive?" Denise moaned as she read the familiar slanting handwriting.

"It came this morning by courier. Well, what does he say this time?" Tom inquired as he looked over her shoulder.

Leaning against his strong arm, Denise responded, "He's either becoming more poetic or more relaxed in his style and familiarity. His earlier letters were a bit more formal. He sounds as if he knows me in this one."

With his arms wrapped around her waist, Tom read aloud, " 'Detective, I trust that you've figured out the significance of the little tornado by now. I'll help you with the biblical reference if you'll attend evensong at the Cathedral with me today. Here's another little charm for the bracelet."

This time, the little package neatly tucked in the corner of the envelope contained a dancing couple in evening clothing. The 18k couple looked like Ginger Rogers and Fred Astaire melded together for all time. Denise could see the man's tiny bow tie and the woman's wrist corsage.

"I wonder what made him select this one," Tom mused. "I still haven't figured out the twister. Have you?"

Smiling, Denise replied, "I got that one when he mentioned winnowing out. You winnow out the wheat from the chaff. Wheat, rye, and barley grow in the flat lands of this country. He confirmed my suspicions when he quoted *The Wizard of Oz*."

"Then what does this one mean?" Tom asked as they returned the heavy books to the librarian and thanked her for the use of the conference room.

"I think we're going to a party. I bet I'll receive the invitation today at church," Denise replied as they stepped into the afternoon sun.

"Why would he invite you to witness a murder?" Tom asked, slipping his arm around Denise's waist.

Responding quickly, Denise said, "I guess it's more fun that way. If he caused all the deaths I think he did, he's getting bored at the ease of the act. He wants a little challenge."

Squeezing her tightly, Tom insisted, "Make sure that you don't become one of his statistics."

"Don't worry. You'll be there to watch my back," Denise smiled as they headed toward the precinct.

They separated two blocks from the precinct door. Although they no longer cared who witnessed their closeness when they were in the public, they did not want to demonstrate it in front of their colleagues. Not only did they think it unprofessional, Denise and Tom knew that they would make themselves the butt of every office joke if anyone saw them together.

Denise busied herself with odds and ends that needed tending before she left the squad room for the Cathedral. She had not attended a service there since her cousin's son had sung in the Choir of Men and Boys. He had the voice of an angel when he was a little boy and that of a frog now that he was nearing adolescence. Denise never knew from one day to the next if he would be able to croak out a welcome. Returning to the Cathedral would be like old home week, even with the murderer among the worshipers.

Before leaving the squad room, Denise turned to Tom and suggested, "Let's have dinner at the diner tonight. I have a taste for carrot cake."

Looking up with a smile, Tom asked, "Should I pick you up?"

"I'll meet you," Denise stated as she pushed her sketchbook into the overcrowded briefcase. "Evensong shouldn't last longer than an hour, but traffic at that hour will be heavy. Besides, I don't know exactly when to expect contact with our perpetrator."

"OK. Take care of yourself, Dory," Tom replied as a worry frown lined his forehead.

"I'll be safe in the church," Denise responded as she started toward the door, leaving Tom at his desk with Molly sleeping on his foot.

"That's what Tomas Becket thought, too," Tom replied with an appropriate reference to the murder of the Bishop of Canterbury in Canterbury Cathedral.

Laughing, Denise waved and took the warmth of the squad room with her. Tom hated to see her go alone to the Cathedral, but she had felt that his presence might stop the suspect from leaving further instructions about the party that might prove essential to their investigation. However, church or no church, Tom worried that Denise might be putting herself in danger.

Finishing the last of his evening work, Tom slipped the leash on Molly, tidied up his desk, switched off the little lamp, and left the squad room. By the time he reached his car, Tom had completely formulated his plans. He would go to the Cathedral without letting Denise know that he was there. He would watch her back even if she did not know that he was keeping his silent vigil. She might ignore the obvious risks of being alone with the killer, but he would not.

Twelve

Evensong started late at the Cathedral because a wedding in the sanctuary ran over time. Denise joined the modest gathering that gazed at the magnificent stained glass windows, the gargoyles, the bass relief ceiling bosses, and the flying buttresses. She did not mind the inconvenience because it afforded her time to wander through the beautifully designed Close that she knew so well but had not visited in years.

On that bright afternoon, the gardens looked especially inviting. Stepping away from the group, Denise strolled through the gate and down the twisting path to see the spectacular display of flowers. She remembered her teacher friends saying that young men from the boys school and young women from the girls campus often met in the gardens for romantic interludes between classes. Today, except for other evensong participants waiting for the service to begin, the garden was silent and a pleasant relief from the noise of Wisconsin Avenue and the bustle of DC only a few yards away.

Denise sank onto a bench in the herb section of the garden. She breathed deeply of the fragrance of rosemary, lavender, and thyme and watched the little sparrows hunting for seeds and insects. Looking over the shrubs, she could see the towering façade of the Cathedral and higher still the bell tower as the sun played on the white structure. Tom would have loved the serenity of the Bishop's Garden. Actually, the carefully clipped topiary would probably have attracted his attention more than anything else. He liked the intricacies of nature, especially when man's heavy hand showed in it.

Once several years ago, Denise had taken a tour of the Cathedral during its spring festival. She had listened to a docent lecture on the structure of the building and the nature of the ornate carvings. The "purple lady," so named for the color of her robe, explained the heating system that ran under the marble floor, the source of the building materials, and the need for patron support for the constant repairs to the structure.

Denise's favorite part of the day had been the tour of the bell tower with the organist. He had taken them into the catwalk inside the Cathedral's framework, leading them down narrow walks and up twisting stairs. Finally, they had arrived at the bell ringing room with its view of Washington. He had explained the process of ringing the gigantic bells and the skill required of the ringers to maintain their balance while striving for the rhythm of the peals.

From there he had escorted the group to see the carillon, still higher in the tower. The view of Washington and nearby Virginia was even more spectacular from this level as birds darted in and out of the curved archways. Every gust of wind made the structure sway ever so gently. Denise had found the bird's-eye view invigorating.

Seeing the others begin to enter the Cathedral for the service, Denise abandoned her bench and memories. She filed into the church and walked down the long center aisle to the crossing and the narthex beyond. With the reredos clearly in view, she slipped into one of the seats in the choir stalls that bore the name of the boy's school headmaster.

As the massive organ began to play, the congregation stood while the boy's choir processed. They looked angelic in their purple robes with white chasuble and white ruffled collar. Denise smiled at the little boy who reminded her of her cousin's son.

The music stopped and the priest began to intone the ser-

vice from the *Book of Common Prayer.* All of his movements
followed the dictates of the rite, the way he bowed, folded
his hands, crossed himself, and invited the congregation to
participate in the centuries-old service. Despite being in the
church on business, Denise found herself being lulled into
a feeling of peace by the serenity, the familiarity, and the
continuity of the worship service.

Denise hardly noticed the gentleman in the black suit who
slipped into the seat beside her as she listened to the brief
sermon. Ironically, the minister spoke about winnowing of
family values as technology made its way into homes. He
reminded the congregation that the care and nurturing of
family should always be more important than the acquisition
of material objects.

As the choir sang the offertory hymn, Denise reached into
her purse for a contribution. Her bracelet briefly caught on
the teeth of the zipper. She struggled momentarily to loosen
it until the man seated beside her silently offered his assistance. Deftly, he eased the little tornado charm from the zipper's grasp. Smiling and passing the basket to him, Denise
returned her attention to the choirboys.

Listening to their divine trebles, she suddenly had a feeling
that she had previously looked into those deep brown eyes
and seen the long thin fingers. Turning toward him as they
rose for the doxology, Denise saw that the seat next to her
was again empty. Only an envelope addressed in familiar
handwriting rested on the seat that the man had previously
occupied.

Slipping the envelope into her purse, Denise scanned the
nave but saw no one. The congregation, choirboys, and priest
were alone in the church. The man who had left the note had
vanished as silently and mysteriously as he had arrived.

When the service ended, Denise pretended to examine the
ornate carvings on the choir stalls as the others departed.
Running her hand over the paneling, she found the secret
door that the vergers, priests, and acolytes used during the
service. Pushing it open, she stepped into the semi-darkness

of the adjacent chapel. Finding it empty, Denise wandered
through each successive chapel until she at last reached the
bishop's robing room and the stairs that led to the undercroft.

Resting her hand against the door to the robing room, she
pushed but found it locked. As she looked up the long aisle,
Denise saw the verger's retreating back and knew that he had
already secured the office. Caring for the priest and the
choirboys was his primary duty. Now that he had locked the
door for the evening, no one would have been able to slip
inside.

Gripping the handrail, Denise descended the cold, slippery
marble stairs to the undercroft. She followed the path to the
right that led to another small chapel and the choirboy's lock-
ers. Hearing their light laughing voices, she retraced her
steps. Stopping only to push on the locked door of the St.
Joseph's chapel, she continued to walk toward the gift shop.

Along the way, Denise slipped into alcoves and pushed
against locked doors that might have given the man a place
to hide. Finding no one, she continued past the last of the
chapels and into the thriving gift shop. Denise had a difficult
time making her way through the thick crowd of shoppers
who examined books, miniatures of gargoyles, religious jewelry, and handcrafted items that would make perfect souve-
nirs of their visit to the Cathedral. Looking but not staring
into the face of every man she met, Denise eased her way
toward the exit. Her last hope was to catch him by the Garth
fountain.

If only Tom had been with her, they could have split up
and covered the area faster and more efficiently. She was
alone, however, so Denise again used an entrance generally
only used by parents of choirboys and priests and escaped
into the late evening sunshine of the Garth. In the center sat
the familiar fountain. The grass around the fountain was always green from the mist that fell onto it. Looking at the
fountain, she still could not decide if it were tulip-shaped or
simply an incredibly interesting shape of nothing in particular.

Years ago Denise had accompanied her cousin to pick up her son. They had waited in the Garth on almost that same spot while the boys rehearsed. When the choirmaster dismissed the, boys her cousin's son had rushed from the choir rehearsal room to plunge into his mother's car for their return home after an especially grueling practice.

Alone, Denise sank onto one of the hard marble benches that lined the perimeter of the Garth. With no one in sight, she opened the envelope and read the card. As she had expected, the man had invited her to attend a gala dinner dance in honor of the local design industry. The suspect had written cryptically in his note, "You really must come. Everyone is dying to attend."

Holding the invitation in her hand, Denise studied the card more carefully. Smiling, she realized that she had attended her high school senior prom in that same hotel and ballroom. She could still remember the turquoise gown that she had worn and the upsweep of her hair. Although she could no longer see the face of her escort, Denise remembered that he had been tall and very handsome, at least that night. In actuality, he had probably been troubled with teenage skin and bad breath. Not that it mattered. In her memory, the evening and the boy had been perfect.

Leaving the Garth, Denise took the long way to her car parked in the lot near the boy's school. Walking past the garden shop, she stopped to purchase a small rosemary plant for the windowsill of her kitchen. The fragrance reminded her of her mother's cooking, spicy and delicious.

By the time Denise reached her car, everyone else had left. The sound of rush hour traffic, the blare of horns, and the screech of tires infiltrated the silence of the Close. The sun sat low in the sky as she pulled from the parking lot and joined the crush of people on their way from DC to the suburbs. Denise did not see the man in the black well-tailored suit and white shirt step from the shadows of the carver's shack. He smiled and quickly walked toward the tennis courts on the girls' school side of the Close.

By the time Denise fought her way up Wisconsin from DC to Rockville, Maryland, she was exhausted and very hungry. She hated driving in rush hour traffic and usually remained at work long past her official quitting time in order to miss the crush of people trying to move quickly on streets too clogged with vehicles to allow more than a snail's pace. She would rather work the extra hour or so than sit in stalled traffic watching her gas gauge fall.

However, that night, Denise had no choice. She had to meet Tom at the diner and felt compelled to arrive as soon as possible even though they had made no definite time commitment. She was anxious to share the experience of the Cathedral with him and to show him their invitation to the dinner dance.

When she finally arrived, Denise did not see his car anywhere. Thinking that he had become engrossed in his work and forgotten to meet her, she phoned the squad room and his cell phone. When she did not receive a response on either, Denise entered the diner alone.

Denise loved the diner. She could not say that the food was the greatest appeal, although she had never ordered anything that did not taste great. Looking from the wait staff in black slacks and white shirts to the counter then to the jukebox and the booths, Denise decided that the thing she liked about the diner was its ambiance. She had dined at more fabulously decorated restaurants, been served by more attentive wait staff, been entertained by a pianist, and sat at a table unmarked by leftover spots of milkshake. However, she had never eaten in a more relaxed or welcoming establishment.

Easing into her seat, Denise perused the very familiar menu. She never knew why she bothered with reading it since it never changed. She had been eating at the diner regularly for three years, and, in all that time, nothing had ever changed. She could always count on fried chicken on Monday and liver and onions on Wednesday. Although she would have to be starving to order the special of the day,

Denise found it reassuring that, if she wanted to sample the dish, a plate of liver would be available.

"Ready to order, Detective?" asked the woman at whose table Denise always sat when she ate at the diner.

"No, thanks, I'm still waiting for my partner. I'll have a soda though, Marge," Denise replied as she consulted her watch again.

"Don't worry," Marge advised with the wisdom gained from having served thousands of liver and onion dinners. "He's probably stuck in traffic. I heard that there'd been a big accident on the beltway. A truck had overturned."

"I'm sure he'll be here soon. Tom sometimes forgets," Denise replied as she pulled the envelope from her bag.

"Like the time he left you sitting here for two hours," Marge laughed. "You were really angry that time."

Chuckling at the memory, Denise responded, "At least he had a good reason . . . his car had broken down. I wonder what it'll be this time."

"I don't know, but I bet it'll be good. Soda coming right up," Marge chortled her way to the soda machine.

Denise remembered that night. She and Tom had just been awarded medals for distinguished police work by the governor and had decided to celebrate with dinner together. They had driven separate cars to the ceremony in Annapolis and would meet at the restaurant. Denise had offered to provide Tom with driving directions or a map, but he had refused, saying that he would be able to find his way to Rockville. She had decided to let him try because, when Tom got into one of those moods, she saw little point in arguing with him. He would not have listened regardless of what she said. When she arrived at the restaurant, she had waited outside in the broiling sun for over a half hour before deciding to ask for a table.

Denise had finally ordered dinner after drinking a pitcher of tea by herself. Still Tom did not arrive. She had almost decided to leave when she noticed the chocolate raspberry cake on the menu. She could not resist. After all, she was celebrating.

Just as Denise was about to take a bite, Tom appeared. He had taken the wrong turn from the city and found himself in Baltimore. Expressions of panic that she might have left him, anger that he had made such a silly mistake, and relief that she was still waiting had covered his face.

Looking out the window, Denise wondered what excuse Tom would offer this time. Even if he had been listening to music at full blast, he should not have become so distracted that he could not find his way. After all, he only had to drive a relatively short distance across a plainly marked, familiar route. They had eaten at the restaurant numerous times together.

Denise heard Marge chuckling over her shoulder and looked up to see Tom standing at the dessert display looking very sheepish. Without offering an apology, Tom slid into the booth opposite Denise. Marge quickly took their orders of steak and cheese subs and left them alone.

"Where were you?" Denise demanded as soon as they were alone.

"Something came up and I couldn't get away," Tom replied as he sipped his soda. He did not look at all concerned that he had kept Denise waiting.

"Would you like to hear my news?" Denise asked when Tom showed no interest in asking about the Cathedral trip.

"Sure. What happened while you were at the Cathedral?" Tom asked without enthusiasm.

Leaning forward and hissing through her teeth, Denise asked, "What's your problem? Did someone burst your bubble? First, you keep me waiting and then you act as if you don't care about this case."

"Give me a break, Dory," Tom replied, not exactly looking upset but definitely not happy. "I've had a long day and I'm tired. Of course, I want to hear about the evensong service."

They sat in silence a moment as Marge delivered the food.

Sensing the tension between them, she quickly placed the plates on the table, added the bottle of ketchup, and left.

"He sat next to me," Denise stated coldly.

"Who?" Tom asked as he nibbled his French fries.

"The suspect," Denise responded, taking a bite of her sandwich.

"What? I was there the whole time and I didn't see him," Tom blurted angrily before he realized that he had wanted to keep that information to himself.

"You were where?" Denise asked incredulously.

"I followed you to the Cathedral," Tom responded shyly, afraid that Denise's famous temper would erupt all over him.

"Why?" Denise asked in a voice tinged with curiosity and anger.

"I'm worried about you, that's why. I didn't like it when that guy said that he'd see you at the Cathedral. I'm even more concerned now that he has come so close to you," Tom stated as he placed his hand tentatively on hers. Not seeing fire emanating from her eyes, he thought that maybe he still stood on solid ground with her.

Melting, Denise replied, "That's so sweet. Sometimes you surprise me."

"I don't know why. You're my partner and my girl," Tom added strongly.

"Yes, I know, but you just do," Denise responded as she linked her fingers with his.

Embarrassment made Tom look away and attack his cole-slaw with uncharacteristic vigor. However, he did not release his grip on Denise's right hand. She had never known him to be so affected by anything. Tom was always the quintessential stoic. Now, due to his feelings for her, he had developed a chink in his protective shell.

To break the tension, Tom asked, "What should we wear to the dinner dance?"

Pulling the invitation from her purse, Denise read, "This says that the affair is black tie. That means that you'll need a tux, and I'll have to buy something fancy that I'll wear only once."

"What makes you think that I don't already own one?" Tom retorted with a chuckle.

"Do you?"

"Sure, I do if it fits and hasn't dry rotted," Tom replied with a dry chuckle. The embarrassment had passed and he had returned to his normal self.

"When did you buy one? Since we've been partners, you've never attended anything fancy enough to need a tux," Denise stated as she surveyed the dessert menu.

"I know. It's been in a garment bag in my closet for years," Tom commented. "For a while there, everyone I knew was getting married. Rather than rent a tux each time, I bought one. It's not flashy . . . just the traditional tuxedo."

Smiling and raising her eyebrows for added emphasis, Denise stated, "I bet you look dashing in your tux. You'll have to model it for me. I can just see you in the tight cummerbund, ruffled shirt, bow tie, and the black patent leather loafers."

Snorting at her comments, Tom replied, "You'll have to wait until the night of the dinner dance for that pleasure. I don't put on that penguin suit unless I have to. What about you? When do you plan to go shopping?"

"Tonight. Would you like to go with me?" Denise replied as she searched the menu for the carrot cake.

"No way!" Tom stated emphatically. "The last time I went shopping with you, we spent an entire Saturday. After following you through every store in the mall, you didn't buy anything. I'll pass on this treat."

Denise and Tom ate in silence as they finished their meal. Both of them were deep in thought. Denise contemplated Tom's following of her to the Cathedral, while Tom pondered the possibility of fitting into the tux again.

"I thought you wanted to spend all your time with me," Denise teased playfully.

"I should amend my previous statement," Tom quipped

as he ate the whipped cream from the top of his sundae with gusto. "I want to spend all my time with you as long as I don't have to go shopping. I felt as if I'd aged ten years by the time we finally left there. I don't want to be like a friend of mine whose girl friend took him shopping every time she went. He even went shoe shopping with her. Everyone was talking about him and saying that she had cooked his goose and was only waiting to serve him up on their wedding day."

"You have something against weddings?" Denise inquired with an edge developing in her voice.

"No, I like weddings and the idea of being married to the right woman," Tom replied, as he glanced quickly at Denise to see if this discussion had landed him in hot water.

"Then what?" Denise asked as she transferred the other half of her cake to the box that Marge had brought to the table with the dessert.

Gesturing with his hands for emphasis, Tom stated, "I simply don't want to advertise to the world that I'm taken. Going shopping with a woman is an admission of being hooked."

"But you went with me before. What's the big deal about going this time?" Denise asked as she watched him scrape the last of the syrup from the bottom of the glass.

"Last time, we were only work partners, so it didn't matter. This time, we're soulmates, and it does matter," Tom said as he pulled out his wallet and verified the check.

Seeing the way he quickly cleaned his glass, Denise asked, "Do you ever taste anything you eat? You eat too fast."

Looking up for a minute, Tom responded, "Sure, I taste it. I don't make love to the food and caress it the way you do. I eat it. That's the purpose of ordering food in a restaurant . . . to eat not to take home."

"I don't caress it; I savor every mouthful," Denise replied looking at the two doggie boxes that contained the other half of her hamburger and the cake.

"Changing the subject, do you think the killer will strike tonight?" Tom asked as he took his turn and paid the check. "He's about due."

Adding a few quarters to his tip as she always did when they dined together, Denise replied, "I was thinking about that myself, but I haven't seen anything in the paper about a special celebrity dinner. I think he's waiting for the dinner dance tomorrow."

Tom walked Denise to her car in silence. The traffic on Rockville Pike had not diminished although it was approaching eight o'clock. People in the Washington area never seemed to go home.

"Are you sure you won't go with me?" Denise asked as she slipped into the driver's side.

"Not even if you sold yourself to me as a love slave," Tom replied dryly.

"That'll be the day," Denise retorted as he leaned into the car for a little peck on the cheek. "See you at work."

Tom waved good-bye as Denise pointed her car in the direction of the nearest shopping mall. Although he would not relax until she phoned him with her usual good night call, Tom was serious about his lack of interest in shopping. He would save that until they were happily married.

As Denise drove down the street, she saw the lights that illuminated the mall beckoning to her to stop and shop. However, Denise did not linger until she found the perfect store. Then, she quickly walked to the evening gown section without stopping along the way to sample perfumes or makeup. She was on a mission and not a very pleasurable one. She enjoyed shopping but not when it meant spending money on something that she really did not want. An evening gown was the last thing she wanted hanging in her closet.

Looking through racks of glittering gowns with spaghetti straps, sheaths that stayed up solely by holding to the wearer's bosom, red numbers with slits to the navel, matronly jacket dresses that covered everything, and form-fitting tubes best left to teenagers, Denise became disheartened and sank into the nearest chair. Her feet hurt from standing and her eyes itched from pollen. She was not having a good time

and was ready to leave when a sales assistant approached
and offered her help.

Grateful for the help, Denise asked, "Do you have anything that's sophisticated yet youthful?"

Smiling, Miss Placket replied, "I saw just the gown in the
back room. It came in only this afternoon. I'll bring it to
you."

While she waited, Denise studied the other shoppers. None
of the other women looked as disgusted as she felt. They
seemed to be enjoying their evening. Whether with friends
or alone, the women fingered the fabric with appreciation,
held the formal wear to their bodies in preliminary size
checks, and carried armloads into the fitting room. Denise
seemed to be the only one not having fun.

She was spending department money and should have
been ecstatic. Instead, she had looked at the gowns by top-
name ready-to-wear designers and had wondered which designer would be the next victim. Her preoccupation with the
case weighed too heavily on her shoulders for her to have
fun. She wanted to go home and read a book, watch a movie,
or shampoo her hair and forget that she was tracking a killer.

Returning quickly, Miss Placket carried not one but two
gowns draped carefully over her arm. She held them out for
Denise's inspection. The first was a very traditional black
gown with thin straps, deep V neckline, slightly flared an-
kle-length skirt, and delicate matching shawl. It would be
perfect and Denise could see herself wearing it. It was her
kind of gown.

The other gown was a golden peach lamé with multiple
tiny straps that crossed over the open back. The designer had
planned for the hemline to touch the floor in the front and
end in a train in the back. A small bolero jacket completed
the ensemble. It was not like her at all. Denise had to have
that gown.

Leaping to her no longer tired feet, Denise willingly followed the sales assistant to the fitting room. Almost before
Miss Placket had closed the door, Denise had slipped out of

her suit and into the gown. It fit perfectly. The lamé hugged her body as if made for her. And the color complimented her complexion perfectly. The flow of the train from the crisscrossed back made her look taller and thinner. She could hardly wait to see Tom's expression when he saw her in the fabulous creation.

For the first time since cutting her hair, Denise wished that it were long enough to pile on top of her head. If it had been longer, she would have been able to pile it on top of her head in big curls. Instead, she would have to be content with a less formal short curly style.

Denise checked the label but did not recognize the name. It was a gorgeous designer gown that could have been made by any of them. She was relieved to see that no one on her list had made it.

Despite the absurd price of the gown, Denise would not consider any other. She hated to change into her suit. The gown made Denise feel like Cinderella, but the suit reminded her of the regimentation of her life as a police detective. Even with the functional black pumps peeking from under the gown, she looked stunning.

Finding Miss Placket standing at the register, Denise simply said, "Wrap it up."

Miss Placket smiled, knowing that she had made another happy customer. Pointing to the shoe department, she instructed Denise where she could find matching shoes after placing the gown in a clear plastic bag. Denise thanked her and walked off happily.

Denise found the shoes as soon as she walked into the shoe department. Actually, the shoes found her. She had been so busy looking at the displays that she had not seen the abandoned shoes on the floor at her feet. Tripping over the box, Denise caused one of them to tumble onto the floor. When she bent to pick it up, Denise discovered that the shoe with the three-inch stiletto heels was a perfect match for her gown. The sparkle at the toe augmented the look.

Carefully laying the gown across a chair, Denise examined

the shoebox to discover that the shoes were her size. Kicking off her pumps and slipping her feet into the heels, she carefully tottered toward the mirror. The height of the heels made her wobble like the first time she wore heels at her confirmation, but her feet felt so glamorous that Denise did not care. She had to have them.

Carrying the box and the gown to the counter, she purchased the shoes. The salesman smiled as he slipped the box into a shopping bag. He seemed to know that Denise would look fabulous in the ensemble.

Denise had one more shopping task to do before leaving the store. Since she never wore makeup, she did not own any. A gown like this one demanded that she look "done" from head to toe. She had already decided that she would wear her hair in large loose curls and now she needed makeup that would draw the entire look together.

She had no idea that she could select from so many kinds of makeup. Denise could have chosen the healthy outdoor look, the professional daytime appearance, the elegant dinner for two and theater makeup, or the Hollywood glamour specialty with glitter as its base. Denise quickly decided that only the full Hollywood treatment would do for the evening and the gown.

Denise could hardly wait to see Tom's face when she opened the door to reveal her transformation. He had looked quite pleased when he saw her in the little Hawaiian outfit and her bathing suit. He would really be knocked off his feet when he saw her in this outfit. She would enter her bedroom a detective and exit a movie star.

Thirteen

The next day, Denise arrived at work wearing her usual dark pinstripe suit, white blouse, and sensible shoes. However, she felt different knowing that the dress hung in her closet. She walked with a more feminine sway to her hips as if she were wearing the high-heeled slippers. Strangely, she felt more like a girl going to her prom than a detective on a murder case.

Tom noticed the change and frowned. He was used to Denise with the sensible shoes and the suits. He did not like the new walk and the new animation of her hands. He could depend on the old Denise, but he was not sure of this one. This version might worry about breaking her nails.

The detectives around the coffeepot stepped aside as Denise approached. Something was so different about her that they had no choice but to clear a space, lower their voices, and drop the profanity. She wore the same kind of suit as always, but she had changed. They liked the metamorphosis although they could not identify the cause.

"What's up, Denise?" asked one of her colleagues. He smiled and tried to carry on small talk but could not think of anything that would interest a lady of Denise's refinement.

"Nothing. I'm still working on the same cases. How about you, Herb? Anything new on the Martinez case?" Denise replied, stirring the sludge they consumed in place of coffee.

"Not yet, but I'm on the verge of something big. I can feel it," Herb responded and then fell silent.

"What about you, Bill? How's the subway robbery case?" Denise inquired as she sipped her coffee.

"We caught him last night as he tried to rob a little old lady we used as a decoy," Bill responded as he backed uneasily toward his desk.

Signing, Denise replied, "I wish I could say the same thing. Maybe I'll get lucky tonight. The suspect has invited me to a big designer bash."

"Yeah, well, you'll do fine," Herb replied and then walked to his desk.

Frowning, Denise returned to her desk. Turning toward Tom, she asked, "What's the matter with them? They're acting funny. Are they afraid that my bad luck on this case will rub off on them?"

Looking up briefly, Tom looked back at his paperwork and replied, "It's not them, it's you. What have you done to yourself?"

"Nothing," Denise stated, feeling quite confused by her colleagues' behavior and her partner's response. "I'm not even wearing that perfume my sister gave me. I haven't changed anything."

Unable to look at her, Tom stated, "Well, something's different. I can see it, too, and I don't like it. You've become a . . . woman over night."

Sinking into her chair, Denise said in total confusion, "I've always been a woman. I don't get it."

"Yeah, I know, but you've got a different air about you this morning," Tom replied without fully understanding their reaction himself. "You're not giving off cop vibes. You have the air of a civilian woman."

"You guys have been adding scotch to the coffee," Denise replied with increasing irritation. "I'm the same me that worked here yesterday. This must be some kind of male time-of-the-month thing."

At that moment, Molly dragged herself to her feet and approached Denise. The dog usually did not give her more than a moment's notice, but now, the beast rested her head on Denise's knee. Looking into Denise's face, Molly seemed to want the companionship of another female.

"See. I told you. Even Molly senses it. She wants to do some female bonding," Tom commented as he pulled the dog away from Denise.

"That does it!" Denise exclaimed indignantly. "All of you, including this dog, are crazy. You're suffering from some kind of delusions. I'm taking a leave day. I'll see you tonight."

"Don't go until you open the envelope on your desk," Tom instructed gruffly.

"Who put that there? I didn't see it when I arrived," Denise demanded angrily.

Tom growled, "Ronda brought the mail while you were flirting it up with the guys at the coffee machine."

Tearing open the envelope with the familiar handwriting, Denise objected, "I wasn't flirting. They're my colleagues. I don't even see them as men."

"That's not too complementary," Tom ,insisted snarling, "I hope that doesn't go for me as well. They definitely see you as a woman. You should have seen their faces when they were talking to you."

Flushing angrily, Denise stated, "All I saw was my colleagues acting as if I have a contagious sign or a scarlet A on my chest. This is ridiculous."

Denise read in silence a few minutes and then tossed the note to Tom. This time, the perpetrator had sent a gold heart-shaped charm with a dazzling ruby in the middle. Denise thrust it into her purse and grabbed her sketchbook.

Reading aloud, Tom said, " 'Wear the bracelet and save the waltzes for me.' What does this mean?"

"It means, dear partner, that you'll have competition for my attention tonight," Denise replied as she walked briskly toward the door.

Something about Denise was definitely different, Tom observed as he watched her walk away. She always walked in a business-like unhurried manner. She walked with purpose but not with haste. Her shoulders were always square and set. Today, Denise walked with hip motion, and she looked softer, more rounded.

Tom made up his mind to uncover the source of the change. He might have to watch more than Denise's back. He might have to protect her from herself, too.

Denise stopped at the spa on the way home. She needed to work off some of the anger that caused her to snap at everyone. She could not understand their reaction or hers to the change in her, but she knew what they meant. She felt different, although outwardly she looked the same.

The dress had caused it. The dress and the shoes and the idea of looking like a well-dressed lady had done it. Denise had forgotten that she was a cop first and a woman second. For a while, she had involuntarily imagined herself as the guest of a handsome, wealthy man who would dance her expertly around the floor. She had forgotten that a killer had invited her to the dance to see him in action. If her colleagues had not pointed out the change, she would have walked into the hotel and become a victim.

Lifting the heavy weights with her legs, Denise began to sweat. It was good, hard, working sweat that glistened on her body as a reminder of her purpose. She was a cop—ready for anything, an expert shot. Tonight, when she slipped on the gown, she would add another accessory that the suspect would not expect to find on her person.

Wiping the sweat from her face, Denise smiled. She looked the same as she had that morning, only the upward curving of her lips that came from her conceit at her appearance had vanished. Now, when Denise gazed at herself, she saw the look of determination that she always wore. She appeared no less feminine, but she looked like a lady with a purpose. She was the Calamity Jane type who would not take stuff from anyone. Tom had better be on his toes.

After arriving home, Denise ate a yogurt and then showered quickly. Toweling her hair and body, she lightly dusted with the slightly glittering powder the sales woman had suggested. Carefully applying the makeup as the cosmetics sales woman had instructed, Denise smoothed a liquid foundation until it faded in the hairline, blended blush to hollow, color, and contour, and outlined her lips and filled in the middle with a deep cranberry stain. Staring at herself in the mirror, Denise liked the results but thought she looked alien, as if a stranger were using her bathroom.

Denise hated the constriction of strapless bras and was grateful that the dress had built-in support. Easing the five straps over each shoulder, she adjusted the skirt over her hips. Reaching over her shoulder, she made sure that the crisscross that played down her back was straight. Slipping her stocking covered feet into the high heels, she surveyed the reflection critically. She looked lovely . . . elegant, sophisticated, and professional, in spite of the makeup.

Reaching into the top drawer and pushing aside a large selection of scarves, Denise pulled out her little handgun. She slipped it into the holster that she wore on the inside of her left thigh. Even her trained eye could not detect a telltale bulge.

Tom arrived promptly at seven-thirty. He stood handsome and tall in a tux that flattered his broad shoulders and narrow hips. In fact, he looked so handsome that, for an instant, Denise almost decided to skip the dance. However, her sense of duty and her desire to show off the new dress propelled her into action.

Carefully slipping the wrist corsage onto her arm, Tom sputtered, "You look great. I'm impressed. It must have taken you all afternoon to look like that."

"Are you implying that I don't usually have my act together or that only a major makeover could make me look like this?" Denise demanded, placing her hands on her hips in mock anger.

"No! It didn't come out the way I planned," Tom defended his statement. "I just meant that you look terrific. You usually look very professional and put together for work. Now you look like a movie star."

Smiling, Denise decided to let him off the hook by stating, "Much better. You look like a million dollars yourself. I'd put you against Denzel anytime."

Looking very embarrassed, Tom said, "Enough of this small talk. Let's go. I don't want to be late."

Taking Denise's elbow, Tom escorted her to the car where she carefully eased in so she wouldn't wrinkle the lamé. She felt like Cinderella going to the ball. Tom looked like her handsome prince. She was living the fairy tale life.

Only, they were on their way to an assignment. They were going to the dinner dance not to enjoy themselves but to catch a killer. They hoped to stop him from using the ergot fungus against another of his competitors.

"What's your plan?" Tom asked as they pulled into the hotel's underground parking lot.

"Not a clue," Denise replied honestly. "The ergot could be in the bread, the pasta, the dessert, or even as the thickener in the soup. I haven't the slightest idea how we'll stop him. I'm hoping that we'll catch him in the act of substituting a roll on a dinner plate."

"But first, we have to identify him. We don't even know how he looks," Tom replied.

"I know. I remember the piercing brown eyes of the man who sat next to me at the Cathedral yesterday. Maybe that will be enough," Denise replied as she allowed Tom to help her from the car.

"You look beautiful," Tom stated quietly. "Just in case I get too busy to tell you later, I thought I should say it now."

"Better than Molly?" Denise teased playfully.

"Definitely," Tom replied quickly as he pulled Denise's body against his. "I'm a lucky man. Got two of the best-looking partners on the force. I couldn't ask for more."

Remembering the pistol strapped to her thigh, Denise asked, "Do you feel anything?"

"Nothing other than my heart pounding, no," Tom responded huskily. "Why? Are you armed?"

"Yes," Denise replied as she planted a very light kiss on

his lips. "I'd be wired too if I could have found a way to disguise it in this dress."

"It fits like a glove," Tom commented. "You can't hide much in there."

"Glad to see you noticed," Denise quipped as they joined the crowd in evening gowns and tuxedos heading toward the lobby door.

"That's my job . . . to notice everything," Tom replied as they walked the long hall that led to the grand ballroom.

"Are you speaking professionally?" Denise inquired with a smirk.

"Both. I wouldn't be much of a partner if I didn't notice everything about you," Tom commented.

"I've certainly noticed you noticing the way this dress clings," Denise added as she surveyed the ballroom.

"So have all the other men," Tom answered as he located the head table.

"I remember this place from the night of my high school prom. It looked larger then," Denise commented with longing in her voice.

"Most things change with time, but don't you. I was afraid that playing dress up had affected you today for a minute. You weren't the Denise I knew at all," Tom said, taking the opportunity to mention the earlier transformation.

"I know and that won't happen again. Dressing up sometimes does that to a girl," Denise conceded. "I'm back to normal now . . . all work and almost no play."

Denise presented the invitation and received their table assignment. Not surprisingly, their seats were in the center of the dining room where they would have a clear view of the head table. The killer had thought of everything. Denise wondered if his previous note about becoming tired were true and if he wanted her to catch him. She decided quickly that he only wanted to be able to content himself with defeating a cop just as he managed to go undetected in killing his competition.

Looking around the room, Denise compared the décor

with that of her high school prom days. Then, the carpet and
heavy drapes had been a deep maroon accented with the
hotel chain's initial in elaborate gold script. The only wood
had been on the large dance floor. Ornate multitiered crystal
chandeliers had hung from the ceiling. Ferns or palms had
sat in every corner to soften the room. Spotlights had cast
their shadow on the brocade-covered walls. The tables had
been covered in white damask tablecloths around which sat
heavy, ornate, red velvet chairs. The room had given the appearance of extreme formality that managed to add a solemnity to the prom.

The latest redecorating had removed all traces of the red
and the solemnity. Mile-long swags of gold and white fabric
draped each window. Smaller ceiling-hugging chandeliers
had replaced the large ornate ones. They had stripped the
wallpaper and painted the walls a shimmering white. Instead
of damask tablecloths and heavy velvet chairs, the decorator
had set each table with linen and pulled up smaller chairs
with bright floral tapestry seats. Plants still brightened the
corners but without the dreadful lights. Now they sat in clusters and swayed with the breeze of the ceiling fan. Everywhere, glistening wood floors invited dancing feet. Although
clients still reserved the room for weddings, dinner dances,
and conferences, it had lost its stuffiness. Instead of hushing
the guests like an old maid aunt, it welcomed their voices.

Denise and Tom had arrived earlier than most guests, giving them the opportunity to study the others with the hopes
of seeing anything suspicious. As they wandered toward the
bar, they noted the ease and familiarity with which people
greeted each other. Many hailed each other from across the
room. Others rushed to embrace a new arrival. The feeling
of genuine caring filled the room.

Yet Denise knew that one designer did not feel the same
warmth toward his comrades and imagined that others might
also have been putting on an act. She hoped that he would
slip and expose himself that night before anyone else suf-

fered at his hands. It was their job to prevent him from committing another murder.

Leaning toward her as they stood near the bar, Tom commented, "I should have known that I'd look dumpy in this tux. Look at these guys. They make me look like yesterday's news."

"Their tuxes are probably the newest styles, even more current than yours. Don't worry about it," Denise replied, "I like the length of the jacket that you're wearing. Some of these others are too long and almost look like dresses."

"I can't tell the designers from the guests," Tom complained. "Everyone looks so done up."

Motioning with her purse, Denise stated, "Look for the nametags. All the designers are wearing them since it's their night to shine."

"Are all designers men? I don't see any women," Tom asked as he continued to study the growing crowd.

"No, look over there. I see three women standing together," Denise replied as she nodded toward the right side of the room.

"Good. I was beginning to think that this was a man's world after all," Tom commented as he continued to scan the faces.

Tom was right. There were few women wearing nametags. Although women had infiltrated the fashion industry, men still appeared to control it. The papers most often covered the openings of the men's new lines in haute couture. The women seemed more involved with providing upscale ready-to-wear while the men, at least according to the press, remained the trendsetters.

Regardless of the venue for creative expression, the gowns were stunning. Denise could not distinguish between the ready-to-wear like hers, the haute couture, and the one-of-a-kind creations. All the women oozed charm and elegance as they strolled around the room speaking to friends. Black gowns were always popular because of their elegance and slimming effect. However, gold, silver, and shades of purple appeared to be the colors of choice. The women wore gowns with little trains like Denise's, ones with tremendous slits up the sides that exposed almost everything, and those that bared the bust and left little to the imagination.

"You certainly seem to be enjoying yourself," Denise commented as she sipped her ginger ale. Being on duty and needing clear heads, they had both avoided spirits of any kind.

"It's like being in a candy store for any male with a drop of testosterone running through his veins," Tom replied without taking his eyes from the crowd.

"That's sexist," Denise whispered teasingly.

"So sue me," Tom grunted. "I'm waiting for that woman's dress to slide off completely. It's nothing but two strips of cloth held together at the shoulder."

"It's glued on her body in strategic places," Denise replied smugly. Tom was enjoying this assignment entirely too much.

"Glued? Maybe she'll sweat it off," Tom commented hopefully.

Chuckling softly, Denise stated, "Not a chance. Look at her. She's as cool as an ice cube. She wouldn't sweat even if they turned up the heat in here."

"I can always hope," Tom insisted.

Smiling, Denise turned her attention to the head table. So far, no one had decided to occupy any of the seats. She wondered which of the twelve people might be the killer. The biblical reference was overpowering. The position of the dais in the center of the table with six chairs on either side further supported that image. This would be someone's last supper.

Looking toward the door, Denise saw a familiar face, one which she had thought never to see again. Nudging Tom and nodding to the right, Denise turned his attention to the crowd entering the dining room. Among them was her companion at the Grand Canyon.

"There's Freda!" Denise exclaimed softly. "I can't believe she's here."

"Which one is Freda?" Tom asked as he studied the faces.

"She's the tall busty blonde in the lavender gown with boat neckline," Denise replied without taking her eyes from the group.

"She's a big girl. How do you know her?" Tom inquired as he drank in the spectacle in shimmering lavender.

Grumbling, Denise replied, "Do you ever listen to me? She's the woman from the Grand Canyon. You know, the one who stopped me from falling and provided the sketch of the killer."

"She's a transvestite, a drag queen?" Tom questioned with disbelief. "She's gorgeous."

"She certainly is, and every female part of her is fake," Denise replied smiling playfully at Tom.

Teasing, Tom said, "Look. She's coming this way. She must have recognized you, although I don't know how she did. You look so different without donkey dust on your face."

Before Denise could respond, Freda had joined them. Embracing Denise in a gentle hug, she gushed, "I'm so happy to see you again. I've brought you two tickets to my show. I was planning to stop at the precinct to leave these, but now you're here."

Denise watched with a smirk as Freda flirted shamelessly with Tom whose face showed his conflicting emotions. He knew that Freda was not really a woman, but his eyes told him that she was a stunning female. Denise could see his confusion increase with every bat of Freda's fake eyelashes.

Rescuing her partner, Denise interjected, "Thanks for the tickets. It's good to see you again. What brings you here?"

Turning her attention to Denise, Freda replied, "The same person who invited you, I'd bet. He sent me an invitation and is paying for all of my expenses."

"I thought you had planned to stay away from him," Denise reminded Freda.

"I had, but I couldn't pass up the chance to come to the DC area and to bring you these tickets personally," Freda replied as she pressed the tickets into Denise's hand.

"You could have held them at the box office for me," Denise suggested.

"I could but then I would have missed seeing all these glamorous people in one place. Stunning. And just look at all those handsome men," Freda simpered, obviously enjoying the view.

"You're living dangerously," Denise replied. "Be careful."

"Don't worry, darling. I'm used to a little danger. It adds spice to life," Freda chirped happily.

"Where are you sitting?" Denise asked as she continued to observe Freda's enjoyment of the gala.

"Table five," Freda replied absently as she searched the room for her assigned seat.

Leaning toward her, Tom replied, "It's in the middle. We're sitting there, too."

Resting her large gloved hand on his, Freda gushed, "This is my lucky day. Escort me to our table. I want to lay claim to a seat . . . next to you."

Denise chuckled at Tom's discomfort. Once again, he had forgotten that Freda was not what she appeared to be. Denise decided that she would go to New York to see Freda's show. If she were this convincing in interacting with people on a personal basis, she would be even better on stage in her professional element.

As the elegant pair, the cop and the drag queen, walked away, Denise turned her attention to the kitchen. Flashing her shield at one of the under chefs, she gained access to the stainless steel center of creativity. Massive refrigerators lined the walls, stainless steel worktables filled the floor, and huge bins of sugar and flour sat on carts for easy access. Meat preparation took place in one location, they made salads in another, and they mixed and baked breads in a remote corner. The dessert chef controlled his own domain. Everything was very orderly and sparkling clean.

Scanning the faces of the chefs and their assistants, Denise did not see anyone who even vaguely resembled the man who sat next to her at the Cathedral or Freda's description of the man who had hired her to buy the charms. Everyone was too busy to have time to plant contaminated flour. An intruder would quickly break the flow of the kitchen and be recognized.

Seeing her standing in the doorway, the chef, dressed in an impeccable white uniform, greeted her saying, "Welcome to my kitchen. What may I do to help you, Detective."

"I was wondering if anything unusual has happened here in the last few days," Denise inquired.

"Nothing. We've been too busy feeding crowds for anything to be amiss," the chef replied without taking his eyes from the activity in his kitchen.

"Have you needed to hire temporary help of handle the number of guests?" Denise asked.

Responding in the negative, the chef said, "No, my staff has been the same for the last few years. If someone is ill, we do the best we can. A substitute would not know our flow. His presence would detract from our routine."

"Have you changed suppliers for the meat or baking products?" Denise pressed, hoping to find something out of the ordinary.

"No, I've used the same supplier for the last ten years without complaint. I don't believe in changing a good thing," the chef replied, apparently anxious to return to his work and not at all interested in her questions.

Seeing that she was only disturbing him and learning nothing new, Denise thanked the chef for his time and left. She had discovered nothing in the kitchen that would help her solve the case. If anything occurred, it would happen in the ballroom.

By the time Denise returned, the curtain behind the head table had opened to show a stage with a backdrop of shimmering fabrics and colors that undulated in the breeze of a fan hidden off stage. Majestic curving stairs led from the stage to the dance floor. Music had begun to play in the background. Everyone, as if on cue, ended their conversations and moved to their seats.

Denise joined Freda and Tom at the table in the center of the room, shaking her head in response to his unspoken question. Suddenly, the room lights dimmed and the lights on the stage began to dance in the colors of the fabric. The curtain parted slightly and an emcee dressed in a deep violet tuxedo appeared. His silver hair glistened in the spotlight. He seemed to float to the right front of the stage on a thin layer of smoke. He motioned for the energetic applause to end as he placed the microphone to his lips.

"Ladies and gentlemen, welcome to the 25th Annual Washington International Designers' Dinner Dance. Tonight, we will celebrate the works of the twelve honorees selected by WID as representative of the best in our profession. We will honor colleagues and friends from as far away as Athens, Greece, or as close as New York. Let's begin by presenting Morgan Volper from Boston."

As the emcee introduced each honoree, the gossamer fabric parted and the designer floated onto the stage accompanied by no fewer than two and sometimes five models wearing his or her creations. The applause was almost deafening as each one bowed, descended the steps, and took his or her place at the head table. The excruciatingly thin models would slither among the tables and out the door.

Although Denise was quite impressed by the spectacle of smoke and lights, she did not forget her primary task of finding the killer. She scrutinized the face of each designer as he or she joined the others at the table. Any one of them could be the killer, although none appeared menacing dressed as each was in tuxedos and shimmering gowns.

Before the white-jacketed wait staff served the meal, the emcee once again took control of the microphone. Standing at the dais, he reminisced about the long history of the fashion industry and the history of WID. Proclaiming the honorees heroes, he predicted a bright future for the industry and especially for the contributors from other than the usual houses in Hollywood, New York, Paris, Rome, and Milan. Then, asking for everyone to join him in a moment of silence for all those designers who were no longer with them, he bowed his silvery head.

Denise studied the behavior of the men and women sitting at the head table. All twelve heads had bowed in silent contemplation of absent friends. No one moved and no one appeared insincere.

As soon as the silence ended, the wait staff went to work. They moved almost silently among the tables, unfolding tray stations that would help with the delivery of the food to the guests. They returned with trays heaped with silver-covered plates. Skillfully, they tossed the Caesar salad with the dressing and placed a portion in front of each dinner guest.

The happy chatter stopped almost immediately as guests plowed their forks into the glistening greens. Background music played by a discretely hidden quintet substituted for conversation. Everyone appeared to be enjoying the evening.

Denise picked at her food, but she did not enjoy it. She was too busy watching the dais and listening to Freda who kept up a stream of conversation. Denise had never seen anyone eat so quickly and talk so much. Tom, however, ate with gusto despite keeping watch on the dais and listening to Freda.

Keeping their eyes glued to the head table, Denise and Tom watched the waiters deliver fresh bread with the main course of Chicken Kiev, asparagus with toasted almonds, potatoes Catherine, and tomato aspic. When her plates arrived, Denise picked at the deliciously prepared meal while keeping watch, yet she saw nothing suspicious. Tom, however, appeared to enjoy every bit of everything except the aspic.

"Aren't you hungry?" Freda inquired as she devoured large bites of chicken. "This food is excellent. Not like hotel food at all. You should eat. You'll get skinny like those models if you don't."

"You're right; it's delicious. I just don't have much room in this dress for food. It's hard sucking in a full stomach,"

Denise responded as she delicately nibbled an asparagus slice.

"Don't I know it," Freda chirped with a chuckle. "Some of my gowns are so form-fitting that I have to wear a girdle if I've eaten too much."

Denise ignored Freda's chatter as she studied the eyes of the honorees. No one had the piercing gaze of the man who sat next to her at the Cathedral. Looking at the waiters, she saw that their eyes were also dull in comparison.

Sensing her frustration, Tom asked gently, "You don't see him, do you?"

"No. Maybe he decided the risk was too great," Denise commented as she pushed away her mostly untouched plate.

"You're not going to eat that?" Tom inquired, pointing to her abandoned plate.

"No, but you can have it," Denise replied as she switched plates with him.

"I don't know how you can pass this up. Even the bread is first rate," Tom stated as he liberally applied butter to another crusty roll.

"You'll be sorry when your cholesterol goes off the charts," Denise advised, continuing her vigil while her partner munched happily on her leftovers.

"At least, I'll die a happy man," Tom quipped without breaking the rhythm he had established with his fork and knife.

Leaning over, Freda joined the conversation, saying with a wicked wink, "I like a man with a healthy appetite for all things."

"Humph," Tom replied as he flagged a waiter from the head table and requested another roll. Almost immediately, the man moved one of the baskets from that table to Tom's.

"Pig!" Denise whispered under her breath.

"Oink! Oink!" Tom responded. "It's obvious that he's not here. We might as well enjoy ourselves."

Ignoring his obvious preference of food to the case, Denise scanned the plates in front of each of the honorees.

The waiters had served identical plates of food, which the designers had eaten with gusto. No one had eaten anything that the main kitchen had not provided.

Knowing that the ergot fungus lived in flour products, Denise could not imagine that the killer could have talked his way into the massive kitchen past the vigilant chef. He would have needed to contaminate all of the flour that they used for dredging the chicken and in making the rolls that Tom enjoyed so completely. To have done that would have meant murdering everyone in attendance. Since only two of the designers appeared on the list that she had compiled, Denise could not see what he would gain from killing all of them since most were celebrating their retirement from the profession. She saw absolutely nothing to gain in killing the guests and other designers. Besides, her investigation had found the kitchen almost impenetrable.

After the wait staff had cleared the tables of all but dessert and coffee, the dancing began. Rather than the ensemble playing music by which the diners could dance, it played an accompaniment for a Broadway-style review. Dancers in costumes created by the honorees strutted their way across the stage in a series of twelve vignettes. All of the guests, including Denise, were mesmerized by the lively performances. It was a delightful end to a wonderful evening.

"I can use some of these numbers in my show," Freda whispered into Denise's ear.

Nodding, Denise could not tear her eyes from the review. With the exception of Tom's little groans from being overly full, nothing could interfere in her enjoyment of the performance. Looking at him briefly, she saw that he had folded his hands over a very full stomach and gone to sleep.

The review lasted a very pleasurable hour with Tom sleeping soundly through it. He had been correct about his ability to sleep through anything, as he had proven while they were in New York. Now, he had missed yet another fabulous production.

As the lights went up, the emcee appeared for the last time

to thank everyone for attending. He reminded each to look under their chairs for little tokens of the evening to take with them.

"Let's hope it's not a goody bag," Tom moaned. "I'm so stuffed that I feel sick."

Beaming, Freda, who had eaten as much as Tom, commented with a flirtatious lift of her carefully penciled brow, "Oh, no! I was going to ask you to take me dancing."

"Some other night," Tom muttered with as much good humor as he could muster.

Looking under her chair, Freda found tickets to a Broadway show. Denise thought Freda would completely loose her composure as she bounced around and chattered merrily. Tom, leaning over reluctantly, discovered a voucher for a new oversized designer label umbrella. Under Denise's chair was a large white envelope.

Pouting, Freda said, "I bet you've got the best gift of all."

Laughing, Denise opened the envelope to find not a coupon or theater tickets but another envelope addressed to her in the familiar handwriting. Rather than being elated by the possibility of spending someone else's money on a trinket or of seeing a show, Denise was frustrated. She had not been able to find the killer, but he had contacted her.

Perusing the note, Denise read aloud, "Before your eyes, but you didn't see. I've killed another. Tee hee! It's a terrible rhyme, but you get my drift."

"He's right, I didn't see anything. No one has died. I don't understand what he means," Denise stated frankly. She saw no reason to hide her dejection and confusion.

Looking from Tom to Denise, Freda said as she waved her long fingers goodbye, "You're both downers. I'll see you the next time I come to DC. Don't forget that you have open tickets to my show. Exchange those for any night you'd like. Bye, dears."

Freda did not wait for them to protest her departure. Turning in her stiletto heels, she tapped her way through the thinning crowd and out the door. They could see her broad shoulders vanish through the French doors on the right.

"Let's go, Dory. It's been a long day, and I need an antacid," Tom said as he linked arms with her and propelled Denise toward the door.

"He must be playing with us," Denise stated as they rode the elevator to the parking lot.

"Either that or he's a magician. We certainly watched everyone carefully," Tom replied, leading the way to the car at a much slower pace than usual.

Denise added as Tom opened her door, "And I checked the kitchen. Unless the chef lied to me, he couldn't have contaminated the flour."

"Look, Dory, would you drive home? I'm really feeling lousy. That's the last time I pig out on rich food," Tom asked as he slipped into the passenger seat and handed Denise the keys.

"I warned you," Denise replied. "I'll take you home and return your car to you at the precinct. You'll have to drive me home after work."

"OK," Tom agreed as he slumped in the seat. "Whatever you want as long as I don't have to look another roll in the eye as long as I live."

They rode to Tom's house in silence. Denise was busy running over the events of the day as Tom sat looking miserable and holding his stomach. It had been a long day, and they were both tired.

After leaving Tom at the front door of his apartment building, Denise drove home. She had been in the same room with the killer and had not seen him make his move. She had not seen anyone who vaguely resembled Freda's description or her memory of the man in the Cathedral. Maybe he was playing with her mind, a sick mind game in which he threatened the lives of others. She would have to wait until the morning paper to learn the identity of the latest victim.

Fourteen

Over coffee the next morning, Denise read the paper in her apartment. The *Washington Post* ran a banner headline about the economy and a smaller reference on the lower right page to the death of Marty Sellars, a renowned ready-to-wear designer who had attended the WID dinner the previous evening. According to the article, his wife had discovered him lying on the floor at 4 A.M. when she had heard a strange sound coming from their bathroom. He had been pronounced dead on arrival at Hospital Center. Doctors had planned to perform an autopsy.

Denise immediately phoned the coroner's assistant, Dan Rivers, who always covered the early morning calls to the office. He had only just begun the autopsy and was open to Denise's suggestions. He agreed to send copies of his report to the CDC and the FBI. When she suggested ergot fungus contamination, he was only too happy to research the possibility.

Although she had worked late and could have used the comp time to catch up on her sleep, Denise decided to go to the office at her usual time. After dressing in a navy blue suit and blue stripped blouse, she took another look at the evening gown. The previous evening seemed so long ago and that dress so alien as it hung to the extreme left of her work suits in her closet. The only memory of the evening was the stiffening of her calf muscles from being unaccustomed to walking in the high heels.

Instead of applying makeup as she had the previous evening, Denise left for work with a freshly scrubbed face. She wore no perfume and certainly no stiletto heels. She had returned to her familiar self and loved it. Makeup and fussy clothes were not her style.

The squad room was strangely silent when she arrived twenty minutes later. No one gathered at the coffee machine to complain about Tom's coffee because there was no coffee. Molly did not sit at Tom's feet because he and the dog were conspicuously absent.

"Where's Tom?" Denise asked Ronda as she checked her messages.

"I don't know. He hasn't phoned," Ronda replied with a little smile.

"You haven't checked on him?" Denise inquired with worry filling her voice.

"No, we thought he might be with you," Ronda responded with a barely veiled expression.

"Why?" Denise asked as she grabbed the phone and started dialing Tom's number.

With an expression that said everyone had expected them to spend the night together after the fancy evening out, Ronda stated, "It's hard to explain."

"You mean that someone has an office pool that says Tom scored last night. Sorry, you lose," Denise answered with anger in her voice. "I drove Tom to his place last night. He wasn't feeling well. I'm going over there right now."

Denise did not wait for Ronda to respond. She ran to Tom's car and made the short drive to Silver Spring. When the elevator took too long to come down from the fifth floor, Denise bolted up the steps two at a time. Using the key that Tom had given her while he had the flu one winter, she let herself into the apartment.

"Tom!" Denise called as she rushed toward the bedroom.

Seeing the bathroom door closed and Molly anxiously waiting outside, Denise knocked and called again. When he did not answer, she pounded on the door. Hearing nothing, she tried to open the door but discovered that something was blocking it. Putting her entire weight into the effort, she pushed until she could make a space large enough for her to slip inside. Molly, whining and whimpering, stayed in the hall.

Tom lay unconscious on the floor, nude and unmoving. His pulse was thready and his coloring was poor. Throwing a towel over him and leaving a very worried Molly to watch over him, Denise dashed to the phone beside his bed to call 911. After giving his address, she opened the apartment door and then returned to Tom's side. He had not stirred in her absence and neither had Molly.

Denise knew that before anyone could move Tom, she would have to restrain Molly. Canine officers would never leave their fallen partners and would attack anyone who came too close and looked threatening. The only reason that Molly had only growled at her was the grudging respect they shared for each other and their mutual devotion to Tom. She quickly opened the closet door, turned on the light, and pushed Molly into it.

"Tom, wake up!" Denise pleaded as she waited for the ambulance. She applied wet compresses to his face in a futile effort to do something to relieve his suffering. She knew that he would not recover unless the paramedics hurried. Already five minutes had passed and they had not arrived.

"Hello!" a voice shouted from the hall.

"In here, through the living room and turn left," Denise shouted the directions to the bathroom.

"Move aside, ma'am. We need some room," the medics instructed.

As they worked, the men fired questions at Denise. "Was he taking any drugs, prescription or otherwise?"

"No, never. He's a fitness freak," Denise replied.

"Does he have health problems?"

"None. He passed his physical a month ago. I think he's been poisoned," Denise stated as she watched them attach an oxygen clip to Tom's nose and start an IV in his arm. He looked so helpless lying there that Denise had to fight back the tears that burned her eyelids.

"Poisoned? What kind?" the man demanded.

"Ergot fungus," Denise responded quickly. She could tell that the medics had never heard of it. "The faster you can get him to the hospital, the better his chances of recovery."

"What's the treatment?"

"Hydration, I think. The CDC will know. Just hurry," Denise urged the men who seemed to be taking a very long time with their preliminary tests. In actuality, fewer than five minutes had passed since they arrived at Tom's door.

Lifting the stretcher, one of the men asked, "Are you his wife?"

"No, he's not married. I'm his partner. We're detectives," Denise responded as they rushed into the hall.

"What's that noise? A dog?" the shorter of the two paramedics asked with concern in his voice.

"His canine partner. She's in the closet. I'll take care of her as soon as you're out of here," Denise stated as they lingered at the door.

"We're taking him to Holy Cross," the tall man shouted over his shoulder.

"I'll be there as soon as I phone the chief and take care of the dog," Denise said to their retreating backs.

"Bring his ID and insurance information with you," the short man ordered as they vanished into the elevator.

Denise stood at the window watching them load the stretcher into the ambulance. When they drove away, she rushed to the closet and released Molly. The dog immediately began searching the apartment and whining for Tom. When she did not find him, she returned to Denise and stared into her face for an explanation.

"Let's go, girl. Tom is sick. I'll take you for a quick walk and then to the hospital with me. You're his partner, too," Denise explained to the dog as she grabbed the leash that lay on Tom's bureau beside his wallet.

Flipping through the worn leather, Denise found his insurance information and his driver's license. She also discovered a photograph of them taken after a successful case. Tom had sandwiched it between the two credit cards and his address book. Smiling, she wondered how long he had carried it. From the number of wrinkles, she guessed that it had been with him since they had first posed for it. She would have to remember to ask him about it later, but for now she stuffed everything into her suit pocket.

Stopping only long enough for Molly to relieve herself, Denise walked quickly to the car. Molly sat without complaint as they waited in the crush of cars, although her ears flicked constantly. The hospital was not far from Tom's apartment, but the traffic seemed heavier than usual because Denise was in such a hurry. At every stoplight, Denise's heart filled her throat and a vice tightened sickeningly around her stomach.

When she arrived at the hospital, Denise parked in the first spot she could find. Trotting from the lot with Molly at her side, she entered the emergency room door. The security guard at the door tried to stop her, but Denise flashed her shield and continued as if she had not heard him. Tom was behind one of those curtains. Nothing and no one would stop her from finding him.

"The ambulance brought in my partner, Tom Phyfer. I'd like to see him," Denise announced as she showed her shield to the woman at the admittance desk.

Pointing down the hall, the woman replied, "He's behind curtain three."

Denise nodded her thanks and rushed in the direction of the examining areas. Physicians and nurses looked briefly as she walked past, but no one questioned the determined woman with the large dog at her side. Glancing at the number over the curtain, Denise found the right one and stepped inside.

Tom lay unconscious on the table. He had looked near death while lying on the bathroom floor, but now he looked helpless and shrunken by the size and stark whiteness of the room. Tubes and wires ran everywhere.

"Miss, you have to leave," a resident in a white coat stated, approaching Denise and Molly.

"He's my partner. I'm not leaving. Is he going to be all right? Have you contacted the CDC?" Denise demanded displaying her shield once again.

Stepping back, the resident replied, "Yes, they suggested abundant hydration. The paramedics said that you mentioned ergot poisoning. Thanks. You've probably saved his life by making it easier for us to identify the substance. We never would have thought of ergot. Migraine sufferers take ergotamine for headaches all the time. It's a common drug."

"I know. That's what the killer's hoping," Denise responded without taking her eyes from Tom's pinched face.

"How did you know about it?" the resident inquired.

Trying to smile, Denise replied, "Lucky guess and from clues the suspect has been sending me. Have any other hospitals reported cases like this one?"

"As a matter of fact, one in DC reported a similar case," the young woman replied. "The patient died. They're sending the stomach contents to the CDC."

"They should tell the CDC to test for ergot poisoning. Tell them to inform the FBI, also," Denise suggested as she continued to study Tom's face.

"The other victim of the poisoning was a fashion designer," the physician muttered more to herself than to Denise as she checked Tom's vital signs.

"I'm sorry. What did you say?" Denise inquired as she stepped closer.

"Oh, I said that the guy who died was a designer," the physician replied. "His wife found him on the kitchen floor with a package of bicarb in his hand. She thought he'd had a heart attack. I heard from a friend of mine at that hospital that he didn't have any signs of cardiac arrest. They tried everything, but he died. He was older and in relatively poor health. Not strong like your partner."

Leaning against the wall for support, Denise breathed heavily with the weight of realization. If Tom had not been a young, healthy man, he would have died from the poisoning. As it was, he was a terribly sick man. Involuntary tears sprang to her eyes and rolled down her cheeks. Molly, sensing that Denise was upset, pressed closer to comfort her.

"Are you OK, Detective?" the young resident asked as she eased Denise into a nearby chair.

"It's just a reaction to the shock," Denise replied as she dabbed at her cheeks with the proffered tissue. "We're trained to feel invincible. If we didn't, we wouldn't be able to do this job. I just never thought I'd see my partner lying there like that. He could have died."

Placing her hand on Denise's shoulder, the woman responded, "He's a lucky man. If you hadn't arrived when you did and suggested ergot poisoning to the paramedics, we probably would have lost him. He'll be OK. You stay here with him, and I'll get you a cup of coffee and some water for the dog."

Denise studied Tom's face. The coloring had improved, but he was still unconscious from the effects of the poison. It would probably take a while before the IV cleansed his system of the ergot fungus.

She had almost lost him. Tom had almost died. She was prepared to lose this handsome man to another woman; that she could fight against. However, she was not ready to let him go to death. He looked so vulnerable lying on that gurney. He had none of his usual spunk, his gruffness, his courage. He was a very sick man, and Denise could not figure out how Tom had been poisoned but she had not.

She had inspected the kitchen and felt confident that no one could infiltrate it. She had eaten food prepared there and suffered no ill results. Rerunning the evening in her mind, Denise remembered that everyone had eaten the same salad, main course, and dessert. Tom had consumed all of his and hers, but it was still the same food. They had randomly selected bread from the same basket. They had consumed the same foods that could have contained ergot.

Suddenly, Denise remembered the difference. Tom had asked for and received a roll from the head table and she had not. Once he had finished all of the rolls from their basket, the waiter had handed him the leftover bread from a basket that had sat on the head table. The killer had planted bread poisoned with ergot fungus.

Forcing her distraught mind to function, Denise tried to remember the name of the designer who had also eaten rolls from that basket. If she could remember, she would have the connection. Ticking off the names from the left, she could picture every face until she came to the seat next to the emcee. Slowly that face came into view . . . an older man . . . gray hair . . . slight build . . . newly retired . . . outrageous designs showing lots of flesh . . . and then the name . . . Christopher Moon.

At that moment, the young resident returned with the coffee and a kidney-shaped pan of water. Thanking her, Denise asked, "Do you know the name of the man who died of the poisoning?"

"No, but I can phone my friend. Give me a minute and I'll have your answer," the resident replied. She departed quickly to obtain the needed piece of the puzzle.

Sitting in the strangely silent emergency room, Denise vacantly watched Molly lapping up the water. Her coffee tasted weak and spineless compared to the brew Tom concocted every morning. This was too sweet and too milky. She needed the stiff, strong, almost lethal substance with which she always started her day.

"Dory?" a voice whispered.

Leaping up and almost falling over Molly, Denise rushed to Tom's side. His eyes fluttered open and then closed reluctantly. A ragged smile lingered on his lips.

Clasping his hand, Denise answered, "I'm here, Tom, and so's Molly."

The smile widened an almost imperceptible amount as he whispered in a very weak voice, "Two girls."

Denise cried. She could not stop the tears that spilled onto his hand. Tom would recover. He would not die from the ergot poisoning. He would not become another victim. Weakly, Tom squeezed Denise's fingers and sank into sleep again. She sat down to wait for him to awaken.

With considerable effort, Denise composed herself. Now that Tom appeared to be out of danger, she could turn her attention to police work. Using the cell phone in her bag, she phoned the precinct and asked for Captain Morton. When he answered, she told him of Tom's poisoning and relayed her suspicions about the connection between his illness and that of the dead designer. She promised to call back as soon as she had confirmation. Assuring her that he would personally follow up with the FBI and CDC in her absence, Captain Morton left her to tend to Tom.

As always, Denise could not sit for long. She began to pace the small space of emergency room three. Periodically, a nurse would enter and monitor Tom's vital signs and say that he was progressing nicely. Denise would thank her and begin to pace again.

She had to do something. She was filled with an energy born of her worry about Tom's health, her anger at the killer, and her frustration at being unable to catch him. He had struck again under her nose just as he had said he would.

Tom had inadvertently provided her with the means to catch the murderer. He had eaten the poisoned bread. As soon as the resident returned, Denise would have the proof she needed.

The resident returned with a broad smile on her tired face. Handing Denise a slip of paper, she said, "Here's the name you wanted. Good luck in catching this guy."

"Thanks," Denise muttered absently.

Unfolding the paper, Denise almost held her breath. If the name did not match her suspicions, she might have to start at square one. If it did, she would be well on her way to catching him. Willing herself to remain calm, Denise looked down at the paper. In barely legible scrawl, the resident had written "Christopher Moon."

Denise's heart skipped a beat and then began to pound. She had the connection for which she had been searching since beginning this case. Since the first note and charm had arrived, she had been trying to tie the murderer's cryptic messages and the little gold charms with the death of designers in the fashion world.

Although she did not know the murderer's name, Denise knew how to catch him. And she would. She would make him pay for his greedy ambition to rank number one in the industry. She would use Freda's sketch and the designers themselves to flush him out.

Freda. Denise would have to phone her with news of Tom's illness. She would have to be on the alert, too, now that the killer had struck so boldly. He might consider Freda, someone who could identify him, as an obstacle to his success and decide to remove her.

"You look like a mad woman," Tom's voice broke into the silence and her thoughts.

Turning to find him smiling as he lay with one arm under his head, Denise felt relief flow through her body. He was awake and becoming his old complaining self. Never again would she call him an old sourpuss. Denise would take him any way she could get him.

Kissing him lightly on the forehead, Denise held Tom's hand against her chest. Looking into his tired face, she asked, "Ready to take on the world?"

"Not yet, but ready to go home," Tom grumbled in a weak imitation of his usual gruff voice.

"Not yet. The doctor said something about running more tests when you woke up," Denise replied, smiling through the tears that rimmed her eyes.

"What was it? A heart attack? I don't remember feeling pain in my chest," Tom asked as he stretched a little.

"No, ergot poisoning."

"What? That's the stuff you think the suspect used to murder the designers. How'd I come in contact with that?" Tom inquired as he pressed the button to raise the head of the bed a bit.

"You ate rolls from the head table. Remember?" Denise stated as she adjusted his pillow.

"Yeah, I ate two from a basket that had been in front of one of the honorees. They were good. A little bitter maybe but good. How's that guy doing?" Tom said as he remembered the previous night's dinner.

"He's dead."

"Geez!" Tom exclaimed studying Denise's very serious face. "That could have been me."

"That's what the doctor said. If you hadn't been young and in good shape, you might have died, too," Denise commented as she held his hand even tighter.

"Do you know for sure that it was ergot poisoning?" Tom asked, unwilling to believe that he had become an unwitting victim.

"Positive. I was pretty sure when I found you on the bathroom floor. You've just had your physical. You're in great shape. The doctors here ran a test on your blood and found the poison. The CDC is running analysis on the stomach contents of the deceased in comparison to yours and the other victims. They'll find the connection," Denise responded, providing the details that would convince Tom.

Tom sat clinching his teeth in anger. Badly concealing his anger, he tried to make a joke by saying, "You told me not to eat so much."

Trying to console him, Denise replied, "At least this time it wasn't the quantity. If you'd eaten one of those rolls at the beginning of the meal, you'd have been equally as sick."

"Now what?"

"First, I'll call the captain to tell him that you're out of danger," Denise replied. "I'm not going to wait for the results to come through regular channels. I'll phone our contacts for the information. I need to get in touch with Freda, too. She's also a likely target. She ran errands for the killer and saw his face. He might want to get rid of her, too."

"How do you think he got the rolls into the baskets? We were on the lookout for him," Tom asked as he considered their options.

"I don't know," Denise conceded shaking her head. "He must have paid one of the waiters to add them to the basket. He hired Freda to buy the charms, appear in the show in Hawaii, and meet me at the Grand Canyon. There's no reason that he couldn't hire someone to plant poisonous rolls at the dinner."

"It probably doesn't matter how he does it," Tom commented. "It's only important that he does. His helpers probably don't have a clue that he's dangerous."

"Freda does now. I told her about him," Denise added.

"Then, she is in danger," Tom replied trying to rub the fatigue from his eyes. "As long as she thought she was just running errands and playing a role, she was OK. Now that she can identify him as a killer, she's in trouble."

A nurse and an orderly arrived at that moment and put an end to their conversation. Smiling, the nurse stated, "You're looking much better, Mr. Phyfer. We have orders to move you to a regular room now."

"But I want to go home," Tom stated stubbornly.

"Not today. The doctors want to observe you overnight. You've been a very sick man. You won't feel so restricted as soon as we get you upstairs and you can walk around," the nurse replied as she and the orderly disconnected all but the IV line.

"Can Detective Dory come with me?" Tom asked pitifully.

"Sure, but not the dog," the nurse answered.

"She's my partner, too," Tom insisted like a small child whose toy someone wanted to put away.

"Not upstairs. Down here, we're not as strict. Upstairs, they won't understand," the nurse stated firmly.

Smiling at his irritation, Denise commented, "I'll leave

Molly with the canine unit and drop in to see the captain. I'll come back as soon as I make my phone calls. OK?"

Showing concern at being alone in the strange hospital, Tom asked, "Will you be able to find me?"

"Sure, I'll ask at the desk for the big, handsome brute of a man who was felled by two dinner rolls," Denise teased to ease his worry.

"Fine, Dory. Poke fun at a sick man," Tom growled with a big smile on his tired face.

As they pushed Tom's bed from the curtained area, the nurse said, "You must have been partners for a while."

"Long enough not to want to be without him," Denise replied as her voice choked on unshed tears.

Denise followed the gurney as far as the elevator. She waved and blew him a kiss. As the doors closed, Tom smiled and pressed it to his lips.

Walking to the car, all the tension and worry that Denise had suppressed in the hospital began to flow from her. The tears welled in her eyes and cascaded down her cheeks. Sinking onto a nearby bench, Denise wrapped her arms around Molly's neck and sobbed. She had almost lost her partner, the man she loved. Nothing would ever erase that feeling of total abandonment, of loss, and of despair from her memory.

Pulling herself together, Denise wiped the tears from her face. Slowly the realization that Tom was safe replaced the emptiness. She would apprehend the man who did this to him. The killer had inadvertently given her the evidence she needed to catch him. Armed with information from the CDC and the FBI, Denise would have all she needed to stop the serial killer in his tracks.

Fifteen

Denise placed Molly with the canine unit until Tom could return to work. Her apartment was not large enough for her cat and Molly under the same roof. Returning to her desk, Denise immediately phoned the CDC and the FBI. Contacts in both agencies confirmed the existence of ergot poisoning in Tom's stomach contents and in that of the deceased. Finally, Denise had a murder weapon—but at Tom's expense.

Denise left a fairly cryptic but meaningful message on Freda's answering device. She wanted Freda to phone her so that she could explain her concerns. Phoning the club at which Freda performed, she left the same message. Between the two, Denise felt fairly confident that she would find Freda.

Her meeting with the captain did not go as well. Captain Morton was not only concerned about Tom's health, he felt under considerable pressure from the chief to solve the case that had taken the life of yet another designer. He paced the office during their conversation and gnawed nervously at his nails.

"Dory, you've got to get a handle on this case," Captain Morton began. "It's beginning to look as if you haven't a clue as to what's happening. Your suspect is more in touch with your whereabouts than you are with his."

"Captain, be fair. I'm doing the best I can under the circumstances," Denise rebutted. "You know there's a leak in the squad room that keeps him informed of my activities.

There's nothing I can do about it. I've taken to making sensitive calls on my cell phone from the sidewalk. I don't even trust my apartment."

Opening his hands in frustration, the captain replied, "I'm sorry, Denise. I know you're on top of things. It's just that the chief is riding me on this one. Now with Tom in the hospital, it looks as if the perp is targeting us, too."

"Not true. If Tom hadn't eaten so many rolls, he never would have fallen into this mess," Denise explained again. "The killer targeted and killed Christopher Moon. Tom was simply an innocent bystander."

"What do you want me to tell the chief?" Captain Morton asked as he sank into his chair only to hop up again.

"Tell her that I'm working on it. That's all she needs to know," Denise replied calmly.

Denise had come in contact with the chief during another high-profile case and knew that she was usually very supportive yet demanding. Now with so many of her associates falling at the hands of a serial killer with a vendetta against designers, the chief was becoming unnerved. Still, she needed to realize that cases like this took time to solve. At least now Denise knew the murder weapon and was formulating plans to catch the killer.

"If that would only work, I'd be the happiest man alive. You know she'll want more. I'll think of something," Captain Morton responded from his spot by the window.

"Has anyone isolated the leak?" Denise asked tactfully. Departmental breaks in security were very sensitive issues.

"Yes. You don't have to worry about it happening again," the captain responded without embellishment.

"Who's the hacker?" Denise probed, sensing that he was definitely keeping something from her.

"There wasn't one," Captain Morton replied. "A monitoring system printed out a list of searched Web sites. The chief assigned someone to do a study of personal use of the Internet on the job. Your ticket reservation activity looked like personal use. When he delivered the report, the chief checked your information."

"So, how did the suspect find out?" Denise asked almost hesitantly.

Clearing his throat, Captain Morton replied, "The Chief mentioned the sophisticated equipment and the time she could save by implementing restrictions on the personal use of the Internet on the job at a cocktail party. I guess the perp heard her."

"Oh, so no leak," Denise quipped, "just loose lips."

Looking helpless, Captain Morton added, "That sink ships or investigations."

"At least that's solved," Denise stated as she walked toward the door. "Sounds to me as if the chief has given you information to use in defense of our investigation, Captain, and maybe get her off your back for awhile."

"Keep me posted, Denise," the captain demanded with a tone of request in his voice.

Nodding, Denise returned to the squad room. On her desk lay the familiar envelope. Instead of only being slightly annoyed by the correspondence, Denise felt anger that the man who had poisoned Tom would contact her. Rationally, she knew that Tom had simply been an innocent bystander, but she could not silence the fury that burned in her heart.

Studying the envelope, Denise discovered that the suspect had sent the note by courier this time. The perpetrator had, undoubtedly, decided to gloat over the successful evening. Although she was not in the mood to read anymore of his sophomoric rhymes, she reluctantly ripped open the envelope and extracted the fine vellum. In his usual loopy handwriting, Denise read, "Detective: Sorry about your partner. He shouldn't have eaten those rolls. They weren't meant for him. Now you know my motive and my method. All you need to discover is my identity. Perhaps this charm will help."

Unwrapping the package, Denise placed the tiny gold charm on the palm of her hand. Like the others, the workmanship was outstanding. One side of the open-weave design showed the mask of comedy and the other contained that of tragedy. It was as if the goldsmith had created sides that were so completely simpatico that it was impossible to distinguish the two. Dividing them was impossible for there was no seam. Denise saw immediately that the suspect wanted this charm to represent the human soul . . . so completely woven in all of its facets that to separate one element from the other would destroy both.

"Now he's getting philosophical on me," Denise muttered to herself as she attached the new charm to the bracelet with the others.

Although all of the charms exhibited infinite care by the goldsmith, the last one was far superior to the others. Denise knew that this was the last one she would receive. The suspect had saved the best for last.

She had to apprehend him now before he vanished. Looking at her composite list of designers, Denise saw that several had retired and had, therefore, removed themselves from the suspect's grasp. Another had died of a heart attack while on vacation with his lover. The killer had removed the others. Only one remained from the original list. Consulting the other ranking sheets, she found his name on all of them. Giles Tilghman would be the next and last victim if she did not stop the killing.

Consulting the list of telephone numbers Ronda had compiled for her, Denise phoned Giles Tilghman's shop in Tysons Corner, Virginia. When his secretary answered, she made an appointment to meet with him later that day. She advised him to eat no flour-containing products prior to her arrival.

Keeping her promise to Tom, Denise returned to the hospital. She found him sitting in a chair and entertaining his roommate with police stories. The young man's eyes were huge with admiration and wonder. Tom's face lit up the room when he saw her.

"Feeling better?" Denise asked as she planted a warm kiss on his lips.

"Much. I'm doing so well that the doctors might let me

come home today," Tom beamed as he slipped his arm around her waist.

"Great! However, a little rest wouldn't hurt you," Denise replied snuggling against him.

"Rest? Who gets rest in the hospital?" Tom exclaimed. "I tried to take a nap and a nurse came in to check my vital signs. I tried to watch television, and a technician appeared to take blood. I decided to doze in this chair, but a resident in poison control woke me up with a whole series of questions. I'm eating and walking the halls. I don't need to be here. Besides, I'd get better rest at home."

"We'll see," Denise commented not wanting to build up his hopes in case the discharge did not come until the next day. Actually, she was not saving Tom the disappointment as much as she was trying to prevent him from being a less-than-desirable patient. Tom, when sulking, was difficult.

"Any news on the case?" Tom inquired as he leaned his head against Denise's chest.

"I made my phone calls. Oh, and I found out about the leak," Denise replied.

"So?"

Chuckling dryly, Denise stated, "The chief . . . seems she's installed new monitoring equipment that prints out reports of all our Internet usage. She wanted to make sure we weren't using too much government time for personal entertainment. Anyway, she checked on the Web sites and found my reservations. By way of casual conversation, she mentioned the new system at a cocktail party. The suspect learned everything he needed to know from her."

"So much for trust. Anything else?" Tom inquired with a scowl.

"The suspect sent this note. I received it this morning along with this charm," Denise responded showing both to Tom.

"He didn't mean to poison me. That's big of him," Tom muttered with venom in his voice.

"He even commented that we know everything except his

identity now," Denise added. "I'm working on a way to learn that, too."

"The charm's real nice," Tom commented as he studied the double faces. "It's the best looking one yet . . . even better than the little tornado with the diamond."

"I think so, too. Sort of his swan song, last fling, final curtain," Denise replied, reciting all the hackneyed expressions that meant the end.

"I get your drift," Tom said, holding up his hand to stop her.

Grabbing her hand, he pressed it to his cheek. Tom was so happy to see her and so glad to be alive. Now that he had had a brush with death, he understood the fragility of life . . . and of love.

"Do you feel up to a walk?" Denise asked, resting her hand on his arm. "There's a sunroom at the end of the hall."

"Sure. Now that I'm free of that IV pole, I can go anywhere," Tom replied as he stood up and stretched.

Holding hands, Denise and Tom strolled the length of the hall toward the solarium. She could feel the eyes of the nurses following them as they passed. The expressions of appreciation were obvious on the face of every nurse and female physician. Denise was not blind to the fact that Tom was a handsome man. His physical appearance had been the topic of discussion among her friends before she became his partner. All the women on the force, regardless of precinct, had heard of his broad shoulders, narrow hips, strong shoulders, and incredibly handsome face. However, they were also aware of his bouts of moodiness, his quick temper, and his obsession with being left alone. Although he was a good catch, none of the ladies could figure out a way to get around his temperamental attitude.

Denise had needed a partner and he had been available. She had heard that he would make a challenging partner. She had decided to take a chance on him, and she had never been sorry. His dry sense of humor and his loyalty made him a perfect match for her workaholic but playful nature.

By the time they reached the solarium, Denise felt as if she had walked miles instead of yards under the watchful eyes. Tom, however, had not appeared to notice the attention and stares. He had spent most of his time looking either straight ahead or at her.

Selecting a seat in the sunshine and away from the other patients, Denise brought Tom up to speed on her plans. She mentioned the connection between Giles Tilghman, the list, and the suspect. Tom listened attentively and silently as she laid out her plans. Only a deepening of the furrow between his brows showed his level of concentration.

"I'm seeing Mr. Tilghman this afternoon. If he'll agree, I'll use him to catch the murderer," Denise said as she fingered the newest charm.

"How do you know that he'll go along?" Tom asked, watching the sun play in her hair.

"That's simple. If he doesn't, he'll be a dead man. I think that'll motivate him to help," Denise replied, linking her arm through his.

Frowning, Tom inquired, "Are you so sure that he's not the suspect? You said that he's the last one on your composite list. He might be the murderer."

Pulling a page from a magazine, Denise produced a photograph of Giles Tilghman. He was tall and thick with blue eyes and starkly white hair. Although in his early sixties, his skin was youthful to the point of looking artificial like a facelift.

"The eyes could be contact lenses and the hair could be a dye job," Tom growled in his usual skeptical manner.

"Not according to his birth records," Denise replied as she pulled out the biographical information Ronda had found on each person on her list. "According to this, Giles Tilghman was born with blue eyes. His college graduation photograph shows him as blond-haired with blue eyes. Besides, Freda described a man with piercing brown eyes. I know that contact lenses can change the color, but I still think he's the likely victim."

"OK, let's suppose that Mr. Tilghman is the next victim. How do you plan to lure the suspect into the trap?" Tom inquired as he studied Denise's face. He found her so beautiful that he often could not take his eyes from her.

Developing the idea as she spoke, Denise said, "Mr. Tilghman will host a party of some sort and invite all of the designers who attended the dinner dance, but none of the press or friends of designers. Maybe he'll rent a boat or a room in a country club. It doesn't matter as long as the gathering is intimate. I'll be the only non-fashion-industry person there."

"How will he know which ones to invite? He might invite all the wrong ones," Tom protested in an effort to poke holes in Denise's plans.

"No, he won't," Denise replied, pulling the past evening's guest list from her bag. "He won't invite any of the retirees since they're no longer a threat to the suspect. Of all the people at the dinner, only twenty were designers . . . many of lesser fame than others. The others were celebrities the designers had dressed or reporters. If he eliminates the retirees and the second string, he'll only invite eleven people."

"You're a pack rat, Dory. You save everything, don't you?" Tom laughed as he scanned the guest list that had been inside everyone's program. He had left his on the table without giving it further thought.

"You never know what'll come in handy," Denise chuckled. "Sounds workable, doesn't it?"

"Except for one part," Tom commented sternly.

"What?"

"You said that you would be on watch. You're not doing this alone. I'll be with you," Tom stated firmly.

"But, Tom, you're not well. You're still weak from the poisoning," Denise objected with concern in her voice.

Standing over her, Tom exclaimed, "Weak? Me? I don't think so!" With that he scooped Denise into his arms and held her at chest level.

They laughed heartily as Tom pressed her close. His eyes

followed the angles of her face and the swell of her bosom as he returned Denise to her feet. She locked her arms around his neck and pulled his face to hers. Their lips collided passionately and held fast.

Denise did not notice the other patients looking at them. She did not feel the sun burning her skin. She felt only Tom's arms around her and his mouth loving her.

Stepping to arm's length, Denise breathed, "I guess you're not that weak after all."

"I'm sorry, Dory. I guess I just got carried away," Tom said with a hesitant smile. He did not remove his hands from her waist.

"So did I," Denise agreed with a smile. "I guess you are well enough to help me on this case."

"Good," Tom grinned. "That's settled. When's your appointment with Mr. Tilghman?"

Dragging her eyes from Tom's face, Denise said with shock, "In thirty minutes across town. I'll come back to see you tonight."

"Not here. I'll take a cab home. Come to my apartment. I'll roast a chicken. You'd better hurry," Tom instructed as he lightly kissed her lips.

Denise waved goodbye as she hurried down the hall toward the elevators. She would have to rush to be on time for her appointment. Pulling her cell phone from her purse, she phoned Mr. Tilghman's shop with the news of her late departure. His secretary quickly changed the time, giving Denise the extra time she needed.

Putting the car in gear and joining the traffic, Denise muttered, "Thank goodness for cell phones."

Fortunately the traffic was not heavy that afternoon as Denise rushed through town. She quickly found a space in a public lot and jogged through the light pedestrian traffic to the shop. Unlike the rest of the shopping area, Mr. Tilghman's shop bustled with activity. Denise had to squeeze past women nibbling tea sandwiches in order to find the secretary.

The secretary pointed toward the crush of people around the tall, handsome designer. Despite his age, Mr. Tilghman was only slightly stooped. His white hair accentuated his dark tan. He looked up and smiled as Denise approached. His blue eyes twinkled with the contentment of financial success.

Denise ingratiated herself into the inner circle around him and introduced herself. The smile never faded from his face as he extended his hand in welcome. His eyes, however, lost some of their sparkle at the mention of the previous night's murder.

Beckoning with a manicured hand, Mr. Tilghman directed Denise to his office. Sitting on the blue and gold tapestry upholstered sofa, he spoke in a voice tinged with a soft Southern accent. "I'll do anything I can to help you, Detective. These murders are simply devastating. So many of my friends are gone because of this man," he said with sadness.

Taking a cue from his statement, Denise stated, "That's why I'm here, Mr. Tilghman. I need for you to throw a party and invite a discriminating selection of your colleagues."

"A party?" Mr. Tilghman replied incredulously. "Wouldn't that be in poor taste? WID only held its dinner dance last night because it's an annual event that's planned far in advance."

"I know it seems that way, but it's the only solution," Denise responded. "I wouldn't ask you to do it if there were any other way to catch the killer."

"How do you know that he'll attend?" Mr. Tilghman asked with a certain amount of skepticism in his voice.

"He can never pass up the opportunity to remove another one of his competitors from the list," Denise replied knowingly.

"I don't understand," Mr. Tilghman stated as he pulled his legs under him on the sofa.

Slowly and deliberately, Denise explained, "The killer has a vendetta against anyone who is his competition for a national ranking. He has made several of the local and specialty lists, but he has never made the coveted national lists. He wants to be the premier designer."

"Everyone knows those lists feed the ego and nothing else," Mr. Tilghman retorted. "The man's a fool. No one has ever received more than momentary fame from being on that list. Certainly nothing monetary has ever come my way because of it. Ridiculous."

"I agree, but that's his logic," Denise replied with a shrug. "He'll continue to kill until he sees his name on that list. You're the only one standing between the killer and the accomplishment of his dreams."

Denise waited in silence as the realization of his imminent demise washed over Mr. Tilghman's face. His eyes stopped twinkling and took on the expression of a deer caught in a car's headlights.

"In that case, I'll do it," Mr. Tilghman agreed. "When do you want me to host this party?"

"The sooner the better," Denise stated without the slightest feeling of satisfaction. "As long as the killer is loose, you're not safe. Don't eat anything that in any way contains flour until we apprehend him."

"Let me see that list," Mr. Tilghman demanded, extending his long, thick fingers.

Denise watched as he scanned the list of potential guests. She could tell from the periodic scowl that Mr. Tilghman was remembering little tidbits about each of them. When he eventually looked up, she could tell that he had mentally organized the party.

"Let's do it tomorrow at eight o'clock," Mr. Tilghman stated. "Many of these people will go to Rome next week, me included. I'll start my caterer working immediately."

Rising, Denise instructed, "Tell him to guard his kitchen and his food well. He should provide only dark rye rolls for the meal and use no other flour in the recipes. He should let no one know that he's catering your affair. He should assign his chefs to another job and do all the cooking himself. We'll provide the waiters, and I'll arrive early to help them. You are to tell no one that you're using him. Everything must be very circumspect."

"Why serve only dark rye? They're so ordinary," Mr. Tilghman asked with distaste written on his face.

"If any other bread appears, we'll know that someone substituted it. We'll have to watch very carefully," Denise replied firmly.

"If it weren't a possibility I'd killed, this would be exciting," Mr. Tilghman beamed. "I love keeping secrets from my guests. My lips and Stephano's are sealed. My home will be the location of an incredible spectacle tomorrow night. Oh, my! I must set my secretary to the task immediately."

Denise left Mr. Tilghman knowing that he would keep his word. Something about being the next to die silenced a man and gave him motivation to keep his own confidence. She knew that he would burst before he would betray this secret.

Tom's apartment building was on the other side of town, not very far from their precinct. The drive was surprisingly easy compared to the mad dash she'd made to Mr. Tilghman's shop. Climbing the stairs, she rapped on the door. Tom, looking healthy and happy, opened on the first knock with Molly at his side.

"How'd you get Molly? I have your car," Denise asked as she looked at the happy beast.

Stepping aside to let her enter, Tom stated, "I took a cab home and stopped to pick her up. I thought you'd never get here. The chicken's ready, and I'm starved."

Denise quickly set the table while Tom served the plates. While they ate, she told him about the meeting with Mr. Tilghman and the plans for the dinner the next day. Tom listened attentively, nodding and making comments and suggestions. By the time they finished their meal, they had planned their portion of the evening. They phoned their friends and made the arrangements to use them as members of the caterer's staff. Denise and Tom would supervise every component of the meal. Mr. Tilghman only needed to supply the opportunity for the murderer to strike again. The dinner would give him the opportunity. Any food he would bring would become the method.

The candles flickered and went out as Denise and Tom planned their strategy. Both were too well known to the murderer to camouflage themselves as part of the caterer's staff. Their involvement would have to come from behind the scenes.

"Let's meet at Mr. Tilghman's condo early tomorrow to find a place to hide. We need to see and not be seen," Denise suggested.

"Sounds good to me, but I'm tired, Dory. I'd better go to bed if I'm to be any use to you tomorrow," Tom stated as he rose and stretched.

"I'll see you at Tilghman's in the morning," Denise replied as she pecked him on the cheek.

"You can stay the night, if you'd like," Tom offered.

Seeing the fatigue play across his face, Denise replied, "No, thanks. We need our rest for tomorrow. We'll have plenty of time for slow romantic evenings."

Denise slipped out the door and into the night. She had been tempted by memories of their passionate afternoon kiss to stay the night. She knew that Tom would have tried his best to recreate the passion that had engulfed both of them in the solarium. She did not want to put him in a position for possible failure. He had almost fallen asleep during dinner. Only her constant chatter had kept him awake. They would have many more days and nights together.

Sixteen

Denise and Tom arrived early the next day to set up their observation stations in Mr. Tilghman's guest bedroom. They arranged carefully labeled monitors on a utilitarian folding table they had brought with them before concealing them in vases in the living room and dining room bookcases and in the kitchen chandelier. They placed tiny microphones under the tables and in the flowerpots to pick up the dinner guests' conversation. After they had finished, they were able to monitor and listen to all conversations in the public rooms and kitchen of the condo.

When Mr. Tilghman complained that he felt that they had violated his privacy, Denise reminded him that the alternative was death. He had huffed into his bedroom and had not reappeared until Stephano arrived with his baskets of food. Although Denise and Tom would have preferred his help in making the final arrangements, they were relieved when they could no longer see the pained expression on his face.

Taking no chances, Denise had removed all grain products from the kitchen. She and Tom carefully inspected the kitchen and the contents of Stephano's baskets and hampers. As instructed, he had brought only brown rolls that he would warm in the convection oven and prepared dishes that did not require the addition of grain flour. He watched in horror as Denise lifted the lid on each partially cooked menu item.

When Stephano could remain silent no longer, he demanded indignantly, "Am I to be supervised all evening or will this insult to my professionalism eventually come to an end? I did not bargain for this when I agreed to Mr. Tilghman's outlandish requests. Think about it, I have not instructed you in the performance of your duties."

Keeping her composure in the face of his anger, Denise replied, "You have been most gracious. However, as you have probably figured out, this is no ordinary dinner party."

Beaming with the possibility of publicity, Stephano asked, "Will someone famous appear tonight? Are you Secret Service? Is the president coming?"

Playing along with the improved humor brought on by his raging vanity, Denise responded in a lowered voice, "I'm not at liberty to answer that right now. It's enough to tell you that you will be doing a great service by helping us to maintain the integrity of this kitchen. If you see anyone other than the off-duty police officers enter this room, you are to summon me at once."

"Gladly!" Stephano promised. "Why didn't you tell me this sooner? I wouldn't have been so grouchy if I had known that this evening would be so important."

"There are some things that are on a need-to-know basis, Stephano," Denise answered with intrigue in her voice.

Pressing his long, thin fingers to his lips, Stephano pledged dramatically, "My lips are sealed. I'll protect this kitchen and the food with my life."

"I don't think that'll be necessary, but I do appreciate your help. I'll bring the officers to you now," Denise replied as she backed from the kitchen.

As she left, Denise could see the glow of Stephano's face almost illuminate the room. He was so excited to be part of the intrigue. She hoped he would not be too disappointed when fashion designers appeared rather than the President of the United States. Fortunately, he would be too busy in the kitchen to notice until the meal ended.

Denise gathered the six officers in the staging room where she gave them the details of the evening. Speaking carefully, she detailed her expectations of them and the killer. She informed them that they were to keep their eyes open not only for the man but also the method. Any slip would result in death. When she had finished, she delivered them, clad in black slacks or skirts, white shirts or blouses, and red cummerbunds, to Stephano in the kitchen.

Stepping forward to great each one, Stephano welcomed them to his kitchen saying, "Ladies and gentlemen, you are about to embark on a sacred mission. You will serve a masterfully prepared meal to some of the most important people in the world tonight. You will present yourselves with dignity and decorum. You will serve the guests silently, with a white napkin folded over your arm at the ready. Although you are police officers by trade, tonight you will wear two hats. Tonight, you will represent your department and my saloon. I expect only the best service to accompany the best cuisine."

Denise and Tom, standing at the door of the massive kitchen, found it difficult not to laugh at Stephano's seriousness. Realizing that he was genuine, Denise decided that he probably gave his own wait staff the same pep talk prior to every event. He was a man who was proud of his work and did not allow anything to soil his reputation.

The grandfather clock in the hall struck eight. Finding Mr. Tilghman standing in the hall anxiously awaiting the arrival of his guests, Denise and Tom nodded and vanished into the bedroom. They would keep an eye on the proceedings from a distance. When the killer struck, they would only be a few steps away.

Gazing at the monitors, Denise and Tom watched Stephano and the wait staff in the kitchen as they prepared the canopies for delivery to the living room. Although they could see a sheen of perspiration on Stephano's forehead, they could tell that he was enjoying every minute as he prepared for what he thought would be a momentous evening for his catering business.

Switching screens to view the living room, they watched Mr. Tilghman usher his eleven guests into the room in which music played softly in the background and the white-gloved wait staff awaited them.

In the dining room, Mr. Tilghman's exquisite china, crystal, and sterling sparkled under the lights of the glistening chandelier. Stephano had folded the white linen napkins into fans and placed them in the center of the dinner plates on their silver changers. The centerpiece, a large arrangement of marzipan fruit, would become part of the dessert. Place cards in the shape of sterling silver pineapples would help to seat the guests quickly.

Denise and Tom watched and listened as the guests clustered in little groups of animated conversation. She smiled when she saw that all eleven had arrived. No one would dare stay away from an intimate little dinner party given by one of their most celebrated colleagues.

"Which one is it?" Tom asked in an unnecessarily soft voice.

"I don't know," Denise replied as she manipulated the camera so that she could study the faces of each guest.

"Does anyone fit Freda's description?" Tom inquired as he peered into the monitors.

"No, not exactly. No one looks like the man who sat next to me at the Cathedral either," Denise replied as she stared at the faces.

"I guess we'll have to wait for him to present himself," Tom stated without emotion.

Without taking her eyes from the screen, Denise asked, "Did I tell you that I received another note this morning? Actually, the suspect left it at the mail desk downstairs, care of Mr. Tilghman."

"No. What did he say this time?" Tom replied gruffly. His good health and humor had returned after a sound night's rest.

"Not much and no charm. He only wrote, 'See you at Tilghman's party,' " Denise responded. "I thought he'd be more direct about his plans, but that's all he said."

"At least we know for sure that he's one of the guests,"

Tom commented. "He's definitely not one of these awkward
waiters."

"Don't talk about them like that," Denise chuckled. "It
was very nice of our friends to give up sleep to help us."

"I know, but Melvin really needs a lesson in balancing a
tray," Tom insisted. "Look at him. He's holding it with both
hands."

Denise looked at the monitor to see their friend Melvin
struggling with a silver tray of brown rolls, trying to keep
them from falling onto the floor, as he headed for the table.
He made a comical sight. But more importantly, Denise was
happy to see that no white rolls had appeared on the tray.

Neither the guests nor Mr. Tilghman seemed in any hurry
to sit down to dinner. Everyone seemed content to discuss the
latest murder. Listening to the conversations, Denise could
tell that the designers were worried about the killer's motives
and his selection of victims. More than one of the guests ex-
pressed concern about becoming the next target of his greed.

Denise waited. She did not know how he would do it or
when, but she knew that the killer wold strike again and at
that dinner party. She had taken all the precautions within
her power to eliminate the possibility of accomplices. Now,
it was up to him.

As she watched the monitors, Denise observed that one
of the guests seemed to be carrying an especially lumpy
purse. Watching her carefully, she noticed that the woman
did not mingle as much as the others. She hovered on the
perimeter, looking at Mr. Tilghman's décor.

"What do you think of that one?" Tom asked as he pointed
to the same woman Denise had been watching.

"She's acting a little suspiciously, but maybe she's just a
loner," Denise replied as she continued to watch Bernie Jacobs. Ms. Jacobs, one of the few black designers to appear
on the national list, had made her name as a fur designer for
the rich and famous.

Bernie Jacobs did not in any way fit either Freda's description of the murderer or Denise's recollection of the man

who sat beside her in the Cathedral. Ms. Jacobs was not tall and thin but short and pleasantly plump. She wore her lightly gray streaked dark brown hair in a bun at the back of her neck while glasses on a chain swung on her ample bosom. She looked motherly not dangerous.

"I'll keep my eye on her anyway," Tom decided as he continued to scan the monitors.

Pointing to the picture of the dining room on the third monitor, Denise stated, "They're finally going in to dinner."

"Yeah, but they're still standing around. Don't these rich people ever sit down to eat?" Tom complained as he rubbed the strain from his eyes.

Laughing, Denise replied, "They will soon. Right now, they're trying to find their seats. Mr. Tilghman used an especially elaborate script on the place cards. They're probably having difficulty reading them."

They watched as their friend Melvin came into view on the monitor again. This time he struggled with the salad plates that he carefully placed on the table. Easing his way between chatting guests, he placed one salad plate at the center of each dinner plate. He looked physically relieved when his tray was once again empty.

Listening to the conversation from the room, Denise overheard the chatter about seats, handedness, and the appearance of the table. Two of the guests were left-handed, posing a seating dilemma for an unaware host. But Mr. Tilghman had thought about everything and placed them on the corners. Others chatted about the stunning dinner service and proclaimed it the most splendid they had ever seen, which, of course, was a courtesy since they all owned fabulous china service.

A tall, thin man with blue eyes and small glasses poised on the tip of his nose had cornered Ms. Jacobs as they entered the dining room. Val O'Connor was well known as an innovator in swimsuit fashions. His attire gave him the appearance of being an absent-minded professor type. His shirtsleeves hung too far below the jacket cuff, his trousers bagged too much around his legs, and his shoes looked well worn. The microphone in the nearest potted plant caught his less-than-stimulating conversation as he helped Ms. Jacobs find her seat. Denise could see the poor woman shrink visibly as she discovered his place card next to hers.

As soon as Ms. Jacobs sat down, she began to pull a bottle of salad dressing, utensils, and seasonings from her purse. Leaning toward Tom, Denise observed, "At least we know what she carries in her purse. Either she's allergic or likes to customize her food."

"I'm hungry," Tom muttered as he watched the guests turn their attention to the Caesar salads Melvin had set before them. Several managed to continue the inane dinner chatter while eating the crunchy lettuce, but most fell silent.

"You'll have to wait until dinner's over and the guests leave," Denise advised as she watched the guests. Although she did not admit it, the aroma coming from the kitchen had made her hungry, too.

"Can't I at least have one of those rolls?" Tom asked pleadingly.

"That's the last thing I would have thought you'd want after being poisoned by one," Denise quipped.

"It's the only thing I know for certain is safe," Tom replied.

"I still think you should wait. I'll take you out to eat after we finish here," Denise promised.

Standing, Tom announced, "I can't wait that long. I'm going to get one."

Signing almost audibly, Denise watched him leave the observation station and venture into the hall. Seeing that all of the guests and their host were seated around the table, she did not worry about anyone discovering his presence. Still, she hoped that he would return quickly. She needed the extra eyes to monitor the guests.

Unable to find a single roll in the kitchen, Tom changed jackets with Melvin. Having seen some extra ones in the baskets on the table, he assumed the guise of an eager, helpful waiter and sauntered into the dining room. He would allow nothing to keep him from having something to eat. He forgot that the killer might recognize him until it was too late and he was already in the dining room.

Denise stared in shock at the monitor as Tom came into view. At first she did not recognize him from the side profile, but, when he turned to leave with a basket of rolls in his hand, she recognized Tom and glimpsed clearly the triumphant smile on his face. Not only had he obtained one roll, he had enough for a feast in his grasp.

Just as Tom reached the kitchen, Mr. Tilghman called out, "Waiter, before you take away the basket, I'd like another roll."

Denise could see Tom's shoulders tense either from being singled out or having to return the rolls. Either way, he reluctantly returned to the table. Several others also wanted seconds. By the time Tom left the dining room, the basket was empty.

"These rolls are excellent!" exclaimed Roger Bird. "Who was the genius who decided to serve these flavorful brown rolls rather than the usual white bread dinner rolls? Wonderful idea."

Mr. Tilghman beamed as if the idea had been his. Speaking humbly, he stated, "I'm so glad you like them. It was simply a whim of mine."

Tom's appearance had caused a rumbling of voices and a stirring of activity at the table. Not even Denise, who had been watching Tom in stunned silence, had seen the almost imperceptible change in Val O'Connor. If she had, she would have rushed from the monitor room and into the dining room.

While Tom's appearance and the disappearance of the rolls she had yet to taste had distracted Ms. Jacobs, Val O'Connor had casually slipped his hand toward her bread and butter plate. No one saw him produce a golden brown rye roll and place it on her previously empty plate. By the time Ms. Jacobs looked again at the table, O'Connor's attention lay in buttering a dark roll of his own.

Muttering to herself, Ms. Jacobs stated, "Oh, I already have one. I must have taken it earlier and forgotten."

Denise's attention immediately turned at the sound of the voice. She had not seen Ms. Jacobs take a roll earlier in the meal and knew that the rolls had vanished from the basket before she could reach for one. Seeing her tear a mouth-sized piece and butter it, Denise sprang to her feet. Shouting into the earphone, she instructed Melvin to stop Ms. Jacobs from making a potentially fatal decision.

Melvin rushed into the dining room while still pulling on his jacket. Seeing Ms. Jacobs with the offending morsel of bread at her lips, he sprang across the table and landed just short of the marzipan centerpiece. Pulling the bread from her outstretched hand and gathering the roll, he righted himself and brushed Bob Franklin's salad from his shirt.

Denise watched as the guests stared at Melvin with frightened eyes. They all knew from newspaper reports that their colleagues had been poisoned by rolls laced with ergot fungus. Suddenly, they all looked a bit green and sick. That is, all except one.

"I've got it, Denise," Melvin shouted over the shuffle of shoes and the clinking of forks.

"Good, Melvin. I'll be right there. Don't let anyone leave," Denise stated as she stood to leave the makeshift monitor room.

"I didn't get a roll after all," Tom stated irritably as he entered the room. "Where are you going? Why is Melvin holding a gun on those people?"

Grabbing his hand and pulling him with her, Denise explained, "You might not have gotten your roll, but you flushed out the murderer."

"I did? Who is it?" Tom asked as he, for once, followed in Denise's wake.

"You'll see in just a minute. Call for a patrol car," Denise instructed as she entered the dining room.

Denise entered a dining room that was more silent than a church. None of the guests moved as Melvin stood guarding them with his service revolver in his hand. Not even the killer tried to leave.

"Stand up, Mr. O'Connor, and back away from your chair," Denise ordered as she stepped to Melvin's side. She could hear Tom's voice in the kitchen summoning the vehicle that would transport the murderer to the precinct for booking.

"I don't understand, Detective," Mr. Tilghman began, trying to defend his guest. "Val O'Connor is one of our most celebrated designers. He couldn't be the murderer."

Watching the tall figure stand as she had instructed, Denise stated, "He has always been celebrated, but, unlike most of you in this room, he has never made the list. He's an also-ran, a member of the second string. Your plan almost worked Mr. O'Connor. It might have if you hadn't tried to slip that roll onto Ms. Jacobs's plate."

Val O'Connor sputtered helplessly as he pushed up his glasses and squinted nearsightedly, "I don't know what you're talking about, Detective Dory. I had nothing to do with that roll or Ms. Jacobs's plate."

"You've as good as confessed, Mr. O'Connor," Denise replied coldly.

"I don't understand," Val O'Connor stated with genuine confusion.

"How do you know my name?" Denise asked as she continued to watch the suspect.

Answering confidently Val O'Connor said, "Mr. Tilghman just used it a minute ago. My attorney will definitely have something to say about this."

Before she could answer, Mr. Tilghman said, "No, I didn't, Val. I only called her a detective. Why'd you do it, Val? So many lives and for what? A place on a useless list."

"It's not so worthless. It bought you this place and the saloon in Paris and the one in London. Need I continue?" O'Connor snapped angrily.

"It might have helped momentarily, but hard work accomplished the rest," Mr. Tilghman responded. "Only hard work and luck make things happen in this industry. You know that, Val."

"It's time for some of the luck to come my way," Val O'Connor barked in a voice so filled with venom that the others blinked in unison. He appeared to stand taller as the anger flowed through his veins.

"Take off the glasses, please, Mr. O'Connor," Denise directed as she watched the change in him.

Without the glasses and the slight slouch, Val O'Connor was almost handsome. His clothes fit better, too, and took on the appearance of the attire the young men wore . . . slightly baggy but still trendy. He looked only at Denise though the cold blue eyes.

"You have me at a disadvantage, Detective," Val O'Connor hissed. "I can't see you."

"Put on your contact lenses. Not the clear ones you usually wear but the others," Denise ordered.

Silently and without objection, Val O'Connor slipped the little case from his pocket and positioned the brown contact lenses onto his eyes. When he looked at her, Denise knew that she had the right man. The familiar steely brown eyes looked back at her. They were the same eyes Freda had described and that Denise had seen on the man in the Cathedral.

"Much better," Val O'Connor stated calmly.

"Too bad you don't have a hat . . . and a wig," Denise commented.

The others stared from Denise to Val O'Connor wondering at the relationship that connected them. Even Tom, who knew his partner's every thought, was surprised to hear the coldness in Denise's voice. It was almost as if the battle of wits had changed her in some way.

"I don't need those tonight," Val O'Connor stated.

"What's happening here, Dory?" Tom demanded. "I don't understand."

"Let's just say that Freda exists only in our imagination. Isn't that right, Mr. O'Connor?" Denise replied without taking her eyes from the suspect.

"When did you know?" Val O'Connor asked in a tone that was almost caressing.

Without taking her eyes from his, Denise answered, "I suspected when I first met her at the Grand Canyon. She looked like the woman I had seen in the hotel in New York and fit the description of a customer the manager of Charming Charms gave me. I remembered that she had big hands for a woman. When I compared the composite I made of the suspect and the sketch I made of her, the similarity was unmistakable. When I saw her again at the WID dinner, I knew that Freda was in some way connected with the murderer. The disguise of being a drag queen almost had me fooled until I tried to reach her and couldn't. A performer would always return calls on the possibility of landing a job."

"And the ergot fungus? When did you isolate that?" Val O'Connor asked smiling begrudgingly.

Returning the smile, Denise replied, "I figured that out after a visit to the library in New York. When my partner ate a roll laced with it, I had the confirmation I needed."

Turning his eyes to Tom, Val O'Connor commented, "The only part of this that I regret is your illness, Detective Phyfer. I never meant for you to ingest the ergot-laden rolls."

"Why don't you empty your pockets, Mr. O'Connor. Let's make sure you don't have any more little treats," Tom insisted as he stepped forward with an empty basket in his hands.

While the others watched, Val O'Connor obediently placed the contents of his oversized pants and jacket pockets in the basket. Along with three more rolls, they found a note to Denise, car keys, and a wallet. Looking at them silently, he pulled the insides out so that they could see that his pockets were empty.

Tom inspected the wallet and discovered the missing link to Freda Maze. Inside under Val O'Connor's driver's license was another for the woman he became with the aide of prosthesis, high voice, false eyelashes, and wig. O'Connor had even obtained an Actor's Equity card to give legitimacy to his other persona.

"Aren't you going to read the note, Denise?" Val O'Connor asked with a warm smile.

"It's Detective Dory," Tom barked as he emptied the contents into a plastic bag and sealed it.

Lifting the flap of the familiar envelope, Denise turned her attention from O'Connor to the sheet on which he had written and read aloud, " 'Good-bye, dear detective. It's been great fun.' "

A last tiny package tumbled into her hand. Opening it, Denise found a tiny crystal vile with a gold top that contained a black grain. Without asking, she knew that it was an ergot fungus-infested grain of rye.

Denise removed the bracelet with its sparkling collection of charms from her wrist. As Val O'Connor watched, she attached the new charm to the bracelet. Opening the evidence bag, Denise added the bracelet to the collection.

The silence in the room was deafening. Only when the police arrived did the others avert their eyes from Val O'Connor. A few managed to watch in continued disbelief as the officer handcuffed their colleague and escorted him from the condo.

Stephano burst from the kitchen as the commotion died down. Standing with a wooden spoon raised as a weapon, he demanded, "What's happening? Has someone killed the president?"

"The president?" Tom queried.

"Yes, isn't that why my kitchen is overflowing with uncoordinated, graceless people who keep dropping things?" Stephano stated excitedly.

Placing his arm around Stephano's shoulders, Mr. Tilghman replied as they walked toward the kitchen, "I'll tell you all about it. Let's serve the main course now, Stephano."

The dinner guests resumed their seats. Despite the reassurance that the brown rolls were harmless, no one ate anymore of them. They concentrated, instead, on the wonderful entrée that Stephano had prepared. While the guests ate family style, Denise, Tom, and the other detectives gathered the surveillance equipment and departed.

Seventeen

Denise arrived in the squad room the next morning feeling rested and at ease. No more notes or charms should arrive. No more ergot fungus rolls to kill unsuspecting diners. Val O'Connor had confessed, and the evidence supported his confession. Denise could rest now that the case was closed.

The squad room smelled like home. Tom's overly strong, overly brewed coffee sat thickly in the pot waiting for her to pour her first cup of the day. Her fellow colleagues gathered around the coffee machine eating donuts, sharing exaggerated stories of cases and photographs of loved ones.

"Hey, Dory!" Dan Thomas greeted her as Denise poured a cup of sludge and added a teaspoon of sugar. "I see you made the paper again. Solved that murder case. Good work."

"Thanks," Denise replied and then added mysteriously, "I wouldn't eat any rolls or donuts for a while, if I were you."

"Why not?" Dan asked with a honey-glazed donut poised at his mouth.

"Ergot poisoning . . . deadly," Denise stated with a wink.

Laughing heartily, Dan said, "Yeah, right!" and took a big bite of his donut.

Molly lifted her head from Tom's foot as Denise approached. Instead of simply returning to her nap, the large dog quickly rose and walked toward Denise. Waging her tail happily, Molly placed her paw into Denise's outstretched hand and waited patiently for Denise to scratch her ears. With a sigh, Denise admitted to herself that she liked the dog. There was room in their partnership for another member.

"About time you showed up," Tom growled without taking his eyes from the report he was writing.

Standing at his desk with the dog at her side, Denise asked, "How'd you sleep last night?"

Looking up and smiling happily, Tom replied with a wink, "Fine, like a rock. It must have been the activity before sleep that knocked me out."

"I wanted to fix breakfast for you, but you had left before I finished my shower," Denise chuckled intimately as she threw her things onto her desk.

Keeping his voice low so that the entire squad room would not hear the exchange, Tom replied, "We'll have plenty of time for breakfast this weekend."

"What's happening this weekend?" Denise asked as she frowned slightly.

"You'll see," Tom replied mischievously as he returned to his work.

"You're certainly acting suggestively this morning for a man who doesn't want everyone to know about our relationship," Denise commented as she turned toward her desk.

Pretending to rise, Tom demanded, "Who doesn't want anyone to know? I'll shout it to the entire squad room. I'll tell all of them that Denise Dory is my girl friend."

Raising her hand to stop him, Denise stated, "No, not girlfriend. You still haven't found a better term than that."

"You don't like 'woman,' " Tom stated.

"No."

"Main squeeze?" Tom offered, studying Denise's face.

"No, too old-fashioned," she replied.

"Ball and chain?" Tom asked teasingly.

"Whatever," Denise replied chuckling, turning her back and concentrating on the mess piled on her desk.

Ronda appeared happily, waving a note for Denise. "This just arrived for you. Now that you're front-page news again, you'll probably get a lot of mail."

"Oh, no, not another note from O'Connor! I thought I was rid of him," Denise exclaimed taking the familiar envelope in her hand.

Tom and Ronda watched attentively as Denise studied the envelope. "This isn't the same handwriting," Denise announced. "It's familiar but not the same."

"Could be a copycat, but it's safe. I've x-rayed it," Ronda stated as she turned to leave the squad room for her post outside Captain Morton's office.

"Well, open it," Tom insisted.

Tearing the end of the envelope, Denise watched skeptically as a package that was larger than a charm tumbled onto Tom's desk. Pulling the note from the envelope, she unfolded it and read aloud, "My partner, my woman, my love, my life . . . and so much more. Tom."

Denise's eyes filled with tears as she looked from the paper to Tom's beaming face. For a man who avoided demonstrations of affection, he was certainly full of surprises that morning. Dragging her eyes from Tom's face, Denise unwrapped the little package. A tiny gold heart locket on a dainty chain fell into her hand.

"It's beautiful, Tom," Denise stated between sniffles.

"I know you don't wear much jewelry, but I thought you might like this. Open it," Tom growled in a hushed voice.

Pressing the little snap, Denise opened the locket. Inside, Tom had carefully placed a photograph of himself on the right and one of him and Molly on the left. Denise chuckled though her tears and hooked the chain around her neck.

"I don't know what to say," Denise muttered as she beamed into his face.

"Nothing. Just wear it knowing that I love you, Dory," Tom replied, looking intently into her face. For once, he did not hide the emotions that filled his heart.

Molly barked happily, wanting her share of the affection. After scratching the dog's ears for the second time that morning, Denise turned to her desk. As she started through the mountain of paperwork on her desk, she fingered the locket and smiled. She did not care what term Tom used to describe her as long as the love lasted between them.

"Damn, it!" Tom roared to the noisy squad room. "Who's the wise acre that hooked my paper clips together?"

Denise laughed and said nothing. She sipped the steaming thick brew contentedly. That was one mystery she had no intention of solving.